JUL -- 2018

IT ALL FALLS DOWN

ALSO BY SHEENA KAMAL

The Lost Ones

IT ALL FALLS DOWN

SHEENA KAMAL

WILLIAM MORROW
An Imprint of HarperCollins*Publishers*

This is a work of fiction. Names, characters, places, and incidents are products of the author's imagination or are used fictitiously and are not to be construed as real. Any resemblance to actual events, locales, organizations, or persons, living or dead, is entirely coincidental.

HarperCollins books may be purchased for educational, business, or sales promotional use. For information please email the Special Markets Department at SPsales@harpercollins.com.

FIRST EDITION

Library of Congress Cataloging-in-Publication Data has been applied for.

ISBN 978-0-06-256577-8 (hardcover)
ISBN 978-0-06-284504-7 (international edition)

18 19 20 21 22 LSC 10 9 8 7 6 5 4 3 2 1

For my mother

1

WHEN THEY ERECTED their first pop-up tents to treat the addicts who wandered in and out like living corpses, I thought: Sure.

When the newspapers ran article after article about the opioid addiction taking the city by storm, it was more along the lines of: No kidding. Nothing slips past you guys.

But when the mental health infrastructure became obsessed with the zombies, I had to put my foot down.

Nobody cared about my griping.

With all these people addicted to addicts now, where are the humble murderers of the city supposed to turn for our mental health support? I ask you. We have been reduced to complaining about it in our weekly meetings. Not that there are murder support groups in Vancouver. I don't want you to get the wrong idea. Alternative outlets for the murderous of the city are sadly lacking. Private therapists can cost an arm and a leg—so to speak—and it's not like you can find community discussion groups on the topic, either. The closest I've found is one for people with eating disorders, but I don't expect people who have done terrible things to their appetites to understand that I killed a person or two last year. In self-defense, but still.

During my share, I settle for telling my fellow nutjobs that I feel like I'm being shadowed by my demons, and they nod in understanding. We are strangers who all know one another's deepest secrets, bonded in the sacred circle of a urine-stained meeting room in Vancouver's Downtown Eastside. They lift their anemic arms in polite applause afterward and we disperse from the collapsed circle. We are blessedly strangers again.

The feeling of being watched follows me from the low-income Eastside Vancouver neighborhood I frequent back to the swanky town house in Kitsilano that I now occupy some space in. I drive with the windows up because the air is thick with forest fire smoke from Vancouver's north shore, smoke that has drifted here in pungent wafts and settled over the city. It doesn't help that we are experiencing one of these new Octobers that doesn't remember that there's supposed to be a fall season and is almost unbearably hot for this time of year.

As I drive, I obsess over still another death. One that hasn't occurred yet. But it will.

Soon.

2

WHEN I GET back to the town house, Sebastian Crow, my old boss and new roomie, is asleep on the couch.

I reach out a hand to touch him, but pull back before my fingers brush his temple. I don't want to wake him. I want him to sleep like this forever. Peaceful. At ease. In a place where the C-word can't reach him. Every day he seems to shrink a bit more and his spirit grows bigger to compensate for the reduction of physical space he occupies. He's ill and there is nothing I can do about it because it's terminal. My dog, Whisper, and I have moved in to keep him company and make sure he doesn't fall down the stairs on our watch, but beyond that it is hopeless. There is a great fire that he seems to burn with now. His body has turned against him, but his mind refuses to let go just yet.

Not until the book is done.

When he asked me to help organize and fact-check it for him, I couldn't say no. Not to Sebastian Crow, the career journalist who is writing his memoirs as he nears the end of his life. Writing it as a love letter to his dead mother and an apology to his estranged son. Also as an explanation to the lover he has abandoned. What I have read of it is beautiful, but it means that he is spending his last days living in the past. Because there is no future, not for him.

Whisper nudges my hand. She is restless. On edge. She feels it, too.

I put her on a leash, because I don't trust her mood, and we walk to the park across the street. There's a man there who has been trying to pet her, so we steer clear of him in a spirit of generosity toward his limbs. On the other side of the park is a pathway that hugs the coastline. Smoke from unseen fires lingers, even here. Not even the sea breeze can dispel it. We walk, both of us feeling uneasy, until we circle back around to the park. I sit on a bench with Whisper pulled close.

The man who has been watching me walks right past us.

"Nice night for a bit of light stalking," I say. "Don't you think?"

The man stops. Faces me. He opens his mouth, perhaps considering a lie, but shuts it again. My back is to the dim streetlight that overlooks this section of the park. Whisper and I are just dark shapes to him, but he is fully illuminated. His coat is open and at his neck there is a long swath of mottled skin running from the hinge of his jaw to his collarbone. It looks like new skin tried to grow there once but gave up halfway, leaving behind an unfinished impression. He's an older man, but I find his age hard to place. Whatever it is, he has used his years to learn how to dress well. Sleek jacket. Nice shoes. It doesn't add up. A man, careful with his appearance, who spends his evenings sitting in a park and following women as they walk their dogs.

We wait in a kind of charged silence, all three of us. Whisper yawns and runs her tongue over her sharp canines to speed things along. He takes this as the threat it's no doubt meant to be.

"Your sister told me where to find you," he says finally.

If he thinks that's supposed to put me at ease, he's off his meds. Lorelei hasn't spoken to me since last year, since I stole her husband's car and ran it off the road and into a ravine.

But I decide to play the game anyway. "What do you want?"

"Damned if I know," he says, with a rueful smile. "Taking a trip down memory lane in my winter years, I suppose."

"And what's that got to do with me?"

"I knew your father once." It's a good thing his voice is soft because said even a decibel louder, that statement could have knocked me on my ass, if I wasn't already on it. "May I sit down?" He gestures to the bench. There's something odd about his tone. His enunciation is too measured for someone confronted by an unpredictable animal. I wonder if the scar at his neck has anything to do with his casual demeanor. If he is one of those men who is so accustomed to danger that it doesn't faze him anymore.

"No. Knew my father from where?"

He pauses in his approach and considers Whisper's bared teeth. "Lebanon. You know he served with the marines there, right?"

I ignore this because I did not know that, but if it's anyone's business, it isn't his. "Doesn't explain why you're following me."

He swipes a hand over his face, the tips of his fingers pause at his scar. He notices my eyes flicker toward it. "From Lebanon. An explosion." He considers his next words carefully before he speaks. "I said I'd check up on you if anything ever happened to him."

I laugh. "You're a few decades too late."

"I'm not a very good friend. Look, I'm retired now and I had to make a trip to Canada. I thought I'd look you up. I had checked on you and your sister after I heard he died all those years ago, but you were with your aunt and everything seemed fine. A couple days ago I managed to track down your sister. She wasn't exactly very forthcoming about you—"

"She wouldn't be." Lorelei and I had not parted on good terms. She had kept her maiden name, though, when she got married, and had a robust online profile. She wouldn't be hard to find, if you had a mind to go looking.

"I told her we were old friends. Took some convincing, but she told me that I could find you through Sebastian Crow. And here I am."

"But why?"

He becomes agitated, fishes out a lone cigarette from his jacket, and lights it. His eyes linger on the wisp of flame from the lighter. "You ever made a promise you didn't keep? I've done a lot of wrong in my life, but how things turned out with your father, in the end . . . I never thought what happened to him was right. I knew he was struggling after the trouble in Lebanon, but goddamn. What a waste."

He looks down at my hand, where my fingers are clenched so tight around Whisper's leash that my nails dig into my palm, leaving crescent-shaped marks.

"I don't know what I'm doing here," he says helplessly. He hasn't taken a drag of the cigarette yet, seems to have no intention of smoking it.

I almost drowned last year. I don't remember a lot about it, only that I must have blacked out at some point. Any free diver or scuba enthusiast will tell you that in the final stage of nitrogen narcosis, latent hypoxia hits the brain. It can cause neurological impairment. Reasoning and judgment are often affected, at least in the moment. But it can also feel pleasant, this lack of oxygen. Warm. Safe even.

It can make you delusional.

I wonder if I'm experiencing a more long-term fallout from my near-drowning. Because I used to be able to tell when people were lying, almost definitively. But now I'm not so sure. After the events of last year, when my daughter went missing, the girl I'd given away without a second thought, I have looked at people differently. Maybe it's my sluggish maternal instincts kicking in, muddling my senses. Or maybe I've lost my mojo. Because when he said he doesn't know what he's doing here, I believed him. I believe that we do things that don't make sense. Even to ourselves.

It's also possible that I am falling into my own hallucinations.

I'm so confused that I say nothing at all in return. The veteran looks as unsettled as I feel. I stare at him hard until he walks away, toward the ocean, and disappears into the dense night. Then I rub some feeling back into my hands. My thoughts are a jumble, until one of them shakes loose.

It isn't just the surprise of someone coming to find me after all these years. It isn't even that he felt the need to follow me in the dark to ascertain whether or not I'm doing okay. It goes deeper than that, and has to do with the things about my father that I didn't know. That there was trouble in Lebanon. With my father.

My father had trouble in Lebanon and then, some years later, he blew his brains out.

3

DEEP IN SPACE, a star named KIC 8462852 flickers for some
unknown reason, while down on Earth an ex-cop, ex–security
agent, ex-husband, and ex–amateur bowler grimaces as he
downs a glass of spinach juice and hopes that his internal organs
are paying attention to the effort he's making on their behalf.

This particular star has confounded scientists the world over
by its constant dimming and brightening, while Jon Brazuca
confounds only himself with his new resolution to be kinder
to his body. He inherited low self-esteem from his spineless
mother and weak-chinned father, both of whom apologized
through life and then on into their retirement.

But Brazuca is over it. This demeaning cycle of "I'm sorry"
and "I beg your pardon" would end with him.

He is turning over a new leaf, and then blending it into a
smoothie.

The evening sun is low on the horizon and he is filled with
chlorophyll and contentment. Brazuca has always been more
awake at night, more alive, and has now turned to astronomy
to help fill in the gaps. He is not a man of science, but wishes
that he were. His mother had once taken him to Spain as a child,
to the cliffs of Famara, and together they had looked out at the
stars reflected in pools of water on the beachfront below.

Thinking of this, he longs for a simpler time, when women he generously pleasured didn't drug him and tie him to a bed, leaving him to be found by astonished maids. Which is something that actually happened to him approximately a year ago. Nora Watts, the woman he'd attended AA meetings with, the woman who had gone and lost a daughter that she hadn't even wanted, the woman whom he felt compelled to help for no rhyme or reason that made any goddamn sense to him—she had left him high, literally, but not at all dry. No, she'd fed him a booze-and-sedative cocktail that put him to sleep and gave his body the little bump it had been wanting for so very long.

And it has taken him months to kick the habit again.

Brazuca stands on the balcony of his apartment in East Vancouver and winks up at the sky, in the general direction of the flickering star he has read about in a magazine. He feels for a brief moment a sort of affinity for the universe. He chugs the rest of the juice and belches in contentment.

His friend Bernard Lam has asked him to come over, and for the first time ever, he feels like hanging out with a billionaire.

"Brazuca," says Lam, at the door of his sprawling Point Grey mansion. If there's a housing crisis in Vancouver, it might be because so much space has been taken up by this single estate. There's an east wing and a west wing, and about twenty rooms in between them. There are outdoor courts for every sport, and a miniature golf course for variety. If you get bored of the saltwater pool, there's a freshwater one on the other side of the property.

Bernard Lam, the playboy son of a wealthy businessman and philanthropist, gestures for Brazuca to follow him inside. His famous charm is nowhere to be seen. His manner is grave and uncertain as he leads Brazuca down a long hallway filled with family photographs mounted on the wall, newer photos of Lam and his recent bride, and then into a study. "What's wrong?" Brazuca asks as soon as the door is closed behind them.

"One moment." Lam goes to his laptop on the desk. There's a bottle of scotch next to him and no photos to speak of here. It is a family-free zone. Lam turns the screen toward Brazuca.

"She's beautiful," he says, glancing at the woman on Lam's computer. In the picture, she's in a sundress on a yacht, laughing up at the camera. She's tall and voluptuous, with a sheet of glossy dark hair and bright eyes.

"Her name was Clementine. She was the love of my life."

No amount of spinach juice can stop the headache that begins at Brazuca's temples at Lam's use of past tense. The woman in the photo wasn't the woman on the walls of the family home. So the love of his life was not Lam's new bride. "When?"

"They found her last week in her apartment. They say it was an overdose. She's . . . she *was* four months pregnant."

"Yours?" Brazuca asks, careful to keep his voice even.

Lam raises a brow, as if the possibility of anything else doesn't even exist.

Brazuca decides not to push. "So what do you need?"

"You're still working with that small PI outfit? They give you any time off?"

"I take contracts as needed. They're flexible." His new employers weren't picky about what work he chose, as long as he took some of it off their hands. They'd even offered to make him a partner in a more formal sort of arrangement, but he'd said no to that. He didn't want formal.

"Good," says Lam. "That's very good. I need you to find out who her dealer is."

"Bernard . . ."

"You will, of course, be generously compensated."

"It's not about the money."

"Then do it for a friend. Do it for me. My girl and my child are dead. I want to know who's responsible."

Brazuca wonders if Lam knows that, with the use of the word *girl*, he has painted both of them with the same brush of idealized innocence. "You're not going to like what comes out of this," he says quietly. "It will bring you no peace of mind." Death by overdose is a nasty thing to deal with. Blame is hard to pin down.

"Who says I want peace of mind?" Lam pours a shot of scotch into his glass and knocks it back. "I'll give you the paperwork and her contacts. They didn't find anything on her phone. The drug she took . . ." He looks away, gathers his thoughts. "It was cocaine laced with a new synthetic opiate now hitting the streets. A fentanyl derivative more potent than what's been seen before, and actually stronger than fentanyl. Called YLD Ten."

"Wild Ten? I've heard of it. Not much. But I know it's out there." It was the stupid name that got to him. Easy to remember when you place an order from your friendly neighborhood drug dealer.

"Then you know how dangerous it is. She was only twenty-five. She had her whole life ahead of her, Jon, and it was with me. I need to know. Please."

"Okay," Brazuca says, after a minute. Because he's not the kind of man who can say no to a cry for help. Turns out, his leaf isn't so fresh after all. "I'll look into it. Do you have a key to her apartment?"

Lam nods. "Of course. I own the place."

"Of course," Brazuca murmurs. "I'll get started right away." He doesn't have to say the "sir" because it's implied. Bernard Lam, whose life he saved several years earlier, is oblivious to this dig.

4

I'M HERE AGAIN at my sister's house in East Vancouver. It's Saturday, and you can only tell it's afternoon by the clock. The haze is not as thick as it was yesterday, but it's still there. Still obscuring the daylight and conjuring frightening images of smoker's lung to the health nuts of the city, who will not quit hiking or cycling in these conditions but will complain incessantly while they do it. I hear there's another forest fire on the Sunshine Coast and the winds are blowing the smoke over this way.

Vancouver isn't on fire, but it sure as hell seems like it is.

I've waited until Lorelei's car pulls out of the drive to approach the narrow gate leading to the backyard. Her husband, David, is sitting on the small deck, contemplating his shitty garden. There are a few herb plants mustering some strength, but they are no match for the mint growing like weeds, even in this postapocalyptic atmosphere. He looks like he's trying to stay positive, but failing. I feel sorry for men like David, the decent, hardworking men of the world. Try as they might, the simplest things seem to overwhelm them. He can't even succeed at coaxing something edible from the earth.

He's drinking a light beer and doesn't bother getting up when I round the corner. The last time we laid eyes on each other, he had thrown some money at me and asked me to stay away from Lorelei for a spell. He doesn't seem surprised now that I have broken our agreement. Then he sees Whisper and a delighted smile crosses his face. Part of the reason I brought her with me is that dog people are so easy to manipulate. She understands her role well enough to trot over and say hello to his crotch with her nose. Bam. Nice to see you.

"Who's a good girl?" He grins, reaching over to scratch behind her ears. "Who's a very good girl?"

And then he looks at me. The grin disappears. I try not to be offended. Good girls are overrated anyway.

"The yellow box," I say. There's no reason to beat around the bush.

He considers this for a moment, then makes a decision. "Upstairs, in the guest room closet. Top shelf."

I walk past him and into their house. My visits to my sister's home are usually of the clandestine sort so, at first, I'm not sure how to proceed. Am I supposed to move differently now that I have permission?

Lorelei's house is much like her personality. Spare, uncluttered, and a little nauseating in its blandness. There's no room for surprises here. The box is exactly where he said it would be. When I come back outside with the yellow shoe box tucked under my arm, I find that things have progressed for Whisper. She is busy enjoying the touch of a man. She's on her back now, and has offered her stomach for a thorough rubdown. The nympho.

"Thank you," I say, when David looks up at me again.

He nods.

"Will you tell her I've been here?"

"Not unless she notices the box is missing. But she hasn't opened it in years, so I wouldn't worry."

I nod, too, and both of us are doing a thing with our necks that is attempting to smooth over the rough patch we've hit. We now have an understanding between us. A secret. My sister's husband and I have agreed that she is not to know that I've been here and that I've taken something from her. I won't tell her because she no longer speaks to me. His silence on the subject is probably due to a misplaced guilt over our tense relationship. Even though it has nothing to do with him. But David is a good man and would not deny me what I have left of my father, all conveniently contained in a box that used to hold a pair of Lorelei's nude pumps, size seven.

I close my legs a notch. The pressure builds slower than I like. Slower than I've become used to. And then it is over, several excruciating moments longer than it used to take. I'm not ashamed, which I suppose is in its own way progress, but then again I'm not much of anything, really.

I still feel like I'm being watched but the angle is all wrong.

As I remove my knees from their indentations beside the stranger's head, I wonder—was it worth the trip over here? The answer doesn't come to me, not when I put on my jeans or even when I untie his hands from the bedposts and make for the door. Like the cliché I have become, the money is in an envelope on the dresser.

It comes when I'm already halfway to the motel's parking lot.

I will sit on your face, says the ad I placed online. *And your hands will be tied. When it's over, I'll leave. NSA. No fuss. No games. My teeth are sharper than yours.*

Then I name a reasonable rate that I'm prepared to pay.

All things considered, it's an insulting ad. I have come to hate myself more than the lonely schmucks who answer it, but I haven't taken it down yet. I come, then I go, and it had all worked out well at first.

My old Corolla takes a minute to get used to the idea that something is expected of it and while I wait I'm left with the unsettling answer. It's not enough anymore. No matter how many strangers whose faces I try to erase with my thighs.

About an hour later, I park next to the restaurant at Burnaby Mountain and head to a spot about halfway up the lawn. The air is cleaner up here, plus the view of the beautiful Japanese wood carvings beneath me and the city of Vancouver to the west can't be beat. I'm at this spot because my journalist friend Mike Starling loved coming to this place to think, or so it claims in his obituary last year, after he was found dead in his bathtub with his wrists slit. To me, Starling wasn't the type to sit around on mountains and contemplate life but, admittedly, my memory isn't the greatest. What I remember the most about him was his disdain for drinkers of multisyllabic coffee and what he looked like in death, in a tub full of bloody water.

My support group friends assure me that I've got nothing to feel guilty about because I'm not the one who killed him—but what the hell do they know, anyway? It's not like their judgment is exactly sound. And what they don't know (because I haven't told them) is that I'm the reason he's dead. He was killed because some dangerous people had come looking for me and he'd made the choice to protect me. He may have even sat here while he thought about it and decided that my life was worth fighting for, and he'd be looking into who painted the target on my back.

I sip at the coffee I brought with me—four syllables—and pour a little on the ground beside me for him. So he'll know the woman he gave his life to save still has a sense of humor. Maybe he did like to come up here, and maybe there's a little bit of him left behind in this place, too, because it seems to me Mike Starling could never walk away from a mystery.

Clearly, I can't either.

5

IT'S LATE. THE contents of the box are spread out on the coffee table in front of me and I'm slumped on the floor, staring at them at eye level. There isn't much there. A love letter. A strip of crumpled blue silk. Five postcards from an address in Detroit. A few faded photographs. One is of a woman in bed, holding a baby. The woman's head has been cropped out, perhaps deliberately, and she's cradling a wrinkled infant in her tanned arms. The date on the back of the photo tells me that the sleeping infant is me.

I put it aside.

The other two are of my father, Lorelei, and me. These photos don't have a date on them, but all three of us have changed drastically from one photo to the next. Lorelei and I are growing with the speed that children do, but my father's aging has taken a dramatic turn. In both, his hair is straight and black, his eyes dark. It's the deepening lines on his face that have changed him. In the first he looks like a content but tired father. In the second, he looks like a haunted man with one foot in the grave. Raising children isn't for everyone.

"What are you doing?" says Seb, from the doorway. My own living ghost has decided to put in a stealthy appearance, his face gaunt and pale.

"Hungry?" I gesture to the box of pad thai that I picked up from his favorite place, just around the corner from the town house. I buy some every couple of days, just in case he's in the mood for a heavy dose of sodium and carbohydrates. I always end up eating it the next morning because he never is. Though he assures me that he eats, I rarely ever see it. I, on the other hand, have put on about ten pounds since I moved in. If there's one thing I can't stand, it's letting food go to waste. Because then you have to figure out how to get more.

He shakes his head and drifts toward the photos. "Who are these people?" he asks, peering over my shoulder.

"My father and my sister."

"And you. Beautiful." When he smiles, the room brightens and I almost forget that he is about to die. "Why the trip down memory lane?"

We keep no secrets from each other anymore. There's no time for that. I tell him about the man from last night and how he claimed to know my father.

"Weird," he says, collapsing on the stiff armchair beside the coffee table. One of the few pieces of furniture that his lover Leo, my former boss, left behind in a scorned rage. "After all this time. Why bother?"

I shrug. "It's just . . ." My eyes skip over the ceiling, the floor, Whisper, anywhere but at the photos.

"Just?"

"We never knew much about his life. After my aunt got sick we were put into care and these things are what I had taken with me at the time. When she died, she'd donated most of what she had to charity and everything else disappeared. We don't have any records of his life left." Or our early life, mine and Lorelei's. I don't say that, though, because it's implied.

"Is that what's bothering you? That you only have this box?" His voice is so light, so gentle that it floats over the tension that has reared up inside me. "Because you've described your dad as a Sixties Scoop survivor. Many children of indigenous heritage who were taken away from their families and put up for adoption knew less about their parents than this. Had less than what you have in this box."

And some had more, and others had around the same amount. Years after the Canadian government implemented the residential school system, it also tacked on a policy of forced adoption that didn't seek to help matters. Out of reserves, out of urban centers, the imposed assimilation came at communities where it hurt. If you think about it, this strategy is always the one that is most used when trying to erase people. In Canada, like it was elsewhere in the colonial world, they began with the children.

I know Seb is probably right that I should be grateful for what I have, but at the moment it doesn't feel like I could possibly know less than I do right now. "What's bothering me is that I can't confirm any of what he said. It's not that I have no information, it's that what I have is incomplete."

He reaches for the postcards. "And what about these? Who are they from?" There is no signature on any of them. Just my father's name, scrawled in a sloping hand.

"He grew up in Detroit. It's where the family that adopted him lived. But he never talked about them to me as a child. We never met. I found out about them from my aunt, but she didn't know much, either."

Seb stares past me, his eyes unfocused. With a sudden burst

of energy, he rises from the chair and grabs hold of my hands. His voice, when he speaks, is low and urgent. "Sometimes these things happen for a reason, Nora. Don't you see? This man comes into your life and forces you to look at what you knew of your father. And, you said yourself, there isn't much. You've been holding on to your memories of him that you had as a little girl and maybe now is the time to get to know who he really was without the childhood blinders on."

But he's dead, I want to say.

I want to tell him to mind his own business and leave me out of his obsession with the past, but I don't. Maybe it's because I normally don't speak of my father out loud. I have built a bunker in my heart around his memory. With concrete walls. Built to withstand a nuclear blast. What is striking in this bunker is not what's in it, but what is absent. There are no answers there, only questions. This is why I have chosen to keep it buried so deep for so long. Because unlocking it only shows me what I don't know.

"Go to Detroit," Seb continues. "Find whoever sent these postcards. Whatever trouble there was, the person who opens the door at this address might know something about it. If you don't go, you'll always wonder. It will haunt you."

Now I see what he's doing. He is trying to save me from making the same mistakes that he has made. I should shut up, but I don't. I don't have any control over what I say next.

"Just like Leo will always wonder," I say. "When you die. He'll wonder why you didn't tell him. And that maybe he should have known that you were sick." Leo, his lover, who was devastated when I left him to work with Seb. Leo thinks it's a professional betrayal, but it isn't. It's a personal one. I'm one of a handful of people who know of Seb's illness and agreed to keep it from the others in Seb's life.

Seb releases my hands as though they've scalded him and leaves the room without another word. Whisper rises gracefully from her spot by the window and trots after him. Like Seb, she refuses to look at me, as if to remind me that I don't deserve either of them.

When I hear his bedroom door shut, I turn off the lights in the living room and stand at the edge of the curtains, staring for a long time at the park across the street. Just because I don't see the veteran, it doesn't mean he's not there.

I call David, who up until now was unaware that I have his number. It's good to have someone around who will always answer the phone when you call. Even if he doesn't recognize my number on his call display, he's too polite to let it slip to voice mail. "Hello?" he says, after the fourth ring. His voice is heavy with sleep.

"It's Nora. Did Lorelei ever go to that address? The one on the postcards?"

There's a pause and I can hear the rustle of the sheets as he gets out of bed. A door opens, then closes. "No," he says, his voice barely a whisper. "She wrote a few letters back in college but never got a response. She didn't have enough money to check it out herself . . . and then she let it go. Are you thinking of making a trip?"

"I don't know," I say, after a moment. "Thanks. Keep doing you." And then, on that positive note, which the first time I heard it I believed it to be a supportive statement about masturbation,

I hang up. It's always good to leave people a little confused. Keep them guessing, so they'll answer the next time you call.

When Seb asked what was bothering me, I talked around it. But it's as simple as this: When a bullet hits a skull, blood and brain matter are expelled forcefully. It tears through cranial bones, connective tissues, and membranes. Depending on how close the muzzle is, there is the chance of burning on the outer layer of skin from the smoke and gunpowder. The end result of a bullet to the brain is death, unless you are unspeakably lucky. My father was not.

What matters to me now, though, is why the trigger was pulled in the first place. Why two young children were abandoned to the system is heavy in my mind. When it comes to fucking over someone's life completely, the motivation is important. And maybe Seb is right. Maybe Detroit holds the answer.

6

SEVERAL MONTHS AGO, when Seb, Leo Krushnik, and I were still working out of the Hastings Street office together, Leo dropped a passport application on my desk with the reasoning that international travel might improve my sex life. "You're not dead below the waist, you know," he told me. "And it's hard to get laid in this city." Then he threw a wistful glance at Seb.

That's when I first noticed the distance between them.

Now I walk toward the office before dawn, much earlier than Leo would ever consider coming in. His new business partner, however, is antisocial and keeps odd hours. I use my old key to get in and wonder that Leo hasn't bothered to change the lock. It's been a while since I've been in here, but the change is startling. A serious decorating overhaul has taken place. Any reminder of Seb's presence has been ruthlessly eliminated. His pastry certification is nowhere to be found on these walls, and it's not at the house, either, which makes me wonder if Leo has done something drastic to the only remaining proof that Seb knows his way around butter and flour.

Despite the office's location in the middle of the shabby Downtown Eastside of the city, the interior is now quite chic. The new decor announces quietly that reasonably priced investigations are done here, rather than screaming it. When Seb gave me a choice to go with him, I didn't hesitate, but for the first time I'm feeling nostalgic. My old desk is still in the reception area, but is almost totally obscured by a large vase of flowers.

Stevie Warsame, Leo's new partner, has moved his good backpack into Seb's office and has set up some kind of complicated computer station in one corner of the room. In the other corner is a second desk, which throws me off balance. Even though this isn't what I'm here for, I can't help but search it. I find nothing but a few spare phone chargers, some surveillance equipment, and a chart that compares the nutritional value of various vegetables when juiced. Leo has replaced me with a vase and given a desk in Seb's office to some kind of juice freak?

"Find what you're looking for?" says a familiar voice from behind me.

Brazuca, my old AA sponsor, is leaning against the doorjamb, eyeing me warily. I haven't seen him since last year, when he told me he forgave me for drugging him and abandoning him in a chalet in the mountains. After I found out that he had been lying to me about his day job, and I was too stupid to realize it.

Now here we are again, both of us still looking a little worse for wear, him slightly less so—possibly due to the introduction of fresh vegetables to his diet. There is more color in his cheeks and his eyes seem brighter. For some reason, I imagine us fucking but it is an unpleasant thought. Neither of us has any give or take. We are stretched too thin, and pressing our sharp bones against each other is the least sexy thing I can imagine. No comfort can be drawn out of us. At least not with each other. If he replied to my online ad, I would have to delete his message. Self-preservation is a funny thing.

"Making some life improvements?" I say, holding up the chart.

He smiles, ignoring the distance between us, as though it is a matter of mere physical space. But as the seconds pass and the distance now expands to an abyss, he sees there's nothing between us but distrust and a single orgasm. "Something like that. What are you doing here? I thought you left to go work with Crow."

"What are *you* doing here? Thought you worked for WIN Security." The security firm that was hired to find my daughter, Bonnie, after she'd gone missing. Hired by a corrupt family they were in the pocket of. I'd been alerted to her disappearance by her adoptive parents, which set off a chain of events that led to my near-drowning.

"Needed a change after last year. You haven't answered my question." He steps into the room. My shoulder still hurts like hell from when I was shot last year, but with physical therapy I have been able to mask my limp, from an ankle injury that never quite healed. For the most part. But Brazuca hasn't been that lucky with his own gimpy leg, a result of a gunshot wound back when he was a cop. Or maybe his injuries aren't just physical. I blame his victim mentality.

"I'm looking for Stevie."

"Warsame is on assignment," Brazuca says, which explains Stevie's silence. "Want me to get a message to him?"

I don't need Brazuca for that. If I wanted to get a message to Stevie, I would do it myself. But what I have to say can't be communicated via electronic means. They haven't created keyboard characters that could encompass it. "I'm gonna be gone for a little while. I need someone to check up on Seb."

He doesn't ask where I'm going and I don't offer any more information. "What's wrong with him?" he says finally.

I tell him about the cancer and the failed treatments. "Leo doesn't know," I add, when I'm done. "I can pay you to do it if Stevie can't."

"Why does everyone think I need money all of a sudden?" he mutters, running a hand through his hair.

I shrug. It might have something to do with his wardrobe, which is several years outdated and, frankly, not tight-fitting enough for the modern man, but I don't mention it. The male ego is a fragile thing.

"How often?" he asks.

"Every few days. The dog walker I hired will do a daily check."

He frowns. "You're not taking Whisper with you? You know what, never mind. I don't need to know."

I walk past him, careful to avoid any accidental brushing of our bodies. The last time we touched I had straddled him and poured liquor down his throat, knowing full well that he's an alcoholic. I've never asked for forgiveness for this. Nor will I ever. I had been able to discern lies before the events of last year, with everyone other than Brazuca. His lies had hurt the most, because I hadn't seen them coming. Maybe I hadn't wanted to. I won't make that mistake again.

"Krushnik isn't going to like this," he says, as I reach the door.

"You can tell him if you want."

But we both know he won't. It's not our secret to share. Leo will find out eventually and we'll have to face him when it's time. For now we agree to keep silent. Another illicit understanding, another man. I seem to be stacking them up these days.

It occurs to me to ask him something, because he is nothing if not observant. "Did you see anyone watching the building when you came in? Who maybe didn't look quite right."

"This is the Downtown Eastside. No one looks right here," he says, looking at me like you would a crazy person. Of which, in the city of Vancouver, the DTES is their muster point. It's mine, too. The destitute, the addicted, the people with demons—we flock here because it is often the only place that will have us.

I nod. So much for his powers of observation.

On my way to the car, I see a group of people huddled around a prone body on the street. I can't help but scan their faces to see if the veteran is among them. He's not, so I turn to the spectacle unfolding. A man is crouching over a woman, speaking to her in a soft voice. She's unresponsive. He takes an intramuscular needle from a kit at his side and draws up a dose of liquid from a marked vial. Then he plunges it into her thigh. There's a gasp from the crowd. Clearly from someone who's not from around here because this is an everyday occurrence in these parts. I don't wait to see if the woman on the ground wakes up from the naloxone shot. There are enough concerned citizens around and, besides, I've got enough problems of my own.

When I return to the house, Seb is in his office with his head pressed against the desk and Whisper at his feet, staring at me with accusing eyes. For a moment my heart stops beating, but then he wheezes in a shaky breath. I am not a large woman, but lifting him requires little effort. He is like a pile of bones in my arms, held together by fragile connective tissues and weak muscles. I lay him gently on the couch and take up my post in the armchair.

Leo has absconded with mostly everything but the books. If he'd known how much Seb needed them he would have taken them, too. But he didn't, so they are still here and when Seb is well enough we reference them as we talk through his memoir. He speaks and writes while I listen and make my own notes, or I write when he doesn't have the strength. We only work in this room and we check all our extra baggage at the door. Everyone needs to have a sacred place, and this one belongs to the three of us. Watched over by the tattered books that have meant something to him over the course of his life.

I am no academic, but Seb's books have been a revelation to me. Nothing moves me like the poetry of Césaire, the political writer from the French colonies who spoke of people's unwilling-ness to challenge their worldview. How easy it was to cast ideas away, as if swatting a fly.

Last week, before the smoke from the northern fires drifted down, I took Whisper to the rocks overlooking the ocean. We had some time to kill while Seb was at the hospital. We stayed there for a long time, long enough to see the circle of life played out in front of us. Just above the waterline, at the edge of my field of vision, two birds of prey circled a certain place in the water. Every now and then one of them made a dive. They called to each other, and the more time that passed, the tighter their circles got. I could only sense what they saw. That the creature in the water, a stray duck perhaps, was getting tired. Its reflexes were slowing. The inevitable was waiting to strike.

It reminded me that disaster swoops down and grabs hold when a creature is at its weakest.

Alone, with two hungry mouths to feed and the knowledge that a woman's love is a powerful thing, but not as powerful as the void it leaves behind when she's gone. Up until that veteran, whose name I didn't even think to get, showed up I had thought my father just couldn't handle the stress.

But now I think of Césaire, and a suspicion lodges in my mind. The idea, he'd said, an annoying fly. Buzzing in my ear. Telling me there's more to my father's death than I'd allowed myself to consider. Upending my worldview.

7

BRAZUCA IS IMMEDIATELY forced to reexamine his biases about kept women as he steps inside Clementine's condo. Whatever bordello he'd been expecting, this isn't it. There is nothing frivolous about this place, besides the cost of living in a condo overlooking English Bay. There is a cozy, warm feel to it, and though the furnishings aren't cheap, they aren't ostentatious, either. Someone with very good taste made a home here.

Soft afternoon light streams into the living room, where Brazuca finds a framed photograph of Lam with his arms wrapped around Clementine. They're overlooking the waters of Deep Cove in North Van, where the Burrard Inlet and the Indian Arm fjord meet. Brazuca has never seen Lam look as happy as he does in that photograph, smiling into Clementine's hair.

There's a noise from farther in the apartment. He turns away from the picture, passes the elegant kitchen, and pauses at the bedroom door. "Hello?"

A young Chinese woman glances up at him, sweeping a strand of hair off her brow and tucking it back into her messy bun. She's wearing sweats with the University of British Columbia logo and is sitting on the floor surrounded by piles of clothing, shoes, and handbags, looking completely lost.

What strikes him is that she doesn't seem to be overly

surprised to see a stranger here. Or concerned for her safety, for that matter. They stare at each other for a moment, then she gestures toward the bags. "Do you know what a designer handbag typically costs?" she says, finally. "Of course you don't. I can tell by the way you dress. You're not one of my sister's regular boyfriends."

Brazuca is amused, despite himself. He crosses his arms over his chest and leans against the doorframe.

"Thousands of dollars," she continues. "There must be at least fifty thousand dollars' worth of handbags in this room alone. What am I supposed to do with these things?"

"We should pool our resources and sell them together. We'd both be rich."

"These labels sell themselves. And I'm not sure what exactly you'd be contributing, whoever you are."

"Jon Brazuca," he says, deciding not to offer a hand. The wary look in her eyes tells him to stay where he is. "A friend of Clementine's asked me to stop by."

She stares at him and he is tempted to step back at the sudden fury in her expression. She gets to her feet. "You mean Bernard Lam? She OD's and he's furious, isn't he? His plaything is dead."

"I don't think Clementine was his plaything."

"Let's get one thing straight," the woman says, jabbing a finger at his chest. "I don't know why she wanted to be called by that god-awful stripper name, but she was born Cecily Chan. She was an English lit major before she dropped out of school to model. She was a person, with a family that loved her."

Brazuca puts up a hand, a gesture for peace. He had a great-aunt by the name of Cecily and understands well why a woman under the age of forty would rather be called anything else. "Okay, I got it. She was loved. I never said she wasn't."

Her face falls. She kicks aside a purse that could be worth more than he made in a month. "I'm sorry. I'm not myself. I hate this. My sister is dead, and all she left behind is a bunch of expensive shit that I've got to deal with now."

He goes to the kitchen and puts on the kettle. A few minutes later, she pads after him with a cardboard box full of designer handbags and drops it next to a pile of boxes already in the living room. Then she takes out a bag of loose leaf tea from a cupboard she can barely reach. Together they make a pot of fragrant jasmine tea and sit at the dining table overlooking the bay.

The room grows dim as the sun sets over the water, but neither of them bothers to close the blinds or turn on the lights. Sometimes he is reminded how beautiful this city is. Why he chose to live here in the first place. He's so lost in his thoughts that it takes him a while to notice that she's staring directly at him. Probably has been for a while now. "I'm Grace," she says.

"Grace. Do you have someone who can come help you sort, um, Cecily's stuff?"

"No, not really."

"Your parents, maybe?"

She shakes her head. "As if they'd ever step foot in here. She and our parents had a falling-out a few years ago. She said she wished they were dead. They told her they could be dead to her, if that's what she wanted. Then she left and they never spoke again. They refused to come to the service when she died because that asshole paid for it. It was just me and some of our cousins. I don't think she had many friends left, toward the end."

Brazuca looks at the cardboard boxes piled in the living room. "Okay, well, maybe I can help move some of this stuff. Where do you live?"

"We live in Richmond . . . Oh, don't look at me like that!"

"Like what?"

Her hands are wrapped so tightly around her mug that she seems intent on breaking it. There is a sudden rage to her, maybe because her sister is dead, or maybe because she's been left to clean up the mess. "Like we all drive sports cars, take violin lessons, and live in Richmond. Like we're somehow taking over your goddamn city all of a sudden. My mom's family has been here since the Chinese came over to build the railroad a hundred years ago, and my dad moved here from the mainland when he was a kid. They're both engineers. We didn't go and buy up property from under your noses. We've got roots here. I'm studying to be an urban planner."

He shouldn't be surprised that she's on the defensive. Housing costs are so high that many blame the influx of Chinese on the astronomical real estate market. Over half the population of the city of Richmond is immigrants, and certain people are uncomfortable with the changing demographic. It is a kind of insidious racism that Brazuca sees seeping through with increasing frequency and he begins to see it now through this woman's eyes. He feels a sudden tenderness toward her. He reaches over and covers her hands with his. "I never said your family didn't belong here. I'm really sorry about your sister."

"My sister, she . . . she let herself be bought and paid for." She turns her hands over and interlocks her fingers with his. Her voice breaks, but there are no tears in her eyes. "You work with Lam, right? You know what those kinds of women are like?"

There is something unsettling about the way she's looking at him. He takes his hands away, but doesn't know where to put them now so just stuffs them into his pockets. "I really just help him figure out problems sometimes. I'm . . . I used to be a cop."

"But you're not anymore."

"No."

She skirts the small table and pushes his mug aside. Then she climbs onto his lap.

"Grace . . . what are you doing?" he says, wondering if he has it in him to throw a horny, grief-stricken woman off his lap.

"I want to . . . I want to feel like she did. Just for a night," she says. Then she pulls his mouth down to hers.

Turns out he doesn't have it in him, after all.

It wasn't a sexy proposal, Brazuca thinks, much later, as they lie entwined on her sister's bed. Then again, his proposals rarely are. He has a knack for attracting women who aren't the least bit interested in a soft touch. His new leaf doesn't seem to be helping him, even in this. They lie in bed, in the dark, for a long time. Brazuca isn't sure if he made her feel like a whore, but he damn well feels like one himself. It is so silent in Clementine's bedroom that neither of them misses the sound of a key turning in the lock. Brazuca catches Grace's eyes and puts a finger to his lips. He eases to his feet and slides on his jeans. He hears rustling behind him as Grace dresses.

Moving quietly into the hallway, he pauses at the entrance to the living room.

He's not sure what he's hoping to find here, but a tiny woman in a fitted pantsuit isn't it. She's standing in the middle of the living room, holding a phone in the air. Her entire focus is on the pile of boxes stacked to the side of the room. He watches from the doorway, Grace hovering somewhere in the hallway, as the woman moves to the box with the designer purses and rummages through it. Her dark hair is so long and lustrous that, even though Brazuca has a slippery grasp on the concept of hair weaves, he is pretty sure that this woman has one. Finally, she pulls out a small vibrating phone from one of the handbags and switches off the call from her own mobile.

"You must be the dealer," Brazuca says.

The woman pauses. She looks at him, saying nothing. He feels Grace's anger building behind him.

He nods to the phone she'd plucked from the handbag, which is a basic burner, the kind you could find easily and fit with any SIM card. "You used a special phone to communicate with her. Kept your number separate from all her other contacts. Smart."

She slips the phone back into the bag. When she speaks, her voice is pleasant and girlish. She has a crooked smile, one that's oddly endearing. "Oh, keeps things neat."

It's the reason he came to the condo. He'd wondered why he couldn't find records of Clem's dealer on the phone Lam had given him. Clementine lived a very isolated life, but she had to get her supply from somewhere.

Grace appears in the doorway. "You bitch."

The woman studies Grace's face. She is so tiny and is smiling so sweetly that he wants to believe that she's younger than she must be. Because her eyes are calculating, however, he figures she must be at least a decade older than he'd first thought. "You're not wrong about that, honey." She glances from Grace to Brazuca. "Bernie probably asked you to come find me, didn't he?"

"How do you know that?" Brazuca couldn't imagine anyone calling Lam "Bernie"—at least not to his face. Lam was a playboy, but there were certain things even he wouldn't stand for.

"Oh, I know everything about Bernie," she says, waving a manicured hand. "You must be Bazooka. Clem talked about you every now and then, but only because Bernie must have. She didn't have much of a life of her own."

He nods. Bazooka. It's the nickname he can't seem to shake. "And you are?"

"Priya." She sighs. "There's no use trying to hide it anymore. If you describe me to Bernie, he'll know it's me right away. I'm the one who introduced them, you know."

"Lam and Clementine?"

"Yup. I help . . . facilitate parties for certain elite clientele. Bernie couldn't get enough Asian pussy. The ones without strings, I mean. And I knew Clem would be good for him." She deliberately ignores Grace. "Funny how people are. Even here, they stick to their own."

Brazuca steps into the room, putting some distance between him and Grace, who looks about ready to spontaneously combust. "Tell me about what you gave her. Did you know?"

"That she would die? Of course not. It's not something I do often, by the way. Clem just didn't trust anyone else and I owed her a favor. She knew I had contacts. But I told her this time would be the last for a while. Her habit was getting out of control and it wouldn't stay hidden if she kept going like she was. Then Bernie would get involved and I'd be in shit. Like I am now, I guess."

"Where do you get your supply?"

"Wait," says Grace, turning to Brazuca. "Is that why he sent you? This is about the drugs? For fuck's sake! My sister is dead!"

Priya glances toward the door. "Seems like you two have some things to sort out."

Brazuca moves closer to her, making sure to exaggerate his limp. It's a cheap ploy, but he's not above using it when it suits his needs. "Maybe we should speak in private." Which, he realizes now, is what should have happened from the start.

Grace crosses her arms over her chest. "I wanna hear this."

"No," says Priya. "You really don't." Then she walks out, holding two designer handbags. One of them, presumably, her own.

Brazuca throws an apologetic glance at Grace as he follows her sister's dealer out, leaving her much the same way that he found her. In the middle of a room, lost and grieving.

He catches up to Priya at the elevator, not bothering to disguise how fast he can move when he really wants to. And only for short spurts of time. "I can't give you a name," she says, as he reaches her side. "You understand, don't you? Bernie won't but you're a more reasonable person. I can tell just by looking at you."

"I think he really loved her. It's more than just the macho bullshit this time. I can't go back to him with nothing."

She nods, understanding. They are all accountable to someone. The elevator doors open and she steps inside. "You a drinking man?"

"Not anymore." Not since Nora tied him to a bed and poured

rum laced with painkillers down his throat. Which he supposes was officially a relapse, but really can't be considered his fault. He had underestimated her and paid the price for it. He'd felt a bit like a whore then, too, he remembers. It seemed to be a common theme in his dealings with women.

"That's too bad. There's a bar in Gastown that I hear is really good. They've got those fruity cocktails with umbrellas in them. The Lala Lair."

The doors close.

Brazuca considers going back into the condo to help Clementine's sister sort through expensive shit and deal with her grief. On second thought, he presses the down button. He has a job to do, after all, and as much as he wants to attribute his conversation with Priya about getting a drink to his sex appeal, he suspects that she had a different motivation. She told him what he needs to know, in the only way that she felt safe.

As for Grace . . . well, he hopes she got what she needed from him.

8

I WAIT FOR Simone in the backstage area of a tiny craft beer lounge that moonlights as a drag club on Tuesday evenings. There are sequins and tassels everywhere. I feel like I'm in a harem girl's gaudy nightmare, waiting for the pasha to come have his way with me. There is a drag queen in the small dressing room I'm sitting in, applying thick liquid eyeliner with the precision of a surgeon. She ignores me completely as she steps into her high-heeled boots and saunters out the door. Seconds later Simone walks in, covered in body glitter and wearing something lime green that is more tank top than dress. It reminds me of the time that we'd first met at an alcoholics' support group. She'd been wearing something similar, possibly in hot pink.

"You haven't been coming to meetings," she says, when she notices me sitting near a rack of accessories and bright scarves.

"I know." It would upset her if she knew I was going to other kinds of meetings. But in my defense, I can hardly keep track of my own issues. How can I expect her to?

She kicks off her heels and sits at the dressing table, rubbing her stockinged feet. "Or answering my calls."

"I don't like talking on the phone." Ever since last year when I'd washed up on the shore of Vancouver Island, after my daughter, Bonnie, had been kidnapped, I have been avoiding

Simone and her perceptive glances. She is fond of talking about feelings. Mostly hers, but she's also occasionally interested in mine, too.

"And now you want me to look into your father's background, is that it?" Off goes the dress. The tightly muscled body underneath it is an advertisement for the aesthetic value of body hair removal. "I got your message yesterday, Nora, but you've been such a bad friend to me that I'm not sure I feel like helping you out this time. You said you found a veterans' organization for the marines in Lebanon? Maybe you should go through them," she says, knowing full well how I feel about talking to strangers on the Internet about anything other than sex.

You wouldn't know it by looking at her, but Simone is something of a computer security expert. She has her own small operation, which she runs as her alter ego Simon, and seems content with living under the radar in gold lamé stilettos. I don't offer to pay for her help because I suspect that it would go badly for me. So I wait while she carefully removes her wig and makeup and dresses in a plain tracksuit over her opaque stockings. The only thing that's left of her drag personality are her long painted nails, which she uses to scratch lightly at her scalp after she's pulled the pins for her wig out.

"Sorry," I say, summoning a smile. "Let's talk about you."

She grins and leads me out of the room. "I was hoping you'd ask. I'm dating this new guy, Terry, but he's still got one foot and half a nut in the closet. It's been a beautiful nightmare."

I cringe at the mental image this conjures and wonder, not for the first time, why when you ask someone about themself in a general way, they see this as an invitation to annoy the crap out of you with an update on their love life. But this is Simone, so I'm more indulgent. "Anyone would be lucky to have you."

"Even you?" she asks, her voice teasing. I hold the back door open for her and she winks at me as she walks past.

"Especially me." It's true. Who wouldn't want a computer security expert as a lover? On second thought, I understand Terry's dilemma. There is nothing she couldn't find out about you if she wanted to.

"And what would you do when I took off my pantyhose and showed you my dick? Could you handle a man like me?"

The question stumps me. Ever since she introduced herself to me as a woman, and one that could sing the hell out of "Single Ladies" at that, I've never thought of her as a man. I'm not sure if she really wants me to. Even in sweatpants, without her wig, her hair cut short, and no makeup on her face, she is the most delicately feminine person I've ever met. She laughs. "Don't look so shocked. Anyway, you're not butch enough for me."

I'm unexpectedly offended. If the alley we're standing in wasn't so filthy, I'd be trying to peel myself from the floor. Not butch enough? How dare she. I consult my female energy, which is as dubious as it has always been. Not butch enough. Huh.

"I'll look into your father, Nora. You know I will. But I can't get started on it for a couple of weeks. Is that alright?"

"Yeah," I say. "I'm taking a trip soon anyway, so email the details when you can."

Her face lights up. "That's new. Going somewhere exciting?"

I shrug. "I hear a bit of international travel is good for the soul."

"It's Detroit, isn't it? You're going to Detroit." Then she sighs and links her arm in mine. "Come on. Walk me to Terry's place. You can tell me all about how your sobriety is coming along."

It's a cloudy night and the smoke hasn't quite lifted yet, so I convince her to catch a cab instead while I take the bus back to the town house. As I reach the front walk, the light blinks on my phone. The light only blinks when I get a message on a particular app I've installed so that I can communicate with Bonnie, the daughter I gave up for adoption sixteen years ago. That she knows who I am is a result of as spectacular an administrative fuckup as there could have been. Welcome to Canada, land of famous bacon, maple syrup consortiums, and egregious clerical errors. One that resulted in Bonnie's original birth papers falling into the hands of her adoptive parents when she was born. Maybe some exhausted office grunt messed up. Maybe it was his first day at work, or maybe the days numbered into the hundreds. Could have been a middle finger to the system on his very last day. The reason that Bonnie's file slipped through the cracks no longer matters because she now knows who I am.

Not only that, she's also got my phone number.

We never call each other. Never hear each other's voices. We only exchange photographs via this app, to avoid incurring extra charges on our mobile plans. The picture she sends this time is of her foot in a stirrup. It's always her foot somewhere and I'm left to assume the rest of her body is, too. She is okay because her foot is. I suppose I'm meant to glean from this that all of her, her whole, is still going about the business of life. Right now getting a pelvic exam, for instance.

Thanks for the update.

I send her back one of Whisper that I've saved for this purpose.

She shows me her feet and I show her my dog and this is what our relationship is. Photos of our lives, but at a distance and masked by melancholy filters.

Inside the house, I find Seb awake and in the office, poring over his latest draft of the memoir. We have just completed his Kosovo chapters and touched on his marriage, back when he was trying to pass as heterosexual. He's always been one hell of a writer, but this book is so emotionally charged that I had to put it down after I'd read his last pages.

I'm worried because he still won't talk about his latest hospital visit. That's how I know it's bad.

"I don't have to go, you know," I say to him, after I've come back from my walk with Whisper. We haven't seen any signs of the veteran since our impromptu conversation in the park. He has vanished into the night and has taken my equilibrium with him. Still, I was uneasy on our walk and Whisper impatient so we turned back halfway through our usual route anyway. She doesn't like staying away from Seb for very long anymore. At the moment she is lying at his feet, idly licking the rug he has buried his toes in.

"Yes, you do. I need to be alone for a bit, anyway."

"You sure you don't need me?"

He shrugs. "It's mostly done. You did a great job with the research and organization of this, Nora. I'm glad . . . glad for your help."

He can't quite meet my eyes.

When dogs know that they are dying, they'll find a comfortable spot and lie there until it's their time. There is no self-pity in their eyes. They don't fight what's coming. It's their people that become fraught with anxiety at the idea that their loved one is about to die. But for the dog there is only a kind of peaceful resignation.

About an hour later I come back into the office. Seb is on the couch with Whisper curled up at the other end, still at his feet, anchoring the thick blanket that covers him. Because he's asleep, I take his thin hands in mine and squeeze them gently. He returns no pressure. Whisper's tail thumps twice, but she refuses to get up. Probably because she senses that I'm leaving them. That my heavy knapsack at the door is a sign that I'm abandoning the pack in its time of need. Even though I've reached out to Brazuca and left instructions—and some extra money—for the dog walker, I still feel guilty. As I look at them, I add fear to the mix.

What frightens me is that she seems as peaceful there on the couch as he does.

But I can't stay any longer. I have a plane to catch.

9

OUTSIDE THE CLINIC, Bonnie stares at the photo of the dog on her phone. Whisper is, as always, looking directly at the camera, slightly bored. A silver BMW pulls into the lot. Bonnie slings her backpack over her shoulder and walks cautiously to the car. She gets in, but is careful not to look at her mother. Lynn doesn't say a word until they leave the lot, but Bonnie has an idea of what's coming. Her mother's shoulders are set with tension. "Why didn't you tell me?"

"I was just gonna take the bus back but I forgot my pass."

"You didn't answer my question. Why didn't you tell me you were pregnant?" asks Lynn, who thought that Bonnie was adjusting just fine to life in Toronto and the only thing she really had to worry about was a mild red cedar allergy Bonnie had developed last year.

Bonnie shrugs. It was an easy procedure, simpler than she'd thought. It's like her insides had been scraped raw, but the cramps were no more painful than usual. "I thought I could handle it, is all."

Lynn deliberately doesn't look at her daughter when she speaks next. "You thought I'd judge you," she says softly. "Because of everything I went through to adopt you."

Neither of them says it, but it's in the air. Because Lynn could not have children. Because Bonnie is the result of an assault against her biological mother. Because Bonnie had a choice where Nora didn't. And someone to drive her home from the clinic afterward.

Lynn pulls onto the side of the road. The unusually warm weather this fall is starting to break. Toronto is cooler now, but not cool enough for snow. Rain splatters the windows as they stare straight ahead, not daring to meet each other's eyes. She puts her hand over Bonnie's and squeezes it lightly. "I would never judge you, sweetheart. Never. It's your body, your decision. Okay?"

"Yeah, I know. I just didn't want to get into it. Can we not tell Dad?"

Lynn sniffs. "Why would we? It's none of his business."

"Thanks, Mom," Bonnie says, somewhat relieved. Her father is still in Vancouver, probably still screwing his boss. She no longer blames her parents for their marriage breaking apart—that was little kid stuff—but that doesn't mean she is any closer to either of them. Especially Everett, who was the parent that she'd trusted the most until she'd found out last year that he'd been having an affair. She had overreacted to the news, in a spectacular way. She had run away to meet her birth father, who had turned out to be a monster. It is a time in her life that she tries not to think about.

"If anything happens, I just want you to know that you can talk to me. That's all." Lynn pulls the car back onto the road. "Are you hungry?"

"It's too late to eat. I just want to go to bed."

Lynn looks at her out of the corner of her eye as they drive to their condo in the artsy neighborhood of Leslieville, but says nothing in response.

Bonnie has an unsettling feeling that has nothing to do with the clinic—or what had come before. That was a relief, more than anything else. This past summer she had seen her old boyfriend Tommy, who wanted to be called Tom now. It was clear to them both that it was over, but they still missed each other. Bonnie hadn't planned on having sex with him, but she didn't regret it. They just weren't as careful as they used to be.

No, she decides now. She feels a bit tired, is all, but she's not unhappy about what happened back at the clinic. Her impulse to reach out to Nora had been a surprise, but it's really Nora's response that's bugging her. Nora usually takes her time to reply. To catch Whisper in good lighting and looking at the camera is no easy feat. This photo came much quicker than normal, as if Nora had been waiting for Bonnie to send her something. As if she had been waiting for it and preempted her response.

As they drive home, Bonnie can't help but wonder why.

10

THE CLOUDS ARE making beautiful shapes just beyond my little oval window. The flight so far has been smooth, the plane cutting through these shapes like icing. I could stay up here forever, but the flight attendant's fuck-me gaze is slowly but surely shifting to fuck-you as I linger over my meal tray. She has tried to snatch it up several times and I've only saved it by latching on with an iron grip. But if there was a fight to the death between us, my money would be on her. I would never bet against a woman who could wrestle her hair into a bun that uncompromising. A bomb could blow this plane out of the sky and among the wreckage they would find a perfect sphere of hair, still intact, with not a honey-gold strand out of place.

When we land, the U.S. border agent seems skeptical that my reason for traveling here is "tourism" but probably can't imagine what damage I could do to Detroit that hasn't been done to it already. From the airport I rent a Chevy Impala and, driving through the city in the late morning light, I can see why he stopped giving a shit. Abandoned buildings everywhere. Run-down streets. People who won't look each other in the eye. It is a violent shock to my system, especially coming from one of the most beautiful—and least affordable—cities in the world, where so many people want to live that almost nobody gets a chance.

To this. Detroit.

It isn't hot or smoky like Vancouver was when I left it, but there is something thick about the air here. Something heavy. It smacks me straight in the nose, like a jab that's come and gone before I've had time to react. Or maybe my mind is playing tricks again.

I check into a cheap motel in Midtown and try to get my bearings. I was told that it was in a good pocket of the city, near the university, but the demolished lots on the block tell a different story. The motel itself seems okay and the sheets are clean but in a faded flower pattern that is unbearably hopeful, given the motel's depressing location. I can't bring myself to get into that bed but I don't want to go outside until I must, so I sit with the curtains drawn, in an armchair that might just collapse under the weight of one more ass. I'm living on the edge, though, so I don't give it another thought.

I dream of a little girl covered in a man's blood, who slips in it as she opens her mouth in a silent scream and scuttles away. Then I wake up feeling like the city of Detroit crumbled while I slept and most of the debris has fallen on top of me. I have not thought of that little girl in a very long time. And I have never, not once before today, dreamed of her. It's a good thing that it's almost evening, and time to pay a visit. So I can push all the happy childhood memories aside for now.

I don't bother looking at maps, because there's too much in the world that seems incomprehensible to me right now to pay attention to street signs and operate a moving vehicle at the same time. I just follow the GPS on my phone until I arrive at the address on the postcards. The two-story brick house must have been nice once, but its glory has faded over time, in tune with the decline of the entire city. From a quick web search last night, I found out that this neighborhood in southwest Detroit used to be a predominantly white area, but is now more mixed than it had been in its heyday when Americans had dreams and the Motor City was the place they came to live them.

The man who opens the door looks as ancient as the paint chipping off the porch and is so heavy that the walk to the door seems to have taken up the store of strength that he has left for this evening. But his eyes are sharp and clear as he looks at me standing in his doorway. Behind him I can see a little girl peeking out. She puts her finger to her lips. A request for my silence.

I ignore her and focus my attention on the man. The sun is setting just over my shoulder, cradling us both in soft pink light. I don't say anything for a moment. Now that I'm here I wonder if perhaps he'll see something of my father's features on my face. I stay silent, a part of me hoping for recognition.

"Who the hell are you?" he says, by way of greeting.

"My name is Nora Watts. I think you knew my dad, Samuel."

His startled gaze sweeps over me, taking in my jeans and hooded sweatshirt, and the way I stand with my right shoulder angled slightly back and my left foot a half a step forward. Like a fighter. He moves back and is about to close the door in my face. "I don't know who that is."

I stick a foot in the doorway to buy myself some time as I search my coat pocket. I pull out the postcards that were sent to my father, held together now by the scrap of blue silk, and show them to him. "Do you know who sent these? They came from this address."

He pretends not to look at the cards, but I know from a tiny shift of his gaze that he has seen them. "Get out of here. I've got nothing to say to you." I take an unconscious step back at the fury in his voice. He slams the door in my face, but not before I see a hint of something that I recognize in his expression. Something that looks a bit like despair. I linger on the porch for a moment, staring at the little girl who is peeking through the curtains at the nearby window. I would bet the rental car that I have recklessly declined to put additional insurance on that he has not only seen the postcards before, but that it was his hand that addressed them.

Because when I asked him if he knew my father, he lied flat out to my face. I'm almost certain of it. It's that little bit of intuition that I used to get when someone lies rearing its head again. The ability that used to come so easily to me now only trickles through in dribs and drabs, but there is enough of it still left to make me wonder at the man who has just slammed the door in my face.

The little girl opens the window and beckons to me. Her brown hair is piled into a messy ponytail at the top of her head and she's wearing eyeglasses with blue frames that keep slipping down her nose. She has a lollipop in her hand, which she now offers to me. I don't know how to assess the ages of children, never having been a part of Bonnie's upbringing, but I think she might be just slightly older than a toddler. Maybe kindergarten age. I take the lollipop, unwrap it, and hand it back to her. "For you," I say.

"Sanks." Her two front teeth are missing and she has a slight lisp. She pokes her tongue through the hole and grins at me. I may have just encountered the most adorable creature that has ever existed.

"Is that your dad who answered the door?"

She shakes her head.

"Your grandad?"

She nods.

"Does he ever leave the house?"

That gets me a deep gut laugh, the way that children do, that is as surprising as it is delightful. If anything could melt this cold heart of mine, it would be a laugh like that.

"We go to school," she says, still grinning. Then she puts her finger to her lips again, waits a moment while she listens to a sound inside, then goes back to smiling at me. It's astounding to learn the young age at which girls start keeping secrets from the alpha males in their lives.

"Do you like it? School?"

Another headshake.

"That's okay," I tell her. "You don't really need it. You've got to make your own way in the world, you know what I'm saying? Don't end up like me. Be your own person. Follow the money."

She nods very seriously at this piece of unsolicited wisdom. I unwrap the blue silk ribbon from the postcards and hand it to her. "Walk extra slow tomorrow when you go to school, okay?"

I step off the porch and head back to my rental car, which I parked around the block. When I get to the spot, it takes me a minute to realize that the Impala is well and truly gone. Stolen. Disappeared. I cross the street toward the bus stop nearby.

The people under the shelter make no attempt to create space. They stand there with their eyes carefully empty, knowing full well that my car vanished in front of them, but nobody's willing to discuss it. Just an everyday occurrence. Nothing special about it.

11

BRAZUCA WATCHES FROM his car as a frail effigy of Sebastian Crow drifts slowly around the park with Whisper at his heels. It's near ten P.M. and they are the only figures in sight. Crow stops at a bench, puts a hand on the back of it for support, and coughs into the sleeve of his jacket for several long seconds. Then he wipes his mouth with the back of his hand and they make their way back to the town house across the street.

Brazuca feels an inexplicable fury toward Nora for dragging him into this. Wasn't there supposed to be a dog walker? He should have just passed the whole thing off to Warsame, who, with a remarkable sense of prescience, has once again gone off the grid on some assignment or another. It takes Crow a full minute to climb the steps to his front door. Whisper waits patiently at the bottom until he's on the landing, then bounds up to join him.

The image of Crow, bent over a bench and in pain, lingers. Brazuca doesn't manage to shake it until nearly an hour later, standing outside the upscale Gastown restaurant that Clementine's dealer Priya had mentioned.

"You going in or what?" says a woman behind him. She's dressed like a showgirl, with big curls and heels so high her feet are contorted at almost a ninety-degree angle.

Brazuca steps aside to let her pass. "Sorry." She doesn't look back at him, though, or even acknowledge that she's heard.

He walks to the twenty-four-hour vegan diner across the street and sits at a window booth with a view of the front entrance and windows of the Lala Lair.

Picking slowly at something called a supergrain power salad, he keeps an eye on the window. Just past midnight, a slim East Indian man wearing tailored slacks and a mock turtleneck steps out of the Lala Lair, careful to keep out of view of the camera mounted above the front entrance, lights a cigarette, and makes a phone call. For the past two nights, Brazuca has been watching the man do this exact thing. Yesterday, however, he'd ordered a quinoa burger instead of a power salad and his stomach has yet to forgive him.

A woman in a slinky blue dress, with a glittering purse, slides into the seat across from Brazuca. "Hey," she says, yanking up the front of her dress.

Brazuca blinks. It takes him a full second to recognize Clementine's sister. "Grace, what are you doing here?"

"Oh, I've been at the Lala Lair every night this week. Such a fun name to say, don't you think? The Lala Lair. Lalalair. Try that three times in a row. Do you like my dress?"

The dress in question is very fitted everywhere but up top and meant for someone with cleavage. "It's nice."

"Liar. It's god-awful. Can't stay up no matter what I do. It's my sister's," she explains. She looks down. "This purse, too. You know, I think I'm gonna keep this one. Anyway, what was I saying? Oh yeah, my sister. Her tits were fake, so she probably didn't have to worry about filling it out."

"You shouldn't be over there," he says, nodding to the upscale lounge across the street.

"Well, I couldn't stay away, could I? I heard you and that other slut talking by the elevators. Yes, I was listening at the door. What was I supposed to do? Not eavesdrop on her dealer? She mentioned the Lala Lair and I figured it had something to do with Cecily. Somehow. What have you found out? And why are you at this hippie diner instead of across the road?"

"A man's gotta eat," he says, his voice flat. She doesn't have to know that he's already been in there, scoped it out, and tried to glean as much information as he could without drawing unwanted attention.

They stare at each other. Under the layers of garish makeup, inexpertly applied, her expression is serious. She pulls a flash drive from her purse and passes it to him. "I have a friend in criminology at UBC who's been looking into drug traffickers for his thesis. He gave me some material on Wild Ten."

"Don't call it that. You're just romanticizing it."

"It is the street name for it," she insists. "He says it's relatively new, but it's catching on. There are these underground drug labs in China that make bootleg fentanyl. They're also playing around with the chemical structure of the drug and creating new versions, as well. Like Wild Ten. Makes it really hard to regulate."

He passes the drive back to her. "Grace—"

"I want to know what happened to my sister as much as you do. And not because I'm collecting a paycheck," she says, clearly unaware that when it comes to digs like that, he's practically Teflon. Everyone's got to make a living. They can't all be urban planners.

The waitress comes over with a bill and Brazuca pays in

cash. When she leaves, he gives Grace a hard look. "You know what happened to your sister. She overdosed and died. End of story. You shouldn't be here or across the street, either. Go home, Grace."

"Don't tell me where I should be," she hisses.

"I'm serious. Don't you have school or something?"

"We had sex once, you asshole. You don't get to talk to me like that. I'm a grown woman. I can be wherever I want." She slides off the chair clumsily, slinging the fancy purse over her shoulder, and curses as the chain strap gets caught in her hair. "Jesus," she says, as she walks toward the ladies' room, attempting to untangle it.

As soon as she's out of sight, Brazuca leaves the diner and crosses the street. With the hood of his jacket up, he stumbles toward the alley, allowing his limp to throw him off balance. Bracing a hand on the brick wall in the alley behind the Lala Lair, he swears as his zipper gets caught and he struggles to get it free.

A sleek BMW pulls into the laneway, picks up a passenger who has just exited the back door to the bar, and honks at him to move. He raises an arm automatically to cover his face from the glare of the headlights and flips the driver the finger.

The passenger window rolls down and the man in the turtleneck tries to get a good look at Brazuca, who is partially shielded by his hood. "Move."

"Yeah yeah, just a sec, dude." Brazuca's voice is gruff, as nondescript as he can make it. He pushes away from the wall and walks toward the street, where he immediately slips into the shadows of a doorway. When the car turns onto the road, lit from a streetlight just off the alley, the license plate is perfectly visible. He snaps a quick photo with his phone. "Gotcha," he says quietly, though no one is there to hear him.

He makes a call to the same number he texts the photo to. The voice that answers the phone is both confused and angry. "What the fuck?" mutters Detective Christopher Lee from the Vancouver Police Department. "You know some of us have real jobs to go to in the morning."

"Nice to hear your voice, too, sweet cheeks. Need a favor. You owe me."

"You gave me one tip in all the time you've been off the force. One."

"Sometimes one is all you need. Sent a plate number to you. Driver picked up the manager of the Lala Lair."

There's a brief silence as Lee turns that around in his mind. "The Lala Lair, eh? Yeah, heard some whispers back when I was in the Gang Unit."

"Find out if there are still whispers?"

"What's that, Your Majesty? You're buying beer this week-end?"

"Yeah, okay," says Brazuca, who never bothered to tell his old partner that he's an alcoholic and, apart from a recent relapse, has been mostly sober for two years. "I'm buying beer. I'll let you get back to your beauty sleep."

"Damn right," says Lee. "Just because you've let yourself go doesn't mean we all have to."

Pulling his hood closer to his face as he rounds the corner,

Brazuca sees a woman in an ill-fitting dress hailing a cab. She's not wearing a jacket, and has her arms wrapped around herself to ward off the chill in the air. Even though it's been a mild fall, it's not exactly weather to forget your jacket in. But it's possible she's not thinking clearly these days. "Gotta go," Brazuca says to Lee.

"You could have waited till morning for this shit."

"You were up anyway."

There's a click on the other end of the line as Lee hangs up. The cab zips past the woman without stopping. "Asshole!" she shouts. When she notices Brazuca walking toward her, she angles her body away.

"Hey," he says. "Wanna make me feel like a whore?"

Grace turns back to face him, narrowing her eyes. "You know, sex work is no joke. It's a lot of people's livelihoods. You shouldn't be poking fun at it." This is said with absolutely no acknowledgment of the fact that she'd started this kind of comment, back at her sister's fancy apartment, paid for by the man Clementine was sleeping with.

"Who's laughing?"

She shrugs. "As long as we're on the same page." Then she slips her small hand into his, he suspects more for balance than anything else, as they make their way to his car parked in the lot down the block. She directs him to the English Bay condo. On the elevator ride up, she opens his jacket and steps into his arms. He can see right down the front of her dress, which is probably her intention.

He could get used to women using him for sex, he realizes. And at least she's honest about it. But still, he can't quite figure her out. She seems like too sensible a woman to let grief overtake her like this. Seems people have become more complicated or he has become simpler. But he doesn't understand how either could have happened without some kind of advance warning.

12

THE CLOCK ON my phone tells me that it's a new day, but my body refuses to believe it. Trying to get back to my motel using public transit last night sapped most of my energy, and now I'm back on it. In the past I have maligned public transportation in Vancouver, which, I now see, was grossly unfair. When it comes to clusterfucks, getting around Detroit takes the prize. And the bureaucratic nightmare that is trying to report a stolen rental car in Detroit has defeated my fighting spirit. I am, for the moment, without wheels. After three buses and a heated argument with someone who appeared to be a transit official, I arrive back at the house.

It was a good thing that I started out before dawn, because I get there just in time to see the man and the adorable imp from yesterday walk down the street, heading in the direction opposite from mine. There is an elementary school about a ten-minute walk away, but the man doesn't seem particularly light on his feet and the little girl has made me an implicit promise that I hope she keeps. On the outside, I have twenty minutes to half an hour to find what I'm looking for.

As I knock out the basement window with a hammer wrapped in a towel I have stolen from my motel, I hope that people on the street will be as unobservant as they were yesterday while my car was jacked. When the man of the house opened the door yesterday, I didn't see an alarm panel by the doorway. Just because I didn't see it doesn't mean that it isn't there somewhere, but there are certain risks I'm willing to take. It's a long way down from the window to the ground and I know my bad ankle can't take the pressure, so I lower myself as far as I can and drop down on my good leg. For the most part, the thick leather gloves I'm wearing have protected my hands from the broken glass edging the frame.

From a quick glance, the basement is full of junk and old sports equipment, so I try my luck up the stairs. On the dining room table I find a stack of bills addressed to Harvey Watts, but nothing in the way of personal correspondence. The little girl has invaded all rooms here with her artwork and her toys. There is no safe place on this floor for a man's personal belongings, so up I go again. There are two bedrooms on the second floor and a third that has been converted to an office. Because I don't have much time, I go straight to the office.

It could be dumb luck that I find what I'm looking for right on the floor by the desk, or it could be that, after I left yesterday, Harvey Watts took a trip down memory lane and didn't bother to put the files away after he was done. Maybe he wanted to have his memories handy, the way that people sometimes do when the past comes knocking.

In any case, here in this battered briefcase are the documents of my father's life. There are several photos of two boys growing up. I realize that the man who slammed the door in my face must be his adoptive brother. I only have enough time to do a cursory check on the briefcase before the door opens and closes downstairs. Outside the windows, the gutters are so rusted I don't think they'll hold my weight. I slip quietly into the hall and down the stairs, hoping that Harvey has missed his breakfast and that I can just head out the front door.

Unfortunately, my luck has never been that good.

As my foot hits the last step, I hear the soft click as the safety is flicked off a gun. In the narrow hallway, somewhere behind me.

My hands go up, the briefcase still in them.

"You know, people get the wrong idea about this neighborhood all the time. We still got a community here, girlie, and people know how to use cell phones when somebody knocks out a basement window."

Well, it wasn't a perfect plan. And it's been a long time since I've had to sneak around like this.

I turn, careful to keep my movements slow and steady. Harvey Watts has a handgun pointed right at my heart. Michigan isn't an open-carry state for nothing. I wonder if he had taken it with him to walk his granddaughter to school. It's not out of the realm of possibility. "You lied to me about my father. You did know him. He was your brother."

Watts snorts and the gun does a little dance. I try not to think about the fact that the safety is off. "Some brother."

"I just came to take what belongs to me, that's all."

"That briefcase don't belong to you. It's been mine since he upped and left, telling me he's off to find his real damn family. Like I weren't nothing. Like we didn't grow up together in this fucked-up house."

"Aw," I say in mock sympathy. If he wants to start in on difficult childhoods, we could be here all week.

His cheeks flush. "You know I've thought from time to time about what Sammy's girls would be like. Never imagined you."

If this was meant as a compliment it falls short of the mark. A compliment is all in the tone. His has all the warmth of a polar ice cap, one that is holding out against global warming. "Look, I just want to know about my dad. That's all."

"Yeah, well, after he left I didn't hear nothing back from him. He said to forward all his mail to his place in Winnipeg, but he never spoke to me after that. Then your sister writes me years ago, telling me he died and could I please tell her his life story. All I got of him is in that briefcase there and good fucking riddance. Take it if you want. I ain't sad at all that he's gone. You tell your sister that. Lauren, or whatever her name is. Just leave me the hell alone."

He puts his free hand on the wall and coughs into his sleeve. "B'fore you go, though, someone is paying for that window downstairs."

He's not joking. I look at the gun. And then I put the few bills of cash from my wallet on the stand in the front hall. I retreat with my hands up, pausing at the door. "Did he ever . . . did he ever say anything about Lebanon? About some trouble he had there?"

"Like he would tell me," Harvey Watts says, his expression dark. "Haven't had a thing to do with your dad in a long time, and that's how I like to keep it. He took off when he was eighteen and didn't come back until after he left the military. Then he was gone again. So I don't owe you nothing."

Maybe it's pointless, but I have to try. "After the military, though. What did he say about that?"

Watts takes a step toward me and I am careful not to make any abrupt motions as I move back, maintaining the space we have created between us. A delicate dance, with a gun as the high school chaperone, keeping us apart. "We're done here," he says. "Get out. And don't come back. Don't be talking to my grand-daughter, either. She told me how you gave her a lollipop. You stay the hell away from her."

The little traitor. You can't trust anybody in this world. She must have kept the bit about the ribbon to herself.

I leave, this time via the front door. Like a normal person visiting her long-lost uncle, with a briefcase full of keepsakes tucked under her arm.

A curtain twitches from the house opposite and I see a shadow by one of the upstairs windows. The concerned citizen, no doubt. Waiting to see how it all turns out.

Me, too, I suppose.

13

THE TROUBLE WITH Lebanon is that there'd been a lot of trouble in Lebanon. During the Cold War, it had been the place where proxy wars by the Americans, the Soviets, and multiple Middle Eastern factions were fought, along with its own internal strife and the civil war that ensued. It's where Hezbollah was born and the point of inception for the world's current suicide-bombing phenomenon. Where refugees from Palestine fled to simmer as the waters around them boiled. Where they'd been massacred in 1982 while a group of foreign soldiers stood by their camps and watched. Hard to figure out exactly what my father might have gotten himself into there but, according to a stack of incomplete paperwork, he was, in fact, a marine.

Maybe I knew that.

I think I must have figured out that he'd been in the military after he left Detroit as a teenager, and before his big move to Canada. Like so much, however, I'd chosen not to look too closely. Him being a marine in Lebanon, in the late seventies or early eighties meant that he'd probably been stationed either at the American Embassy or with one of the peacekeeping missions there. The public is not generally aware of this benign overture toward stability in the Middle East. Not that those peacekeepers ever did much for stability in the region, but at first there was a kind of youthful optimism about it, like the beauty pageant contestants who stand onstage with their tits on display and wish for world peace. No matter how many bikini-clad young women or uniformed soldiers or gray-haired bureaucrats wish for it, peace is a hard thing to pin down. But if he was in Lebanon, my father must have been part of the attempt. In his own way.

I add the contents of the briefcase to the contents of the box and spread them all out on the floor of my motel room in a circle. In the middle of the circle I sit in a desk chair with wheels and walk my feet around to move the chair. I saw this once on a British television program and it resulted in a spectacular breakthrough by the lead investigator. But it doesn't work for me. I get rid of the chair and just sit in the middle of the circle. I focus on a photograph of my father in uniform with three other men, their arms slung around each other. The photo isn't dated and there's no other identifying information on it. My father didn't, after all, flip the picture over and write down the names of the men with him. I stare at their faces and, even given some leeway for the decades that have passed between now and the day this photo was taken, I don't see the veteran who was following me. He must have missed the memo for this photo op.

After a few minutes of thinking about it, I post the photo on a comment section of the website for the Marine Corps veterans of Beirut, on the off chance that someone might recognize my father, or one of the others. From what I've seen of their online discussions, they're a pretty active bunch.

I wish I knew more about his time in the military, but his life had defied documentation. If he had managed to accumulate any at all, this little I have in front of me is what is left of it.

It's not enough, even, to put in a request for his military records. Not even a service number. I close the webpage for the online requisition form. There are too many required fields still blank for me to continue, so I turn back to the contents of the briefcase.

There's another scrap of faded blue silk here, cut like a ribbon. Just like I'd found in the yellow shoe box.

At the police station a few hours later, I run the ribbon through my fingers as I stand in front of the desk officer on duty. It doesn't seem possible that he was admitted to the Detroit Police Department based on the stellar results of his personality test. If he's ever had an ounce of sympathy, he's used it all up on the person before me.

"And the vehicle was stolen yesterday?" he says, frowning.

"Sometime between six forty and six fifty-five in the evening. Do you want me to write it down for you?"

"Well, why didn't you call yesterday?"

"I did. My phone battery died while I was on hold." A world war could have begun and ended in the time I was on hold. Mountains could have crumbled. Glaciers melted. I think about mentioning these things to the officer, but he has chosen this moment to lose himself in whatever's on his screen. Which, because he seems like the sadistic type, I imagine to be a video of a kitten climbing out of a cardboard box.

"Okay, have a seat. Someone will come take a report."

"But I thought that's what you're doing?"

"No. I'll get someone for you."

"I've waited twenty minutes just to speak to you!"

"Ma'am, please calm down." The modulation in his voice

doesn't change. He's clearly dealt with far worse threats than me. He disappears down the hall.

My phone rings and on the call display I see it's the dog walker, Sunil. "Everything okay?" I say when I answer.

"Yeah, yeah. It's just . . ." He coughs nervously.

"What's wrong?"

"Mr. Crow . . . looks terrible . . ."

I frown. Either the connection leaves something to be desired or Sunil hasn't learned how to hold a phone properly. "Call an ambulance and get him to the hospital."

"He refuses. Says he's got . . . appointment tomorrow and he's going to wait for that . . . sure he's fine," he says.

And I'm sure he's lying. But before I can respond, he continues quickly. "I had some trouble reaching you earlier—"

"My phone was dead."

". . . Okay. It's just . . . Maybe I can have the number of the place you're staying? Just in case I need to get a message to you?"

I give him the name of the motel and tell him what room I'm staying in, and what to do if Seb gets worse, and how to handle Whisper if he does. There could have also been a few tips thrown in on how to survive a zombie apocalypse with Seb's and Whisper's safety intact. Sunil hangs up in the middle of it. Minimum wage isn't enough money to deal with this kind of shit, even for a college student.

After failing to get him back on the line a few times, my phone loses its will to fight the good fight. The screen goes blank. I can't even send a message to Brazuca to check up on them. I slump against the hard chairs in the waiting room, feeling like Hamlet. Pathetic. In limbo, with the ghost of my dead father hovering over me. Stuck between doing what I know is right, which is leaving this town, and wasting time in my own personal hell. The desk cop comes back into the room with a mug in his hand and continues to pretend I don't exist. I suppress my murderous instincts and continue to wait it out. Like a confused asshole.

14

IT'S LATE BY the time I get back to the motel. I charge my dead phone and take a lukewarm shower because that's all the highest heat setting will get me. When I emerge from the bathroom, there are half a dozen new emails in my inbox. All of them are in response to the photo I put up, speculating on the identities of the men with my father. None are from any of the marines in question.

I'm left with a problem that a multitude of women face every day: how to find a man in America. Being Canadian, I'm out of my depth. I don't think kinky ads will help me here. Online searching only gets me so far, and I'm looking for a number of men. I am also looking for specific ones. Marines who presumably served with my father. Only one of the names suggested by the helpful citizens of the Internet seems to be in the Detroit area. Two of the men in the photo have obituaries that I've unearthed. I'm not sure how useful tracking down the marines in this photo will be, but I send the names to Simone anyway. Maybe she can help me figure out how to get in touch with their families.

Then I do what any normal woman would do when the menfolk are scarce. I go to a place where people drown their sorrows.

The bar is just gearing up for the evening, so the crowd hasn't gotten too raucous yet. A few tables are scattered with people, but the barstools are filling up. It's a working-class joint, but not necessarily a rough one. People seem largely to be minding their own business. I zero in on an older man at the far end of the bar, in the corner. He's settled comfortably, watching the news crawl and ignoring everyone around him. There's an empty stool next to the man sitting beside him, who is roughly my age, so I hoist myself up on it and order a virgin piña colada with an umbrella. The bar man stares at me hard until I revise it to cranberry juice. "Want some vodka in that?" he asks.

"Do I look like a pussy? I take my juice straight up. I'd inject it raw if needles weren't so damn expensive," I say, tapping my veins. He takes this as his cue to give me my drink and move to the other end of the bar before I can try to communicate with him some more.

I look at the man beside me, who has the fashion sense of a long-haul trucker. "What's the point of any of this, am I right?" I say, with a hand gesture that is meant to say "life" but only ends up upsetting a menu stand.

He gives me a disgusted look and edges away. But he's on a stool and there's only so far he can go.

"I mean, my ex, that loser. He gets out of jail, shows up at my trailer at six o'clock in the goddamn morning and I think he's looking for sex, but that's not what's on his mind. He's come for the dog. Can you believe it?"

He sighs. "Can't get no peace nowhere," he mutters, downing the remainder of his cheap whiskey in one long gulp. He puts some money on the bar and leaves.

I take the opportunity to move onto his empty stool and settle in. The older man looks at me. "You sure do have a way with people."

"It's my good looks and shining personality. You a regular here?"

He laughs. "S'pose you could say that."

I don't crack a smile. "I hear this bar is owned by Mark Kovaks, used to be in the marines?" Kovaks was the remaining name on the photograph. The only one I'd managed to locate, who conveniently had a bar in downtown Detroit to save me some trouble.

The smile disappears and he takes a good long look at me. "Yeah. He's been gone about a week. Went to Jersey to see his grandkids. 'Spect he'll be back soon."

"I think Mr. Kovaks served with my father in the marines. Thought he might remember him. He died when I was a child," I add, conversationally.

"Sorry to hear that. In the line of duty?"

"No. After." In the long mirror mounted over the bar we can see a mic and amp being set up on a little stage in the corner. "I'm looking for information from anyone who might have served with him. Maybe something happened that's not online. He was from here. Detroit. I was hoping Mr. Kovaks could help me out." I don't tell him about the list of names.

"Take shots in the dark, do ya?" We watch in the mirror as the MC does a sound check. It seems we are to be blessed with an open mic night.

"Apparently."

"What's his name?"

"Samuel Watts."

"Never heard of him 'round here. What rank?"

The MC announces a cash prize to the winner of the night, which distracts me for a moment. "I don't know."

"Battalion? Unit? Postal code?"

"Not any of that, either."

"Well, good luck to you," he says, his voice heavy with doubt. "You don't seem to have much to go on."

"You're telling me."

"Would help if I could, but I wasn't even in the corps. Bad heart." He downs his beer and signals the bartender for another. His heart may be shoddy, but his liver appears to be hanging in there. "My brother was. Used to come here with him till he kicked it. Served in 'Nam, survived hell, gets hit by a drunk driver. Life."

"What's the point of any of it?"

On this positive note, we avoid eye contact and watch the performances, if they could be called that, in the mirror. After half a dozen god-awful renditions of pop songs, a collective groan ripples through the room. And I thought it couldn't get any worse. A young black musician who looks to be in his late twenties perches himself on a stool. There's a little smile on his face, but it's not directed at anyone in particular.

"Calm down," the MC tells the crowd. "Y'all didn't bring it so we're gonna have a repeat of last week and the week before, and the week before that. This is on you." But, funnily enough, he doesn't sound unhappy about it.

For a moment after the MC leaves the stage, the man on the stool just runs his fingers over the strings of his acoustic guitar. Absently plucking here and there. Just getting started. I'm not much of a guitar player, but I know enough about it to appreciate what he's doing. He's beginning the story right now, from a place of apparent carelessness. If you watch closely enough you can see that there's nothing careless about it. This is all for our benefit, so we can see what he puts into it. So we appreciate it before the first note even plays. And he doesn't strum. He picks, which is a skill unto itself. The chords form into something unpredictable and magnetic. Then he opens his mouth and sings a song about being in love with a woman who is trouble personified. I've never heard it before but his smooth voice makes every note resonate in some part of me. It may be an original and, if that's the case, I wonder why he's not a huge star. Because that's what's onstage right now. Raw talent and star power. He breaks into an incredible guitar riff in the middle and it's all I can do to keep myself on the seat. It's that good.

I stand up at the end of the song. The MC takes this as some kind of cue, even though I'd just meant to leave on a high point in the night. "And we've got another contender!" he announces.

The crowd shakes off the residual enchantment, not sure if they're in the mood to hear something else. They eye me with a kind of hostile curiosity. "Go on, honey," says my friend on the barstool.

I take a few hesitant steps toward the stage. Pause. What decides it for me, I think, is the look on the bluesman's face. So sure. So confident that he has something that I don't. I'm not above playing dirty. He is barely off the stool when I take the Martin leaning against the amp and lower the mic.

"What are you going to do for us?" shouts the MC.

I don't reply. Like the bluesman, I block him out. Being onstage is about presence. You can either give it away or take it for yourself.

I'm not much of a giver.

The young bluesman raises a brow at me. I ignore him, too. My focus is on the guitar.

When he found out I could play, Seb dug out an old acoustic guitar that one of Leo's friends had left behind when she moved to Paris. I'm not half bad. Because I'm in a bar, and because I'm feeling perverse, I start the chords to "Rehab." Pints of beer pause halfway to thirsty mouths. Partially because of the dire warning in the song about the dangers of alcohol consumption, but also because it is a truth universally acknowledged that nobody in their right mind should ever do an Amy Winehouse cover. Because you can't listen to Amy Winehouse without being deeply unsettled by the lyrics. You can't help but wonder what the world lost because she had said no to rehab, thrice. Also, when the man in the song asks her why she thinks she's here and she says she's got no idea, that is all of us, at any given moment of the day. On any given day of our lives.

My voice, low and raspy to begin with, catches on the word *Daddy* for just a fraction of a second, but it becomes much too real, much too fast for me. A change comes over me as I sing now, and it has nothing to do with wanting to show up some cocky young bluesman. I'm not fine, and my daddy will never know it. So I sing about that and it is my way of reliving what that little girl saw on the day she came home from school, the day that changed her life forever.

The sweaty pile of cash is inevitable.

As the MC hands it over, I wink at the bluesman. He laughs when he catches me at the door. "I set that win up for you. You can at least buy me a drink," he says, catching me before I reach the door.

"Buy it yourself."

"Would, but someone jacked my pot, which I thought was a sure thing. A couple days a week I do this open mic. Was counting on the prize money."

I've also been a broke musician, so I know what that feels like. I wave to the bartender, who pretends to be so totally immersed in stacking glasses that he can't be bothered to come over. "I'm Nate," says the bluesman, holding out a hand. We shake. His voice when he speaks is a little rougher than his singing voice.

He nods to the bartender, who brings him a beer. And reluctantly pours me a cranberry juice. "Vodka?" the bartender asks hopefully. I tsk and shake my head.

"Never seen you in this joint before," Nate says, looking out at the crowd. They are mostly working people here, likely clocked out from their day at the factory—if there still are factories here in Detroit.

"Never been. Came in looking for a military man."

"Well, look no further," he says, grinning. "Did some time in the army, myself."

"Sorry, should have said a marine."

He sighs. "Everyone's a critic. Why a marine?"

I'm becoming something of a chatterbox in my winter years, so I tell him about my father. He sips at his beer for some time afterward. "Long time to be hanging on to that hurt."

When I used to work for Leo, every now and then an elderly lady would wander in with photographs of her long-lost cousin Mathilda, who ran away in the seventies. Leo would sit with her for as long as it took for the story to come out, then he would gently guide her to the door. There's no point in taking cases that are more than a few years old, he would tell me. And he's right. The trail is so cold by the time they've come to us that there's little chance of generating fresh leads. The client is never satisfied. Now that the client is me, I agree. "I'm like an elephant. I never forgive."

"Never forget, you mean?"

"That, too." There are some people who can remember and forgive. But I'm not one of them.

We finish our drinks and he drives me back to my motel. Which I only allow because I can't bear the thought of another delightful Detroit public transit experience right now. He switches off the ignition when we get there. There are no hugs, no handshakes, no polite pecks on the cheek. "Want to see my studio?" he asks, as I reach for the door handle.

"No," I say. Then I get out of the car before he gets the right idea about me.

15

THERE ARE SOME things that go bump in the night that can be chalked up to the imagination. Or are simply the result of an old house settling, or someone on the floor above you going to the kitchen for a midnight snack. Perhaps the long-married couple next door has decided to give the old bedsprings their biannual workout.

But then there are some things bumping about because they're searching through your things as you walk through the door. Because I've approached from the street and not the back parking lot, and because I'm dressed to be run over in the dark, the man in my room doesn't see me coming. It's fair. I didn't see him, either. We stumble upon each other like teenagers on prom night in the backseat of a car that his father let him borrow with a wink and a knowing smile.

And in the end, there's a little blood, but it's from the guy's nasal cavity as I slam the heel of my hand reflexively into his nose.

Okay, there's a lot of blood.

"Oh, God. Oh fuck," he groans, disoriented, as he tries to grab hold of me with one hand and keep his nose intact with the other. We are both slippery with his blood, but he's bigger than me and manages to knock me to the ground.

I roll out of reach, but he's between me and the door, so I

wrench the bedside lamp from its socket. It was the only light I'd left on in the room, and now we're plunged into darkness. I hold it in front of me while I bang on the connecting wall to the room next to me with my free fist and shout "Fire!" at the top of my lungs to whoever is sleeping there.

My voice, having been warmed up from the open mic, is particularly sonorous tonight.

The robber apparently thinks so, too. He's out the door before I can take another breath, his back illuminated for a brief moment in the harsh security light outside my room as he pulls up the hood of his dark sweatshirt. A moment later, a second set of footsteps clatter off behind him.

Doors from the other rooms open, and then Nate comes crashing in. "Saw a couple guys take off. You okay?"

I hit the main light switch and check the tiny bathroom, then I sit on the bed. "Yeah, I'm fine."

"You got . . . there's blood on your hands."

I get up wordlessly and wash them in the sink.

Nate stands in the doorway, unsure of what to do next. Other budget travelers come wandering by in their nightclothes and try to look past him into the room. "Can someone get the manager?" he says to a woman in a red velour sweat suit.

She doesn't move. "Where's the fire?"

"No fire. You're fine."

"But what about those guys who were running away from here?"

"Just let the manager know we need to talk to him." Then he closes the door firmly in her face.

It suddenly hits me. The intruders, whoever they were, had been seen and I'd shouted "Fire!" at the top of my lungs. "There'll have to be a police report, won't there?"

"I'm guessing so."

"Damn it." I'm having the worst luck today.

"Don't worry," says Nate. "You can come stay with me after we get this sorted out."

I bunch the hideous bedsheets up in my hands and stare up at him. Does Nora go home with Nate after the adrenaline high is over, after the motel manager offers her another room, this one with a small lockbox inside, at a thirty percent discount? After the detective, who had inexplicably turned up right after the uniformed cops in their patrol car, takes her report almost an hour later and casts aspersions on her meager belongings?

"So nothing was taken?" asks the detective, whose name is something like Sanchez. He's in his fifties and looks exhausted. I would feel sorry for him, except I can't imagine anyone in the world feeling more tired than I do right now. What is keeping me up at the moment is imagining myself pressing my thumbs into the deep dimples on his cheeks. He would be adorable except for the frown on his face.

"No."

He looks at my knapsack on the bed. "This is all you brought with you? Did you check everything twice?"

"I checked three times." And then I tell him about my rental car being stolen and, really, they've got to do a better job at protecting tourists.

"Not a great area for tourism," he replies, writing down the details. "Tried Ann Arbor?"

I would go over the bridge, across the border, and into Windsor to get away from this conversation if I could. But I just nod and say, "That's a great idea."

"I'll be honest with you. You didn't give us much to go on here. There've been a string of break-ins in the area that I'm looking into, but this doesn't fit the pattern."

"There was a tattoo," I say, suddenly remembering the robber pausing in the doorway of the room, just about to pull his hood up. I hold my hair off my nape and point to the base of my neck. "Right here."

Sanchez hesitates for a moment. In the mirror above the dresser, I see his gaze linger at my neck. "What was the tattoo of?"

"It was too far away to say for sure. But definitely at the base of the neck, like a barcode."

"Was it a barcode?"

"No. I would have recognized that."

A flicker of something crosses his face. He's about to say something, but decides to keep it to himself in the end. He nods. "Alright then. Stay out of trouble while we look into this. Seems to be following you around, ma'am. Stolen car and now this? You gotta be real careful in Detroit," he says, as though you don't have to be real careful everywhere. He hands me a business card. On his way out he casts a suspicious glance at Nate, my guardian angel, who hasn't left the room.

"Your car got jacked?" Nate grins, after the cop has left. "Girl, maybe Detroit ain't the place for you."

"Yeah, no kidding. You got a couch at your place?"

"A small one. My grams used to call it a love seat. Would that do?"

I stare at the bed and assess my options. "Does it sag in the middle and have some kind of flower pattern?"

"The ugliest kind of flower pattern you ever saw."

"Then I'll be right at home."

So she does go home with Nate after all, I think, after we get back into his car. "This is the east side," Nate says, after a while of driving in silence.

"It's not as bad as people say it is," he adds, seeing my dubious expression.

"I'm not scared," I say, as he pulls into a darkened driveway on a street full of dark houses interspersed with lots that seem to consist mainly of piles of rubble. The front of the house is dark—surprise, surprise—but I can see a light on toward the back.

"It actually is that bad, though. You should be shaking in your boots. Here." He hands me a screwdriver from the glove compartment. "Keep that close."

"Wait—" But he has already left the car.

I'm not sure if he's joking or not. I slip the screwdriver into my pocket anyway because I'm not one to take a dire warning lightly. I follow him toward the back of the house. I hear low voices inside, but Nate doesn't seem concerned. "My brother Kev and his girl Ash sometimes have meetings in here." Before I can ask what kind of meetings we're talking about, he lets himself in the back door with a key and we step into the kitchen. There is a chorus of Hey, Nates, but we are mostly ignored as we remove our shoes because whatever they're discussing is heating up.

There is a young man who looks a lot like Nate sitting on

the kitchen counter with his legs spread wide. A woman with a septum piercing is between them, leaning her back against his chest. This must be Kev and Ash. Clustered around the kitchen table are a handful of mature students from a social studies class. Lifelong students, it seems, because they're all pushing thirty and talking about the political implications of living in a postcolonial landscape of oppression. I understand maybe three words of every ten. By the alarmed expression on his face, Nate is in the same leaky boat.

"But how do we tell allies from appropriators?" says a man in a Prince T-shirt, who is not white or black but is not something immediately identifiable, either. They all nod sagely at this question and pass a joint along to help the intellectual process.

"Basement," Nate whispers to me, nodding to the door just off the kitchen.

Both Nate and I hustle downstairs before their politics become airborne and we are made to know more but understand less about our postcolonial landscape of depression. "I try not to see them too much outside of gigs," he explains to me. "They got me playing some of their events."

"Please tell me you don't do 'Redemption Song.'"

He laughs. "Right after 'Imagine,'" he says, locking the door at the top of the stairs and shrugging past me. "Got a set with them at an Angel's Night rally coming up next week. Bigger crowd than I'm used to."

"Angel's Night?"

"Yeah. Longstanding Detroit tradition. Night before Halloween when assholes would go crazy and set fires. Used to be called Devil's Night but the community took it back in the nineties and put a different spin on it. Now we've got community patrols and events to keep the streets safe."

These kinds of patrols exist in pockets of Canada where violence or addiction have taken entire neighborhoods by storm. But I have always wondered if walking the streets armed with little more than good intentions is beneficial for one's mental health. "Does it work?"

He considers the question for a moment. "Ah, a little bit . . . We got less fires . . ." Then he gives up. "We try." He unlocks the keypad deadbolt at the bottom of the stairs. The staircase and hallway are dimly lit and dingy, but smell strongly of disinfectant. He turns on the light in the room and leads me into his inner sanctum. I step inside and take in the tiny, neat studio with a bathroom off to the side. There is a desk with a brand-new MacBook Pro gleaming like the Holy Grail. A beat-up old Fender Strat is holding up a wall covered with newspaper and egg cartons. Strangely I feel no fear as Nate locks the door behind us and it's only then that I put it together that the makeshift soundproofing on the walls is the source of the blessed silence we are cloaked in now.

"Some fire hazard you got here." I nod to the cartons, trying (and failing) to keep the excitement out of my voice. There is a midi keyboard and a condenser mic set up in the corner of the room.

He puts his guitar case down carefully and takes up the Strat. "I know. Beautiful, ain't it?"

I don't know whether he's talking about the guitar or the room, but it is beautiful. Even the Martin, which must have seen better days, looks like all I'd ever want to come home to.

The hideous flowered love seat is in the corner of the room, but instead of detracting from the setup, it adds a certain lived-in feel to the place. There's nothing sterile or haphazard about this room. It is a piece of his heart.

"You're the first person I've let come in here," he says, tossing me a bottle of water. I catch it reflexively with one hand. "There's another bathroom off the hall outside, if you need it. I record in this one."

He types his password into the Mac and opens up Pro Tools. I watch in silence as he plugs the guitar into the computer, runs the cord into the bathroom, then closes the door behind him. When he starts playing his distinctive finger picking style, I know instinctively that he's sitting in the tub with the Strat in his lap. The acoustics in a bathroom can be amazing, with the reverb bouncing off all the porcelain and tiles. The first chords of his original tune that he played at the open mic come through the space at the bottom of the door.

I close my eyes to the raw, haunting melody that is being played in a bathtub and recorded on his laptop. It's the first time ever that I've been lulled to sleep by the sound of live music. Right before I fall into oblivion, I wonder what I'm doing here in Detroit at all. How I'd convinced myself that I needed answers to the questions around my father's death. How I convinced myself that they could be answered. I should be shaken by the fact that my car was stolen and I was almost mugged in my own damn motel room. I should be at the town house with Whisper at my side, watching Seb die. Instead, I am on the ugliest sofa I have ever seen, thinking about men and death and the blues.

16

THE NEXT MORNING, Bernard Lam takes a long look at Brazuca's disheveled hair, his wrinkled clothes from the night before, the lipstick stain on his collar, and lets him into the Point Grey mansion without a word. A housekeeper doesn't pause in her polishing of the entranceway table as he and Brazuca pass her by. She blends into the background as easily as the potted plants in the corner, as she was no doubt meant to do. Lam gives her a friendly smile before showing Brazuca into the study.

"I'm just about to fly to London," says Lam, closing the door.

"Business?"

Lam sighs. "Some function or the other. I'm to represent the company at my father's side. To let everyone know that he's had sex at least once, I'm assuming. What do you have for me?"

This time it's Brazuca who goes to the window and looks out at the stunning gardens stretching to the basketball court. He could have waited until he was showered and dressed, but he has a feeling of disquiet that he can't seem to shake.

"Clementine's dealer gets her supply through a bar in Gastown. Classy joint. Had a friend investigate it and he says we're looking at the Khan crime family. They call themselves the Triple 9s because they've got connections to the UK—and it's also a term for cooperating with the cops, which is some kind of inside joke. But here's the thing. The Triple 9s went quiet. There'd been a turf war about ten years ago, but things have changed. Now it seems like the bar is doing well and the Triple 9s are diversifying. I hear they're into real estate these days. Business as usual for the gang, but they're keeping quiet."

"Business as usual," Lam repeats.

Brazuca curses himself silently. "I didn't mean to imply that Cecily's death was—"

Lam holds up a hand. "She hated being called that. It was her grandmother's name, and she couldn't stand the old bat."

"Sorry."

"How could you know? So tell me, who's the dealer?"

Brazuca shrugs. "Can't rightly say. Saw someone leaving Clementine's condo but couldn't get an ID. Followed the trail and it led to this bar. Made the connection." He's not sure why he's protecting Priya, but suspects that it has to do with Lam more than anything else. Lam doesn't seem like the type to lay a hand on a woman, but Brazuca spent enough years in law enforcement to know that you can never really tell. Plus, Priya didn't have to give up the bar, and by keeping her out of it, he could use it as leverage if he needs more information from her later.

"You never saw this person again?"

"No."

"Okay," Lam says, frowning. "Can you find out more?"

More? Unlikely, Brazuca thinks. "I think it's time to let this one go, buddy. Before it was the Triple 9s, that gang was led by someone else. Now they're diversified, and this time they're smart enough to stay under the radar. You could be spinning your wheels for years looking for someone to hold accountable.

I found her dealer and traced it to the Triple 9s. Now you know." He lowers his voice. "I think it's time to move on."

"Don't tell me what to do," Lam snaps, reminding Brazuca of Grace. He buries his head in his hands. "You know what I never understood?" he says, after a full minute of silence. "Why she turned to drugs."

"Hey—"

"I gave her everything. She had everything, Jon. Somebody took advantage of her and I want names. I want to know every fucking person involved. These Triple 9s or whatever they're called have got to get their supply from somewhere." Gone is the devastated lover. Lam doesn't raise his voice, but he is almost shaking with anger.

"Then you've gotta find someone else because this is above my pay level." Brazuca has already been shot once on account of Lam. Friendship does have its limits.

"I'll pay you more," says Lam. Then he names a figure so absurd that Brazuca has to sit down to absorb it.

"That's ridiculous."

"Plus expenses," Lam continues, as if Brazuca hadn't spoken. "You dig up the supply chain and then take your money and go live your life however you want to do it. Buy a cabin in the woods or a condo in Seattle. Point a giant telescope at the sky. Whatever floats your boat. And you'll never have to do this again."

Lam senses Brazuca's wavering, his growing interest in the sum named, and his voice becomes urgent.

"You're the only person I can trust, do you know that? Everyone else is connected to my father or his business in some way.

This . . . this is for me. I want to know every single fucking person responsible, Jon. Because I swear to God, Clem wasn't an addict. Someone did this to her. Took advantage of her and messed with her mind. She was happy."

If that were the case, neither of them would be here. The love of his life wouldn't have needed to relax with a little synthetic bump. Wouldn't have relied on a deadly combination of chemicals to trigger her brain's opioid receptors. Artificially spike her dopamine levels. But Lam isn't yet ready to accept this. Which is likely what has inspired his sudden generosity.

Brazuca stands and tries to hide the pity in his eyes. Women have divorced him, drugged him, tied him to a bed, broken his heart, walked away. But none of them has ever killed herself to get away from him. He thinks of his bad leg. Of his new leaf that is withering right in front of him. Of selling out and cashing in, because opportunities to become set in life are few and far between.

Who is he to look a gift billionaire in the eyes and refuse?

17

I WAKE UP to the sounds of Gary Clark Jr. playing softly in the background and my phone vibrating, almost to the bass line. "Just a sec," I mutter to Simone, to the strains of "If Trouble Was Money." Through the open bathroom door, I can see Nate asleep in the tub with his coat rolled up under his head. His uneven snoring is a testament to the truth that sometimes even the best vocalists can be pitchy.

I pick up my things and leave as quietly as I can. "Yeah?" I say into the phone, once I'm out of the room.

"Well, hello to you, too, sunshine."

So she's still a little bit upset with me. I wipe the sleep from my eyes and sit on the bottom step. The staircase isn't lit. Given the headache building at my temples, I'm grateful for these small mercies. "How's Terry?" I ask.

She laughs. Even though with the time difference she's three hours behind, she seems to be far more awake than I am. Probably hasn't even gone to bed yet. "Nora, you are something else. Let's talk about Terry when you get back. I've managed to track down a couple family contacts for two of those names you sent me. If you want to go that route. Texting them to you now, but not sure how far you're gonna get with these. They're landline numbers. Who has a landline these days?" She is unable to keep the scorn out of her voice.

"I'll try them anyway. Thanks."

"How is it going so far? Any other developments?"

I could tell her about the stolen car and the attempted robbery last night, but I don't. It would only worry her—or worse, annoy her—and I need her on my side right now. So I tell her about Kovaks instead.

"What are you gonna do until he gets back?"

"Been thinking a lot about tattoos. Might be looking into one."

"Right," she says skeptically. "Make sure you get a piercing or two to go with it. I hear nip rings are making a comeback." Then she hangs up on me. Within seconds her texts come through.

I leave the house as quietly as I came in, stepping over the detritus in the kitchen on my way out, left over from the party the night before. Despite the headache, I feel strangely well rested. I have been thinking a lot about tattoos, to be honest. About how distinctive it is to have one at the base of your neck, like a barcode from a sci-fi flick. And how when you describe it to a cop and he pauses for a split second, a flicker of recognition on his face, maybe it means something. That he knows something about the man who was rifling through my stuff.

And, just like a motherfucking cop, he left it up to me to figure out what that something is. If trouble was money, indeed, I'd be a millionaire.

18

I HAVE NO luck with the first number that Simone sent me. The number, with an Atlanta area code, has been disconnected. The phone continues ringing with the second one, but there's no answering machine to pick up. Cory Seaper's family is still living in a landline era, somewhere in Florida. At least their phone is still connected and, while I wait at Mark Kovaks's bar for him to return, calling it is as good a way as any to pass the time. It is hard to stay sober, recovering alcoholic that I am, but I've got the barman's attitude to keep me in check. Whenever I think of adding a splash of vodka to my fruit cocktail, his obvious angling for an upsell keeps me on the path to sobriety.

After the initial flurry of response from the veterans website, interest in the picture has died down and there are no new suggestions in my inbox. Seb has been suspiciously silent, as well, and has ignored all my calls since I've gotten here. He texted *Everything is fine* to me last night, which means that it isn't. He knows full well that if I give up looking for information about my father's death, it would be for him.

The man sitting next to me at the bar has been giving me the eye, watching me make call after call and leaving no messages. "He stand you up, doll? Man don't deserve the honey, he does you like that."

I stare at him, then at the phone in my hand, and see the connection he's made.

"Yeah," he continues. "You can do better, baby. If you're feeling lonely, I could be a friend. When was the last time you had a friend take care a you?"

I have a funny feeling he's not talking about just a friend, and his interpretation of "taking care" probably wouldn't be similar to my own. But I decide to play along anyway. "Last month," I say, with a morose shake of my head. I tell him about the ex just out of jail and the dog. "But all he wanted was old Brutus in the end. He was just trying to butter me up by using his body."

The man becomes grave. "My Opal just passed last year. Cancer. Still can't get over it. I didn't even know she was sick." He stops to wipe a tear from his eye. "How's a man supposed to live without his dog, you tell me that?" He knocks back his whiskey and stumbles out of the bar. All thoughts of improbable friendships have disappeared.

When he leaves, I try the Seaper number once more and am about to hang up after the seventh ring when someone on the other end picks up, muttering a breathless "Hello?"

I'm so thrown by hearing another voice on the line after repeated calls that I don't reply immediately. She says it again and is on the verge of disconnecting when I suddenly say, "Yes, hi. I'm calling about Cory Seaper." I put some money down on the bar for my drink and make my way outside.

"He's dead," the woman on the line says flatly.

The late morning sun shines on the overgrown lot next to the bar. A group of teenagers ride by on bikes, on their way to school, no doubt. Better late than never. "I know that. I think he might have served with my dad. There's a picture of him with three other men. I'm trying to identify them to see if maybe anyone remembered my father. If maybe any of the families remember his name mentioned in conversation?"

She is silent for a long moment. "Can I see the picture?"

I have a photo of the photo stored on my phone, so I hang up and text it to the mobile number she gives me. She calls back from the new number within a few minutes. Her voice, when she speaks, has lost its impatient edge. There is a catch to it now. "Yeah," she says. "That's my dad, alright. Third from the left. God, he looked so happy. And young."

They all did, in that picture. Cory Seaper was shorter than the rest of the men but heavily muscled, with close-cropped blond hair and a wide grin. "Mine is on the far right."

"He was good looking."

It's the first thing that comes through in the picture, how attractive my father was, with his dark hair and dark eyes. Like mine. His smile that was shy and sweet, not like mine at all. He still looked like a teenager here. Young and hopeful. "Yeah, he was. His name is Samuel Watts. Does that ring a bell? Did your dad ever talk about him?"

"No. My dad was private about the time he served. He was at the barracks bombing in Beirut." According to Seb, Beirut had stood out during the tumultuous eighties. Not in the public eye, because the public memory is shit, but in history. A suicide bomber drove a truck filled with explosives through a security checkpoint at the marine barracks located at the Beirut airport.

He killed close to two hundred and fifty American soldiers and service personnel. Another truck targeted the French soldiers, killing over fifty French peacekeepers.

"Was he hurt?"

"No. He wasn't injured, but my mom always said he lost something that day. He used to be a pretty happy guy, before. He got out of the military not long after and did sales for the rest of his life. Cushy desk job was all he ever wanted after that."

"Was there any kind of trouble that he was part of before that? Something that he let slip?"

"He was there when a fucking barracks blew up! How much more trouble do you want?"

Neither of us speaks for a moment. "Sorry," she says finally. "Guess it's a lot to deal with right now."

She talks a bit after that about how she's sure her mother was a little bit frightened of her father, and for him, too. That he flinched at loud noises, but kept a robust gun collection regardless. He'd slapped her once as a child, very hard, and then never allowed himself to get too close to her afterward. That she'd grown up with him cold and distant, except at her wedding, when he walked her down the aisle. He was even quiet in his heart attack, which happened one night when he'd gotten up for a glass of water and her mother found his body the next morning, not having a clue that he'd fallen during the night.

I wonder if I should tell her about how I found my father, but I can't get a word in edgewise. Then she says, "I've got to go. Sorry I couldn't be much help. Thanks for the photo." She ends the call before I have a chance to respond.

Back indoors, the barman continues to ignore me. I wave a

twenty at him. He exchanges glances with a man at the other end of the bar, shrugging nonchalantly as he takes his sweet-ass time coming over. The baller attitude turns quickly to astonishment as I write my number on a cocktail napkin and hand it over, along with the twenty. "Can you call me when your boss gets back from Jersey?"

A look of relief crosses his face when he realizes that I'm not hitting on him. It's not totally out of the question that our intense mutual dislike could lead to potentially explosive sexual chemistry. But he is grateful nonetheless not to confront it face on and gives me a terse nod before walking away. The day drinkers in the room cast curious, if slightly glazed glances my way before turning inward again. There's nothing sinister about the way that they look at me, nothing like the feeling I had before I confronted the veteran, but I still feel the weight of their eyes. I have reconciled myself to the fact that this feeling of being stared at is here to stay. Like a persecution complex, but the stares feel more judgmental. A woman can't live like this. Senses heightened at all times. Constantly playing defense.

19

"YOU'RE NOT TRYING to get in my pants, are you?" says Detective Christopher Lee, from the deck of his North Vancouver house. The lights of Vancouver are in the distance, surrounded by the dark, calm ocean. The view is incredible and almost makes up for the fact that the house itself is structurally unsound and one winter storm away from collapsing around the grumpy homicide detective who lives there. "Because it takes more than a couple beers to hit a home run with me, dude." Lee belches quietly and opens a second can of beer.

"That's not what I heard." Brazuca takes a drink of his own and grins over at Lee, who, with his designer clothes and well-used gym membership, is known as something of a ladies' man.

"You been talking to my ex-wife again?"

"Nah, your priest."

"Don't bring him into your sick world, you fucking heathen. Why are you here?"

"We're talking about gangs. In Vancouver. Lala Lair, remember? I'm working a drug overdose with a connection to the Triple 9s?"

"Jesus. Anything but that shit. You realize that this is my day off, right?"

"Look at you, taking the Lord's name in vain. Who's the heathen now?"

Lee waves his hand, as though magically dismissing the thought that he, with his alcoholism, womanizing, and profanity, could ever be considered anything less than God's perfect servant. "What the hell do you know about it? I'll go to confession next week. Did you tell your client that an overdose is a blessing, that his junkie can exit without stringing him along for life?"

Brazuca is careful to keep his expression blank. "I tried to tell him there was no point in going down this dark alley, but it was the love of his life. She was pregnant."

"Ah, fuck. Fentanyl?"

"Cocaine mixed with Wild Ten."

"And you figured that my experience in Homicide would help out?" Lee looks at Brazuca for a long time. "For a PI, you got shitty contacts on the force if I'm the sum total of them."

"You were in Gangs for a while," Brazuca says easily, masking his anger. He used to have great contacts with the police department—when he'd been on the force himself. But after he'd gotten shot, he flamed out spectacularly and nobody but Lee wanted to have anything to do with him. Not even his wife. Which was something that no amount of stargazing could smooth over.

Lee sees past the deflection and takes pity on him. "Well, hasn't changed that much. You got the bikers, the mixed gangs, the Latin cartels, the Eastern Europeans, the Asians, the South Asians . . . They're all here, man, and they're all into real estate and drugs. Apart from some low-level street squabbles it's been pretty quiet lately. They've got their systems down pat. Violence is bad for business."

Brazuca nods. The surprisingly thorough files on Grace's flash drive suggested the same thing. The streets have seemed calmer, but that doesn't mean there was nothing going on. "Can you find out about the Triple 9s?"

"What are you looking for?"

"Drugs came from them, so who's their connect?"

"I heard . . ." Lee looks away and frowns. He finishes his second beer and opens a third can.

Brazuca watches him for a moment. Grows impatient as Lee makes no attempt to continue. "What?"

"Jesus. This is between us."

"You're kidding, right?" Brazuca says, unexpectedly offended. Lee has never hesitated to share anything with him before.

"I mean it."

"Don't be an ass."

"Hey, this is serious. Need to hear you say it, man."

"Fine. What you tell me is between us."

Lee raises a brow. "And you keep my name out of it."

"And your name is nowhere near my report, as if it would ever be, and I won't even put this in my notes. Plus, I'll take it to my grave and have it written on my tombstone that you and I officially never had a conversation on this lovely day in October, this year of Our Lord, et cetera."

"That wasn't so hard, was it? When I was in the Gang Unit, I had a source who swears that someone from the Triple 9s met up with Jimmy Fang's second. Triple 9s were connected, but we didn't know they were connected like that."

"Jimmy Fang . . . as in Three Phoenix triad Jimmy Fang? Jimmy Fang who disappeared ten years ago?"

"The same, baby. So when you say you're up on the Triple 9 connects, that's what I think of. I think of Three Phoenix, and the fucking heroin junkie who whispered something in my ear one time. The junkie who wouldn't stand up in court and we couldn't prove shit. That kid disappeared right before I transferred out of Gangs and I never knew if they found out he was talking to us and took care of him."

"Shit. Three Phoenix . . ." They'd been famous for some brutal hits on the Vancouver streets some twenty years ago, but hadn't made the papers much since. Even Grace's files had contained some references to them, but they were dated. "Jimmy Fang was years ago. Any new triad activity that's been making the rounds?"

"Come on, man. New triad activity? Triads came from tongs, which have been on the west coast for nearly a century, initially to protect a population that's faced discrimination from the get-go—by the way. Ever heard of the Chinese head tax? Discriminatory housing policies? Underground organizations have been operating here for a very long time. Whenever law enforcement gets a handle on what's happening, they're already two steps ahead. Now with technology being so globalized, we don't stand a chance. If there's one thing Asians are good at, it's technology."

"Uh-huh," says Brazuca, who is well familiar with Lee's perverse sense of humor. "You're Korean and from what I can remember, you can barely use a computer. You used to call IT every week because you kept forgetting your own password."

"I spend so much of my free time doing math that recalling

specific number combinations is difficult. Also, I've been hit in the head a lot because of all the tae kwon do I practice," replies Lee, who, to Brazuca's knowledge, has never done tae kwon do and can barely figure out how much to tip after eating out. "Point is, I couldn't tell you what's new, and I bet to holy hell no law enforcement operation in this country could, either. But if you want information on organized crime in Vancouver— any organized crime, by the way—then look in front of you." He waves expansively to the dark ocean in the distance. "You gotta figure out who's got access to the port. Let me give you a hint. Port unions have been infiltrated for a long time now and they don't even seem to care. So, guess what? It's everybody."

Brazuca stands. "Thanks." Vancouver's ports were notoriously porous, but Lee confirming it hasn't given him any peace of mind. "You've been a ray of sunshine, as always." He tosses his can at the open recycling bin and misses.

Lee laughs. "Didn't realize we were dating. I'll be on my best behavior next time." He reaches for Brazuca's can and is about to toss it into the bin when he catches a glimpse of the label. "What in holy hell is iced kombucha?"

Brazuca shrugs. "Who knows."

Lee stares at him. His eyes are as clear as they'd been before he'd started in on the beer that Brazuca brought. He may be a borderline alcoholic, but he's a high-functioning one. "You know, don't you?"

"Shut up," Brazuca says, unable to explain fermented tea even to himself.

"Don't worry. Us Koreans are experts in fermenting shit,

buddy. Ever heard of kimchi? Big Bad Bazooka," Lee says, laughing again, "drinking his kombucha."

"You're an asshole. Don't quit your day job." Brazuca lets himself out from the back gate.

"My mother thinks I'm a catch! You Catholic?" Lee shouts after him, still grinning like an idiot. "Call me!"

20

I NEED SOMEONE to complain to so I try to reach Veterans Affairs. No one returns my calls. If anyone has ever had an encounter with the VA, they would not be surprised. A veterans' crisis center a block down from my old motel is empty. The sidewalk in front of it is a strip of rubble, razed for some reason long forgotten, perhaps to let the veterans standing outside the empty suite of offices know as clearly as they can that they'll find no firm ground here. I have sent an email about my father to the Marine Corps Research Center in Virginia, but the message has disappeared into the ether along with my phone messages.

I still have some pent-up energy left, though. I call Seb again, but he doesn't answer. I could complain to Simone, but she'd warned me not to expect much, so I doubt she'll be understanding. Cory Seaper was another dead end, which was to be expected on this seemingly fruitless mission to find out the truth about my father's death. I feel like a morbid character in a children's book. Did you know my father? What about you? Do you remember seeing a man who was sort of like me but better looking?

If I had taken to foster care or it had taken to me, this might not have been a problem. When it comes to my dad, maybe, like Lorelei, I'd have looked for a little bit when I was young and given it up when I got older because, ultimately, there were better things to do in life than keep an eye on the rearview mirror.

But foster care and me didn't agree with each other.

In yet another way that the Canadian child welfare system has failed, the families that took me in—there were four in total—didn't teach me to look forward. They cashed their stipend checks while showing me that belonging is a thing for other people. Part of it is what is shared. Home. Language. Traditions. Certain spiritual beliefs. Broad, sweeping mythologies and the smaller origin stories that occur within every group of people who share a family tree. It's not something that applies to a single person. It is not something that applies to me. You need at least two people, three is even better. I reconciled with this lack of belonging very early on in my life, because it suits my personality. I've never expected anyone to give me the keys to unlock who I'm supposed to be because I've assumed other people know as little about the subject as I do.

But my father must have been a hopeful man. He left whatever he had here in Detroit to go backward, to find out if he had a home that had miraculously waited for him for decades.

Or maybe something drove him away, says a voice in my head. One that sounds suspiciously like Seb, who won't answer my calls but will offer imaginary opinions regardless.

I'm tempted to stay here and watch some more people drink their problems into sweet oblivion, but I can't take it anymore. I have to know what happened in the fucked-up house my father grew up in. It has taken a while for that phrase of Harvey's to sink in, but now, with no other leads and nothing else to do but wait for Kovaks to show up, it's all I can think about. I can't lie. The physical, sexual, and emotional abuse that had been revealed in recent years by some Sixties Scoop survivors about their adoptive homes has played a part in my willful ignorance. Some kids were reminded in the most grotesque ways imaginable that they'd been bought and paid for, with money handed over to adoption agencies and kickbacks siphoned to crooked government agents.

Money saved, too, from fewer people who could—or would—claim Indian status.

It was a messy business, one that most people, myself included, don't really want to look too hard at. I don't want to know that bad things happened to my father, but I'm left with little else to go on. So I am, once again, going back to his childhood home.

Hopefully this time I'll make it past the front door without having to break in.

21

EVERY NIGHT, THE supposed head of the Triple 9s is driven from the Lala Lair in Gastown to a quiet residential street in North Vancouver. Brazuca has learned several things from watching this man and his driver. One, operations at the bar are so locked down that it would be almost impossible to get to him there. Two, his North Vancouver house is also gated, with security cameras mounted around the perimeter. Three, it would be a stroke of blind, stupid luck to get a break in this case. An unexpected shift in routine, someone messing up, something out of the ordinary.

So, yet again, he's in the back alley by the Lala Lair, in the shadows, watching the BMW as it idles nearby. He's been here too long tonight with absolutely nothing to show for it. There's a chill in the air and it's cloudy out, so there aren't even any stars to look at while he waits. He's about to slip away when the Triple 9 driver gets out of the BMW to stretch his legs. At that moment, someone from the kitchen sticks a head out of the back door and calls out to the driver, who reluctantly goes inside, taking his sweet time about it.

For a split second, Brazuca can't quite believe it.

He moves out of the shadows. Strolling past the car, he stoops to tie his shoelace, ducking out of sight of the security camera mounted over the entrance. It takes almost no time at all to attach the small black box he's kept in his coat pocket to the rear bumper, hidden from view. It's the first time since he's been watching the car that the young driver has left it unsupervised.

After testing to make sure the device is secure, he walks away like a man without a care in the world, or one who is about to come into some serious money. Unconsciously mimicking the slow gait of the BMW driver, he takes his time getting back to his MINI. If the tracking device is discovered, the Triple 9s will no doubt increase their security measures and he'll likely never get another chance like this to dig up a lead in their supply chain. But Stevie Warsame, Leo's partner in his current PI company and something of a gadgethead, has assured Brazuca that this model is the most secure and unassuming one that Warsame's worked with. So Brazuca feels slightly more comfortable taking the risk. He has to do something to speed things along so that he can get Bernard Lam the answers he so badly wants and the financial freedom that Brazuca has only seen on the faces of happy retirees featured in bank commercials. He could be a happy west coast retiree, and why the hell not?

The funny thing about it, though, is that he can't seem to picture himself with a cabin by the water, a kayak strapped to his roof rack, and a granola-munching woman at his side. He sees Lam, in his grief. Grace, with her unhealthy obsession over her sister's death. Leo, in the dark about his ex-lover's illness. And, after a moment, Nora, whom he can't picture in old age no matter how hard he tries. Him and Nora, that's what drew them together. There may be happy endings at the hands of dead-eyed masseuses at seedy parlors around the globe, but the real ones, the ones where you get to keep your dignity and self-respect, aren't for the likes of the two of them.

Now that he thinks about it.

Brazuca pushes thoughts of Nora from his mind and spends the next day tracking the car's movements. He's waiting for another stroke of blind, stupid luck. Another sign that his life is turning around. Some aberration in schedule that will give him a lead. Instead of looking up at the stars, he stares at his phone, on which he's set up alerts for the tracker. He's hopeful, not stupid. The device will be discovered eventually and he'll be fresh out of leads but, for the moment, he's got nothing else to go on.

In a moment of boredom, he returns to Clementine's apartment and finds Grace sleeping in the bed. She mutters under her breath and turns toward him, but doesn't wake. While he stands there, deciding whether to slip into bed beside her, the phone in his pocket buzzes. A new alert on the tracker. It tells him the BMW's current location isn't one that's been visited yet. He feels a small creep of premonition, a tiny thrill of anticipation skating up his spine.

This is it, he thinks. His aberration.

He turns and departs quietly, locking the door behind him. Leaving Grace to her restless sleep.

22

THE CURTAINS AT the house across the road have been twitching at me for almost an hour. I'm out on Harvey's front porch, waiting for him to show up. I know that I've been seen and maybe a call has been made to him. If there's one thing I hate more than talking to cops, it's talking to snitches who do it for anything other than money. But I try to keep this to myself as I cross the road and knock on the door.

The twitch morphs into a nervous flutter.

"I know you're in there," I say loudly, into the mail slot at the door. "I just want to ask about my father, Samuel. He used to live in that house across the road. I'm wondering if you knew him."

After a moment of silence I sit on this porch for a full five minutes, hoping this swapping of stoops will get me some answers. If nothing else, it affords me a good view of the house my father grew up in. It was probably nice, once. There is a little yard, now overgrown, and the cracked yellow paint must have been pretty a few decades ago.

The curtains are motionless. I'm tempted to give up this futile quest of mine and do some sightseeing. Maybe go see the murals painted by Diego Rivera at the Detroit Institute of Arts. And I might have been tempted, if I hadn't already had my fill of those images on convenience store postcards. In the murals he depicts the wonders and horrors of a machine revolution. But he has not taken into consideration the drug epidemic, has not seen like I have a woman so high she stood on the street in her underwear just to explain something indecipherable to passing cars. I've been told by tourist websites that I should visit the Motown house and the music lounges. I should talk to the ride-share drivers about the decline of the city they still live in. Eat a locally sourced organic sustainable meal that costs more than the average resident's weekly food budget. I should try to forget the city's past glory because it is long gone, having been sold by titans of industry years ago. In a world of Somebodys and Nobodys, Detroit is a Nobody that used to be a Somebody and is feeling rough about it. Like today. There aren't many people on this street, but the ones that pass by can't spare anything but a suspicious glance for me. I try not to take offense. I'm feeling similarly.

Five minutes pass. Soon it becomes ten. Just as I'm about to leave, a tan Buick pulls up to the curb and a woman around my age hustles out with a paper bag in hand. She almost runs me over on the porch before pulling up short and blinking down at me.

"Hi," I say.

"Hiya." She looks from me to the front door, and then back again. A hand goes to her hair to whip her long braids back over her shoulders. "You waiting for Retta? 'Cause I can tell you for a fact that the old bird is in there. She ain't been seen out of this house since the nineties." The woman seems almost shocked that anyone would want to talk to Retta with the curtains, but her voice is kind so I take a chance.

I wave in the general direction of Harvey's yard. "My dad

grew up across the street. He died when I was a kid, though, and I guess I wanted to clear up a couple things about his life here. I was hoping Retta would know something about him."

The woman frowns. "Oh, she knows. She knows everything about this damn neighborhood. Don't you, you old witch!" she says, shouting the last bit at the front room windows, one of which has mysteriously opened a crack in the time I've been talking to the woman from the Buick.

"Get off my porch, tramp!" comes the reply, loud and clear. A pale, wrinkled face appears at the corner of the open window. "And tell that goddamn criminal that I don't got nothin' to say to her!"

Now I know who called Harvey when I broke into the house.

"Is that right? You want your barbecue, you'll tell this nice lady about her daddy. Or I swear to God, I'm gonna eat this right here, turn around, and never come back. I'll tell the pastor you died and he won't make me come see your scruffy porch ever again!"

There is a noisy, almost theatrical gasp. "My porch is clean as a whistle, you godless jezebel!" comes the furious response. Then a weighted silence.

The woman sits beside me. "I'm Melissa," she says.

"Nora." We shake hands. "Why did she leave the house? In the nineties?"

"Oh, that. She heard there was a new church down the way and came to service. Shoulda seen the look on her face when she realized it was a black church. Ha! Pastor makes us do neighborhood outreach to the old crusties, though. Says she's my cross to bear. Want some cornbread?"

She opens up the paper bag and pulls out a large square wrapped in wax paper. We sit there companionably, sharing a hefty piece of heaven on earth. "Mmmm," Melissa moans, orgasmically. "So good."

The front door opens. "Get away from my food," says the old woman standing in the doorway. She is wearing a pressed dress and matching hat. She must have put all the makeup she owns on her face, because I can't quite imagine that any of it could possibly have been left over. Retta from across the road fiddles with a pearl necklace at her throat, while eyeing the crumbs of cornbread on our laps.

"Not until you help this lady," says Melissa.

"No respect for elders." Retta frowns at her, then looks at me. "You can't come in here but you want to know about that other boy that grew up 'cross the road? He was not terrible, that one," she says, grudgingly. "Stopped a couple of hooligans from trying to break in here once. Everyone liked him a lot better than the one that lives there now. Even the parents, too. Both of them gone now. Almost killed them when the one they liked better left for the army."

"Marines," I say, standing to face her.

The old woman snorts. "What's the difference? He up and left when he was eighteen; didn't tell nobody where to find him. Came back years later and the parents were both gone. Car crash. The other one had to take care of everything, even though they didn't leave the house to him. Left it to their favorite, didn't they? I don't like that other one, but he ain't all that bad. For them to treat him that way . . . damn ungrateful if you ask me."

Nobody did, but I'm glad for whatever information I can get. It takes me a moment to sort through all the ones and other ones in her explanation. "My dad owned that house?"

She nods, sending the bobbles on her earrings clattering together. "Heard that one gave it to the other one, then disappeared. He knew. Knew what was gonna happen to this city. Got out while he could. Smart boy."

Melissa clears her throat. Staring at us from the sidewalk is a large man, clutching the hand of a little girl in a soccer uniform.

"What," says Harvey Watts, his voice low and furious, "the hell do you think you're doing?"

23

I'M SITTING AT his kitchen table as Harvey makes pasta for the little girl opposite me. The girl, whose name is Darla, of all things, stares at me with frank interest as he slams things down on the counter, bangs cupboards closed, and makes all the noise that it is possible to make boiling water. I'm reminded of last year, when I sat at my sister's kitchen table, trying to connect with her after I'd stolen her car and crashed it. After Bonnie had gone missing, I was desperate to find her. I sat at Lorelei's table and tried to explain myself, for once.

This moment is imprinted in my memory because it was also the time she called me a slut. Harvey couldn't possibly have opinions on my sluttiness, but from the way he's clanging the pots and pans, I have a feeling that he might harbor a few suspicions.

Under the table Darla holds out a lollipop for me to unwrap, but I'm not falling for that one again. I ignore her and continue my observation of my father's adoptive brother, imagining what it's like to be the natural son of parents who preferred the boy that did not spring from their loins. The one they brought over from Canada. I've also been looked through enough in life to know how that eats away at you if you give a fuck. I try to put myself in his shoes, being passed over for a mere Canadian, and it's a tough sell.

I'm about to feel sympathetic until he starts speaking. Not to me, though, to the space somewhere around me.

"You wanna know about your dad?" Then, without waiting for a response, he plows on. "They got him from Canada, when he was two years old. Paid the agency ten thousand dollars for him. My mom couldn't have any kids after me, but they wanted me to have a brother that was about the same age. We grew up together, but he left as soon as he was eighteen for the marines and only came back after he was discharged. No money, no nothin'. Didn't even know Moms and Pops were gone. It was just me here, doing everything in a house that I goddamn grew up in but belonged to him now."

"Why did they sign it over to him and not you?"

He looks out the window. "I was . . . I had a habit," he says, absently scratching the inside of his elbow. "Took me a long time to kick it, but I did. Stuck around while I got straight, too. I coulda left like everyone else. Coulda hightailed it outta here, but I didn't."

"Where would you go?"

"That's the damn truth! Lived my whole life in this city; never wanted to be nowhere else. But he did. He didn't want to live here anymore. Gave me the house for nothing. I offered to buy him out. I was working then—coulda done it but no. He met that Arab woman that lived in Montreal and took off to Canada to find his birth family. He'd found some work in Winnipeg and they moved there because that's where he'd been born."

"Did he find them?" I ask. "His birth family."

"No. He only found out he was born to a single mother in

Winnipeg, but he was never able to find her. Didn't stop him from going, though. Last I heard he was still in Winnipeg, but he never returned my calls or replied to my letters. My own brother. We didn't really have no one else besides each other. Was never good enough for him, was I?" He can't keep the anger at bay anymore. His fingers clench into fists. Darla bursts into tears.

"What Arab woman?" My voice is a little louder than I'd anticipated, and the question falls like a hammer on the table.

"What?"

"You said an Arab woman. What Arab woman?"

He stares at me blankly for several long seconds, like he's never truly seen me before this moment. "Your mother. Who did you think I was talking about?"

Darla, her face streaked with tears, holds out the lollipop again and in my distraction I unwrap it for her and hand it back. What is building inside me isn't excitement, per se. I am back under the water, feeling a weightlessness that isn't at all unpleasant. When I built my bunker for my father, I hadn't thought to include my mother in it. I have no memories of her to put in. I try for all the control that I can muster before I speak again. "He met my mother here?"

"She was in Dearborn for a wedding but they met here in the city while she was visiting. Don't you know any of this?"

"No. She left after my sister was born. He died and then his sister—"

"That woman was not his sister!" he says, jabbing a finger at the air in front of me. He has, for a moment, gone into his upper register and is not particularly comfortable there. "Goes and meets her at a friendship center where they connected. They were both adopted but wanted to find their other families. She was looking for her little brother and he was looking for anyone. But she wasn't his sister. She was . . . he had a way with people, Sam did. People just wanted to be near him. He didn't even have to try."

He grasps the edge of the kitchen table with both hands for support. Though he is looking through me, searching somewhere in his memory, in his own past, I see him now. What he's been hiding. It isn't a grudge that his parents loved my father more than they did their own flesh and blood. Not that they left their adopted son their house, that they yearned for him to come back home from military service. To use anything to get him to come back home to them. It's that Harvey must have loved my father in the same way.

"That's why you sent the postcards. You wanted him to know that you were still there for him."

"He called me when your mother left him, you know. He'd been laid off at the factory he was working at. Wanted to borrow money."

"Did you lend it to him?"

"No. I was between jobs back then. Still trying to kick my habit, too. I said he could come back here and live for free if he wanted. There was still work here at that time—and he needed it. My daughter was staying with me back then, she coulda used some cousins to grow up with. He said no. He said . . . he said his family was there. When he was with your ma, I could understand. That woman . . ." He shakes his head. "I never seen a good-looking woman like that before. But I never understood why he didn't come back after."

All his earlier bluster seems to go out of him. I can see how tired he is as he puts a plate down in front of Darla. How old and alone. I wonder what happened to his daughter and why he's raising his granddaughter by himself. I wonder if he always loved my father, even from the beginning, or if it took a while for that bond to form. One that was so unshakable for Harvey and so easily dismissed by the child his parents brought home one day. These thoughts flit through my head in an instant, but what I hold on to isn't about him at all.

"Do you have a picture of her?"

He looks up from his studied observation of his grand-daughter eating her dinner. "What?"

"My mother. You said they met here? Did they leave behind any photos that weren't in that briefcase?"

"Hang on." He leaves the kitchen and, moments later, I can hear him on the stairs.

"Hi," says Darla, waving her fork at me. A little bit of pasta sauce splashes on the table. Neither of us moves to clean it up. We stare at it for a moment, then she grins at me, the gap in her teeth a form of ice-melting kryptonite.

"Hey," I say, somewhat grudgingly.

She reaches into her pocket and shows me the strip of blue ribbon. "Shh," she says, her eyes comically wide, her finger to her lips.

"Yeah, well, I'm not the one with the problem keeping my mouth shut, am I?"

I absurdly hold on to her earlier lack of discretion. I'm tired and both thankful that there are so few windows in here to keep an eye on and exhausted by the energy that thinking like this takes up.

Harvey reappears with an old newspaper clipping, kept in a clear plastic shield.

"Lebanese Politician Involved in Hostage Crisis Has Roots in Dearborn" reads the headline of a large, national paper. I'm not sure what I expected. There are two photos in the article, one is a head shot that shows a tall, clean-shaven politician, Ali Nasri. Who, according to the article, still had a hand in Lebanon's political scene during the hostage crisis in the eighties—even though his family mostly lived in Michigan by then. The other picture was taken at a wedding where Ali was standing next to his son Walid, Walid's bride Dania, and about half a dozen assorted guests.

"I saw this in the paper once, back in the eighties, and she's there. That's her," says Harvey, pointing to a woman standing off to the side. "Sabrina Awad."

Her body is angled partially away, but her face is turned to the camera, her expression one of consternation mixed with surprise. Even though she is at the far edge of the photo, no-where near the newlyweds, she draws the eye. Her beauty is so singular. In a room full of attractive women, made up as though glamour were going out of style the very next day, her simplicity stands out. In the photo, she has long dark hair, left loose over her shoulder, and a kind of symmetry of features that you can't fake, even with makeup. The cut of her dress shows off slim arms that I recognize from another photograph from my past, one where she is holding me. It's held up by delicate straps that are accented by little bows made of ribbon.

I have a feeling that if this photograph were in color, the dress would match the blue ribbon that Darla has hidden back in her pocket. "Can I keep this?" I say to Harvey.

He nods. "Yeah." It isn't until I reach the door that he speaks again, almost as an afterthought. "You know, you don't seem nothing like him, but your voice. Something about it. Sam . . . he sounded a bit like you, I guess."

Maybe there's something in the wistfulness of his tone that makes me ask my next question. "Did my father . . . did he seem like the type to take his life?"

"God, no. But I didn't know him very well, toward the end. I thought we were close when we were growing up, but I guess that was a lie, too. You hear stories about people coming back from war, about how it changes them. Being in the military changed him, too, I guess, but the Sam I used to know wouldn't have done that . . . What the hell do I know, anyway? My own daughter died of an oxy overdose a couple years ago. I thought I knew her, too. Started to believe becoming a mother had turned her life around." He looks at Darla as she slips from her chair and puts her plate in the sink. The anger in him seems to deflate. "You can . . . I mean, if you're thinking . . . You can come back, if you want."

My grunt could be taken as confirmation, I suppose, but I leave the kitchen knowing that I'll probably never come back here. That a little girl who has no connection to me or my mother has this tiny piece of her. And that somehow, I don't mind at all. Some little girl should have something of my mother's. One who is not either of her daughters, both of whom hate her for leaving them and not coming back. Never. Not once. Not even when their father died.

As I walk away from my father's childhood home I realize that I'm hungry. My first thought is of a falafel. But that's inappropriate. I bury the desire to send a message to Bonnie. Heads up. It is more complicated than you thought. Do you love falafel and have you been wondering why?

I look over my shoulder as I walk away from my father's childhood home, because something inside me tells me that my departure is being tracked. Harvey is at his window and his nosy neighbor is at hers. Darla wanders out to the yard, under the watchful eyes of them both. She waves at me as I look back at her over my shoulder, but I ruthlessly suppress the instinct to wave back.

We could have been family once, maybe, but it's too late for that. Harvey Watts just confirmed what I've always believed. My father went to Canada searching for his roots. He never found them. He was just as lost as I used to be until a few minutes ago when, for the first time in my life, I saw a photograph of my mother's face.

24

STEVIE WARSAME EASES his large body into the car without speaking. He pours himself some coffee from a thermos and grimaces at the first sip. "You make shit coffee, Bazooka," he says to Brazuca, who's staring at him from the driver's seat.

"You're breaking my heart." Brazuca starts the engine and pulls away from the line of parked cars on the road. He glances back for one last look at the unassuming two-story house that the BMW's tracker led him to. It's on a quiet, tree-lined street, with plenty of yard space. Which means that, though it doesn't really look like much, the Burnaby neighborhood they've been watching must be an expensive one. He'd even caught a glimpse of a pool in one of the backyards. A backyard pool. In Vancouver, a place where it was a luxury to have anything better than a shitty, overchlorinated indoor pool—the kind that Brazuca swims in every morning.

Warsame, who has just walked by the house for a closer look, is unruffled, as always. "You want to hear the good news or not? Seems like your average private residence but there's a camera above the door and in the driveway. TV's on inside, so someone's home. What's the deal with this case, anyway? Cheater?"

"Just some surveillance for now," Brazuca says, not wanting to get into it just yet.

Warsame doesn't like this. "What exactly are we surveilling? Way I see it, I'm doing you a favor."

"I'm paying you!" Lam's pockets are deep to support hiring outside help, but Brazuca hasn't yet told Warsame who the client is. To get the Somali ex-cop to do anything, however, you need to make it worth his while.

"Yeah, so what? I don't have to be here, bro."

There is a directness to Warsame that comes with his easy smile. He'd lived through a war in Somalia, had his childhood upended to move from a Kenyan refugee camp to Canada, learned a new language in order to enforce the laws of his new country. He had seen more than any person ought to have, all before he grew out of childhood. You could not dissuade him when he wanted something—or convince him that your needs were greater than his. His unwillingness to let anything slip past was what made him such a good investigator.

Brazuca sighs. "Friend of mine asked me to look into an OD. Dealer's connected to the Triple 9s. A lead set me up on this house."

Warsame's incredulous look mirrors Lee's when Brazuca told him the same thing. "You're digging up a supply chain for an OD? What the fuck for?" It was dangerous work, best left to the police—as Warsame well knows.

"Favor, mostly. Just seeing where it goes." Brazuca isn't fooling anyone with his feigned casual tone, especially not Stevie Warsame, but he's still glad when Warsame decides this is enough information for now.

But by his look, he's not going to be put off for much longer.

"I'm gonna grab some food. You need me later?" Warsame asks, when Brazuca drops him back at his car a few blocks away.

"Yeah, stick around if you can."

Warsame nods. "Your dime. Let me know if you want me to bring some more guys on for the job."

"Yeah, thanks, man. I want to see how this plays out a little first."

Warsame doesn't come cheap and Brazuca has a feeling that his guys wouldn't be, either. He's not ready yet to start contracting more work without a better idea of what he's dealing with. He waits until Warsame pulls away in his two-door sedan with tinted windows before mixing a protein shake from a container that he now stashes in his glove compartment. In this moment, drinking his healthy shake and thinking about his muscle mass, he is not aware of just how much he resembles another field operative, one who had surveilled Nora's daughter, Bonnie, last year. A gun for hire.

He circles the neighborhood and is about to pull into a free space with a decent view of the house he's been watching when the garage door opens. A brand-new Toyota pickup truck backs out onto the road. As it passes, giving him a honk to get out of the way, he catches a glimpse of a bearded man with a baseball cap pulled low. Brazuca waits in his MINI Cooper until the pickup turns the corner. Before he follows the truck, he sends a text to Warsame: *On the move.*

In separate cars, they tail the truck to the bearded man's place of work. Watch him park his car in the employee lot.

"Surprise, surprise. Looks like you found your Triple 9 link to the Vancouver port," says Warsame, over the phone.

Brazuca grins. Maybe this will be easier than he thought. He ignores the nagging suspicion that nothing ever is, certainly not for him. But maybe, just for once in his goddamn life, his luck has changed for good.

25

IT'S STILL LIGHT outside when I hit up the hipster café located inside a general store and run by a young man I assume is Amish. That, or he's trying to bring back long sideburns and vests, which, given the neighborhood, isn't completely unthinkable. I open the MacBook Pro that had been a gift from Leo before he and Seb split up. The exterior of it is a little worse for the wear, but it works just fine as I boot it up and continue my search from the last few days.

There's a new message from the veterans group, but it's from an administrator outlining the process of retrieving my father's military records. I'm tempted to do it, but being driven to madness by bureaucracy isn't my idea of fun, so I nix the suggestion almost immediately. I keep looking until I come across an odd story archived in the forum. Someone was joking about a piece of radio equipment falling overboard while stationed in the Mediterranean in '77, and how the marine responsible for it got reamed out. Another commenter asked if he got brig time for losing cryptographic material, but the response was negative. Doesn't seem like enough to make a man want to kill himself, but I still file it away for later.

In my search I make another unhelpful discovery. Hideous neck tattoos are surprisingly popular in criminal circles. Back at the motel, I didn't see much of my would-be robber, but I saw enough to note that his skin color wasn't dark. But it's not a lot to go on, since "not dark" is a pretty broad category. I debate asking Simone to look into it, that maybe some obscure database or the other has a breakdown of gang tattoos and why someone would possibly want one creeping into their hairline—but if I did that I would have to tell her about the robbery attempt at my motel. And, too chickenshit to face her disapproval, I stop myself before I send the message.

It's getting late, and the café is closing down for the evening. My phone rings and there is a moment of brief hope as I think of Seb, finally getting back to me, but it's not him. The number has a Detroit area code, and isn't Nate's.

"Hello?"

The man on the other end of the line clears his throat. "Yeah, the boss is back," the bartender says gruffly, and disconnects before I can thank him for the call. It's just as well. My mouth is dry and I can feel a headache growing at my temples. I've spent an inordinate amount of time at the bar since I got to Detroit, driving myself crazy watching people indulge in my favorite forbidden pastime and it's time for it to pay off.

Before I go, though, I use the last few minutes before the café closes to do a quick search on the family that was featured in Harvey Watts's newspaper clipping. The Nasris. There are no more pictures published publicly on that wedding, no more information on the bride or the groom, or the unnamed guests that were so prominently featured. No trace of the woman who gave birth to me.

26

THE BAR IS lively tonight. There is some kind of televised sporting event happening and team pride is out in full force. People are wearing jerseys, some of them yellow and some red. I don't know what it means and would ask the bartender, except he has been busy since I walked in here. I do manage to catch his eye and he nods to a hallway toward the back of the bar.

In the small office at the end of the hall, there is a man sitting at a desk going through a stack of papers. He's well into his sixties, but looks healthier than everyone I've seen at this bar, including myself. "Low on whiskey. Next shipment won't be in till tomorrow, so get ready for a riot," he says, without glancing up.

"I'll get my bear spray out," I reply, standing just inside the doorway.

He peers at me over the rims of his glasses. "You're Sam's girl. Alastair told me that you've been looking for me." Before I can wrap my head around the idea that the surly bartender is named something as whimsical as Alastair, he gestures to the chair across from him. "Sit down."

I close the door behind me and take a seat. It's only a fraction quieter in here. The office is clean but shabby in the way of dive bar offices around the world. I have a feeling that it's worse than it looks, and that the most offensive parts are covered by god-awful red banners that seem to match some of the jerseys seen outside. Something about the logo on the red jersey makes me pause. It takes me a full minute to realize that it's the Detroit Red Wings, and the sport in question is hockey. Suddenly I feel more comfortable. If there's one thing all reasonable Canadians know, it's how to handle a hockey enthusiast.

I nod to a photo on the wall, of a much younger Kovaks at a game. "What are the chances of the Red Wings making playoffs this year?"

He shakes his head. "Don't even get me started. It's game night and we got assholes to keep an eye on. What do you want to know about your dad?"

So much for that. "I want to know about Lebanon."

I slide the old photo of my father with the other men across the desk. He stares at it for a long time. "I remember this. This was taken in North Carolina. That's me, your dad, Cory Seaper, and Juan Gutierez. When we first started out we all rented a house together near Camp Lejeune. This was taken before we all got separate deployments and had to give up the house." He sighs, and his voice turns wistful. "They're all gone now. I think I'm the only one left."

"Yeah?"

He's still absorbed with the photo. After a moment, he rises and clears away a pennant hanging from a set of deer antlers on the wall. Underneath the pennant is a photo of my father and Kovaks clinking shot glasses together below the sign to the bar. Here they're older than they were in the photo with Seaper and Gutierez, but not by much. "This was when we were both back to civilian life and I took over my dad's bar. God, we were so young then. World was a scary place. Cold War was gearing up and there was so much fear."

"Wonder what that's like." I'm still trying to absorb the picture of my dad in front of the bar. A few minutes before this I was at that same entrance, looking up at that same sign.

He glances at me. "Ha. You got that right. We don't seem to get past fear, do we? Not much difference now than it was back then. Used to be the Nazis, then it was the Vietcong and the Russians. Now it's coming at us from everywhere." He looks away for a moment. "Got an old journalist friend who spent some time reporting in Lebanon. From what she's said, information was the currency of the day. Doesn't seem that much has changed, to be honest, but Beirut used to be a place it got disseminated before the civil war, maybe after, too. There were agents everywhere. Double agents." He laughs. "Triple agents."

"Quadruple agents?" I say, because when you take people back to the past, it's best to sometimes remind them that you're still in the room with them.

"Don't be silly," he says, frowning. Now I know that quadruple agents are where he draws his line. "If you want, I could get her to give you a call."

"Sure." Information never hurt anyone. But interesting as this all is, I don't see what it has to do with my father. "You see much of him after he became a civilian?"

"Yeah, a bit. I left the service before he did. That wasn't the career for me. I just thought it would be an opportunity to see the world. Was trying to run as far away from this place as I could, but my dad got sick. Needed help with the bar. It's been in my family since my grandpa, so I didn't have much of a choice back then. After he left, Sammy would come by every now and then. Then he said he was moving to Canada with that fox of his . . . sorry," he says. "That was your ma?"

I shrug. Since I was shot last year, the one shoulder doesn't go up so well, so it ends up looking like an awkward range of motion, with only one side of my body involved. "I guess so."

His keen eyes skim over me, note the tenseness in the one shoulder. I'm pretty sure he'd also seen the slight hitch in my step when I walked into the room. I get the feeling there isn't a lot that he doesn't see, and that's probably why my attempt at distraction with hockey small talk bombed.

"She left when I was a kid," I explained again, to yet another stranger. You'd think that by now I would get the hang of it, but I haven't.

"So you got mommy issues to go along with your daddy issues, do ya, darling?"

"My name is Nora."

His expression softens. There is so much understanding in it that I'm once again reminded of Seb, even though I've been trying not to think about him lately. I realize that I don't know what to do with kind men. Simone would say fuck them, but that's out of the question. Leo might say feed them, but I wouldn't know how to start with that. Instead I look at the hockey paraphernalia in the room while I try not to think about my mommy and my daddy issues. If I'm being honest with myself, I've got some sister issues, too, but I'm sure as hell not going to let him in on those.

"So, Nora," he continues, this time a little gentler. "What can I do for you?"

I tell him about what the veteran said. About Lebanon and my father. When I finish, he taps the desk with the end of his pen and frowns at me. "There was trouble in Lebanon at that time, but that's not very specific. Was your veteran talking about the civil war? The Syrian invasion? The Israeli invasion?"

"I don't know what he was talking about. He left before I got any answers."

Kovaks shakes his head. "I'm afraid I can't really help you. Your dad never stepped foot in the country, far as I know. He would have told me, too, because we talked around the subject a few times in regards to your mother. He was stationed on a ship in the Mediterranean. Worked support in comms."

I sit up straighter in my chair at this. "He stayed on a boat off the coast? He never went into the country?"

"Not when I knew him. I mean, one time his ship rescued some Palestinian refugees out of Lebanon when their boat got in trouble. Syrians were shooting the shit out of them as they left the port in Sidon and the boat took on a lot of water in the middle of the journey to Cyprus. They would have died out there at sea if your father's ship hadn't found them. It stuck with him. Those poor people, starving, pissing themselves, crammed in tighter than Red Wings fans at the bar during the playoffs. Almost on top of one another. He talked about that a bit. Never seen anything like it. People so desperate to get away from home that they did anything they could for a better life."

He notices my silence, my turning inward. "Look, I was born in Detroit. It's as shitty a place to be from as anywhere else, and I'd never tell you otherwise. But at least I knew my family. I could point to this god-awful neighborhood and say, that's where my granddad grew up. Then point to that ugly-ass strip of buildings and say, that's where my mom got mugged one December and we couldn't afford Christmas presents that year. But at least I have that. Your dad never knew his place of birth. He had a homeland and didn't know a thing about it. Never been there as an adult. And there on that boat in the middle of the ocean were these people who could never go back to their homeland. He changed after that. Still a nice guy, just less . . . happy-go-lucky. Wasn't surprised he went for a Lebanese girl, to be honest. Something about that experience on the water made a connection for him."

Inside all of us is a little child who wants to hear the story of her parents' romance, even when there are more important questions to be asked. I try to keep her at bay, but fail miserably. "Do you know how they met?"

"At a little falafel shop around the corner from here. Can you believe it?"

I shake my head. I just can't. The thought is too ridiculous to stomach.

At the door, I hesitate for a moment. I get the sense that he's held himself in check, that there is something still left unsaid. I can see by his expression that he won't offer it up on his own, so I ask the question that has been on my mind. "What was he like?"

Kovaks pauses. He lifts his gaze from the window and stares at me. It's the small kindnesses in the world that undo us. The kindness that is now in his voice. "He was a good guy, Nora. The best." Then he pauses and looks away. "I never thought he would . . . it's a shame that he did what he did. Lotta guys, they come back from war and they can't adjust. You know, it's hell out there and some people just can't move past what they've seen. Your dad . . . I was shocked when I heard how he died. It still gets to me."

Does he sense my confusion? All the things I'm trying to keep tamped down inside my gut? Of course he doesn't, and this ability to exist like this, hidden in plain view, is not unique to me. Women do it every day. Keep things hidden not to relive pain, but in order to stay under the radar. With our aging, aching bodies, stuffed every which way into support garments, propped up on miniature stilts that make it impossible to walk and still maintain some equilibrium, we don't want them to see the rage that simmers just beneath the surface.

Something occurs to me now, something that I hadn't really thought of before. "How? How did you hear he was dead?" According to Harvey, my father had cut ties to this place. There was no record of a relationship with Kovaks in the stuff Lorelei had collected. He had left the photo of Kovaks at Harvey's house when he moved to Winnipeg.

"Old friend of your mom's came by looking for her. He saw a report in the paper on your dad's . . . his death. He'd wanted to make sure she got the news from a friend because he'd heard your parents split up. He said you girls were with your aunt, but that your mother deserved to know. Sad thing, though, when a woman leaves her kids like that."

If there was a report in the paper about my father's suicide, it's news to me. Lorelei had looked for any information she could possibly find on the subject and had not come up with anything in the paper. Even though, by all accounts, he deserved some space. He was a good guy. A good guy whom I never knew past childhood. A good guy who'd had no reason to kill himself. Because I can see now, there had been trouble in Lebanon but not with him. Which begs the question. Why, exactly, did he die?

If there was no trouble in Lebanon before he left the marines, then what the hell was that veteran talking about? It has come upon me slowly, this realization that I'm in over my head here. I'd come to Detroit to find out why my father took his own life, expecting some kind of tragic story of something he'd seen in combat, in a place that was oceans away. But the more I dig, the more people I talk to who used to know him, the more it seems that he didn't. Take his own life, that is.

And if he didn't take his own life, well . . . then someone else must have put a gun to his head that day.

27

BONNIE HASN'T FORGOTTEN the tattoo.

She'd been drugged. Her blood was taken and sent off for testing to see if she was a possible match for her dying half-brother. She hadn't been in her right mind then, but things have been coming back in flashes of blurred memories. She hadn't been meant to see the tattoo at all. They had kept her drugged, mostly, but every now and then she'd rouse and see the man who said he was her father and the bald man, both hovering over her. The bald man wasn't old, but his entire head had been shaved for some reason. He had been furious at her father for the tattoo, because her father hadn't understood it, didn't deserve it. They spoke in a language that she didn't know, but matters were made perfectly clear when the bald man yanked up the sleeve on her birth father's shirt and pointed at the tattoo.

She had been frightened of the bald man. Sometimes she'd wakened from a deep fog to find him watching her with cold eyes. Her supposed father was quick to laugh and become angry, from what she'd observed, but the bald man had not showed any sign of excitability until the tattoo incident. When the bald man noticed she was awake, he'd left the room, her father following after him. The door slammed shut and Bonnie was alone again. Scared. Weak. Passive. She swore then that she'd never be in that position again. She would find out everything she could about her father's family and the people who'd taken her as if she meant nothing.

She has been thinking about this a lot. In a way, she is nothing. Not this or that or the other. She has realized that her birth mom, Nora, has no clue, either. They're both confused and in the dark, so what does it really matter the history that brought her here. Over time—not much, she's still a teenager, after all—she felt less and less like nothing and more and more like part of everything. Nothing was hers, so everything was hers. It made no sense, not really, so she's never mentioned this to her mother Lynn or her other mother Nora, or her father Everett or to Tom. She doesn't really have friends in Toronto yet and she doesn't talk to her best friend from Vancouver much anymore, so there's no need to worry about keeping things from them, thank God. She just has to keep it to herself because it sounds crazy even to her.

She is her own.

Just like Nora, she doesn't belong to anyone. Thinking about Nora, she experiences a pang of regret—or something like it. She'd sent the photo at the clinic, with her feet in stirrups, because she'd wanted to share that moment. It was just like last year, when she went to see Nora at the hospital. She had wanted her birth mother to know what she went through to find her. The pain, the fear, and everything else that had happened. But Nora hadn't even recognized her then.

Thinking about that time only gives her nightmares, but she can't help herself. She hasn't slept through until the morning in . . . well, since forever, it seems. Drawing is the only thing that helps get her through the night. She gets out her sketchpad and pencil. After the incident last year, her therapist encouraged her to use art as therapy. Her sketches and paintings were almost always of shadow faces hidden in landscapes. Hidden so deep that it became a game to set scenes that were not obvious at first glance, but once you saw them you could not forget. It added an energy to the pieces that could not be explained unless you could see what was underneath. Every now and then she'd draw a symbol that she'd seen inked on her father's arm. The symbol was dripping with blood. She mostly drew the blood.

28

THEY'VE BEEN WATCHING the Burnaby house that the GPS tracker led to for the past day and a half, and Brazuca can't remember a time when he's been this bored. Picturing the loads of cash he'll make when he closes this case for Lam helps, but only if he conveniently forgets about Warsame's fees. Which hasn't been easy, since Warsame can't seem to drop the subject.

"So . . . ," Warsame begins, yet again, over the phone. "How does this work? Do I invoice you or Krushnik? He knows I'm on this, right?"

"Yeah, I told him. He's just working on a background check, and wrapping up an insurance fraud case. We're good for a bit."

"So I invoice you, then?"

Brazuca remembers now why he hates teamwork. He sighs. "You invoice me. Any sign of the mother?"

"Nah," says Warsame.

Brazuca turns onto the street and pulls into a spot a few cars down from Warsame's sedan. Property records show that the house they've been watching belongs to a retired schoolteacher named Greta Parnell, who doesn't seem to actually live there.

But her son Curtis does. Curtis Parnell, the bearded man that Brazuca had followed to the port, who also happens to be a card-carrying member of the longshoremen's union.

"But," Warsame continues, "I have seen two idiots coming in and out since this morning."

Brazuca frowns. This is the first time anyone else has been spotted at the house. "What kind of idiots?"

Warsame's sigh comes through loud and clear on the line. "The most basic kind. Young. Jacked. Bad haircuts. Pretty sure they're carrying. You know, assholes."

"Assholes and idiots aren't the same thing."

"I dunno," says Warsame. "Why be an asshole unless you're an idiot? Point is, think I saw a flasher."

Jackpot, Brazuca thinks. A flasher was a badge that climbers in certain motorcycle clubs get while they're on the program to move up to full member.

"Did you get a shot of it?" As Brazuca learned when he asked about GPS devices, Warsame loves his toys. He would put trackers and cameras in everything he comes across, if he could. He's also an amateur photographer and has a fondness for talking about the most tedious fucking things, like composition and lenses. He'd almost refused to lend Brazuca one of his old cameras today, a tiny Canon, until Brazuca agreed to pay his rental fee. Which was steep.

"Nah, man. Lighting was off." Warsame then launches into an explanation of his camera gear as the two idiots in question emerge from the house and take off in a brand-new Ford Mustang.

"I got this," says Warsame, pulling onto the road after them. "Parnell at work?"

"Like the good boy that he is." Curtis Parnell didn't just show up to work at the Vancouver docks today, he made a point to get there early, too. Which means that Brazuca had also been at the port this morning. Bright, early, and undercaffeinated. Watching the other members of the longshoremen's union trickle in and noticing that what identified them as a group was their look. Not "dockworker chic" like the hipsters that have invaded Gastown. Authentic dockworker. Their jeans were not fitted, their plaid shirts likely didn't cost more than a few dollars on sale, and their beards existed to keep their faces warm while they worked outdoors, as opposed to being merely a fashion statement to hide weak chins.

Parnell blended in well, but there was no doubt in Brazuca's mind that he'd found the Triple 9 associate at the port. Whoever sold to Clementine's dealer, this was the connection it came through. The connection that Bernard Lam is so desperate for. He's sure of it. Now he just has to find out where, and who, the product is coming from.

Warsame yawns. "Parnell can't be all that good if he's got those two assholes coming and going from his house."

And he isn't. According to Lee, not only is he somehow affiliated with the Triple 9s, but Curtis Parnell is a full-patch member of a biker gang linked to the Hell's Angels. Two years after a police informant brought down a rival gang, he and his buddies went quiet. "All of a sudden it was like they found Jesus and became respectable citizens," Lee had said.

"All of a sudden that seems like bullshit," Brazuca replied.

"You should be a psychic, Brazuca. Quit your day job and put an ad in the paper. While you're at it, try calling someone other than me. Fake-ass wannabe cop." Lee hung up. He was very cranky at six thirty in the morning.

Still, the dig about Brazuca being a fake cop hurt. And yeah, maybe he was a wannabe, but at least he was getting paid enough now to create some options. Maybe he won't have to be a fake-ass cop forever.

After Warsame leaves, tailing the two idiots, Brazuca gets out of the car to get some blood back into his aching leg. Since Lam mentioned it when he dropped the bomb about how much he was willing to pay to keep Brazuca on the case, Brazuca can't stop thinking about telescopes. He's got his eye on a beauty over in Whistler. Just a short drive on the stunning sea-to-sky highway and a state-of-the-art telescope is all his. He's also been thinking of where to park his brand-new toy, maybe a nice little condo with a balcony. Or a house like Parnell's—unassuming and hedged in by a low tree line, protecting it from the street, but leaving an open view of the sky.

His mind still on telescopes, he finds himself walking down the street toward the house. When he gets close to the discreet security camera mounted above Parnell's front entrance, he pulls the brim of his cap lower. Something on the driveway by the garage catches his eye. Keeping his head down, he moves closer and finds a cell phone. He picks it up but, before he can pocket it, hears the unmistakable sound of the slide racking on a semi-auto.

He turns his head.

Sees Curtis Parnell looming over him, his expression cold.

Just like that, his luck evaporates.

He opens his mouth to speak, to protest, to scream—but with a swift movement, Parnell slams the gun into his skull. He falls to the ground.

All that's left now is silence.

29

WITH NOWHERE ELSE to go, I end up at his back door again. No surprise there. If there's anything that I've learned from my years of living in Vancouver without paying rent, it's that I'm a back-door kind of gal.

"Didn't think I'd ever see you again," says Nate, when he opens it up.

"Yeah, well." I hesitate, feeling somewhat guilty I hadn't even sent him a text when I left. "Can I crash with you?"

"Depends," he says, crossing his arms over his chest. "You gonna pay the toll?"

I look past him at the flyers scattered on the kitchen table for Kevin's annual Angel's Night rally. The room is filled with a surprising mix of young people, except that in addition to the social studies students, there is a fresh group of earnest young men and women in cargo pants and fringed ponchos.

Ah, hippies.

I know them well, because the west coast is like their Mecca and each summer they come in droves to wander around in their own stench, hefting their heavy backpacks, ostensibly searching for clean water and fresh beginnings but too stoned to find any or even make a real attempt. But poverty hasn't ground them down yet and they still spew words like "that's so meta" and "the universe is trying to tell you something." I've chosen to interpret that as a cue from the universe to get the hell out of that conversation, but it doesn't seem to matter to them. They just shrug and continue on, clad in hideous sandals and high as fuck.

I have an almost magnetic repulsion to hippies, but can't stop picturing Nate's cool, silent studio beyond the door. "Want me to put up posters?"

"Nah. They got these guys for that," he says, jerking a thumb toward the motley crew behind him. "From you I want something else."

I give him a hard look at this, but his smile isn't salacious. I've witnessed flirting enough times to know when it's happening, but it's not something that I'm well familiar with on a personal level. My interactions with Alastair, Kovaks's surly bartender, are a testament to my lack of skills in that department.

Nate's smile disappears. "I want you to come sing with me, that's it." He steps back to let me inside. "You're free to say no. I just like your voice, is all. I want to work with you."

My hesitation is brief, but the draw of what he's offering overwhelms any remaining reservations. It's my soft spot he's appealing to now. The desire to sing again, which I cradle so closely. And I can't stay in the doorway forever. Somebody behind Nate has just said, "If you put it out there in the universe, that energy is gonna come back, like, a thousand times." Which is my exit cue.

"Sing what?" I say as he leads me downstairs to the blessed silence of the basement studio.

"What else?" he says after shutting the door behind us, handing me the lyrics to the song he'd played at the open mic night.

The same one he'd been plucking his way through in the bath-tub while I fell asleep.

There are some people who are so persuasive that you will ask them a favor and subtly end up on the hook for far more than you'd reckoned. It is only when we are in the bathroom to-gether, me in the tub and him sitting beside it with what has to be a four-thousand-dollar microphone between us, that I start to remember why I don't ask for favors. But I'd be lying if I said it's unpleasant to be here. I am tired, my throat is sore from all the chatting I've been doing, and I'm far too aware of his body so close to mine. The mic, a silver condenser, has an old school look to it, and even though it's rather large it does nothing to sever the thin line of tension that vibrates between us now.

"We'll have to share," he says, holding up a pair of head-phones, the newfangled ones where the ear cups rotate outward so that two people can comfortably listen without smashing their heads together. He kicks the door shut and now it's noth-ing but us and his music. So we put our heads together as that slow burn of a guitar intro starts up. He takes the first part and I can't get over how rich and buttery his full voice is. I join him on the chorus, my tone so much lower, thrumming just under-neath. His falsetto on the hook is like cotton candy, so airy and light it practically floats through the ceiling. Then it's my turn on the second verse. We spend about half an hour like this, sing-ing to each other and listening to the playback on his laptop.

"Still liked the first one the best," he says, stretching out the kinks in his back. We've run out of bottled water, so for the time being we're done. Neither of us wants to venture upstairs to scrounge around for some more.

"First time can be magic."

An awkward pause follows. Neither of us is pale enough to blush, but I'm sure that the blood rushing to my face is giving it a shot.

"If you make it big, will you ever leave Detroit?" I say, to fill the void.

"I'd go play other places, sure. But this is where my roots are. My aunt, she was a singer here, too. Still comes back, time to time. My family, we're scattered all over this city. It ain't perfect, but it's our home."

Apart from this studio and Kovaks's bar, Nate's home doesn't seem that great to me, but what do I know?

"You ever think about leaving Vancouver?"

"No," I say, after a moment.

"See, that's what I'm talking about. We all have to be from someplace." He stares at his computer for a bit, then says into the screen, "I've been thinking about why you're here. Figuring about your dad and all that. Seems a bit crazy to me, but I get it. My mom's side of the family is American born and bred, but my dad was an Indian man from the Caribbean. He died of a heart attack when I was about fifteen."

I can tell from his tone that sympathy is not what he wants right now. He doesn't expect me to apologize because his father is dead. Doesn't even want to hear it. "He was Amerindian?" I didn't know that they were still around in the Caribbean anymore.

He shakes his head. "From India. I think the Amerindians were wiped out, mostly. Indians came to the islands as indentured laborers after Britain abolished the slave trade. They called them coolies. When my dad was growing up in the Caribbean he used to ask his parents where they were from in India, about their parents and his grandparents. They told him that his people were merchants, but he always thought they were lying. Nobody wanted to be associated with coolies because they were like slaves. Nobody wanted to be so poor they were almost black. Even though that's why they came to be there in the first place. So he never knew where in India his folks were from. That part of their history was lost."

I'm well familiar with this kind of creative reconstruction. For a long time in school I used to tell the other kids that my dad was in the army so he couldn't ever pick me up in the afternoon. When they asked about my mother I would say that she was a nurse and she worked the night shift at the hospital. I had no idea what it really meant at the time, I just heard some other kid say it in relation to her own mother's noticeable absence at school functions and it had sounded good. Then my foster brother told everyone in the schoolyard that I was an orphan while he held me up by my throat and shook me. As soon as I was free I punched his lights out. I learned how to keep my mouth shut after that. Reinventing yourself has its downsides. For me it was my foster brother. For Nate's family, it was a breach of trust when his father realized that they were liars. Pretense can only take so much scrutiny before it comes apart.

He puts on our song, which is how I've come to think of it. The conversation falls away while we listen. It's been a long time since I've heard my voice recorded. It's not false modesty to say that I can sing. It's a fact. This is the one thing that you couldn't take away from me if you tried. Nate can sing, too. Even better than me, maybe. Right now I'm amazed at what we sound like singing together. I want to ask what he intends to do with the song, but don't want to spoil the moment. Like the pretense of our pasts, what I'm feeling now can't be held up to the light. After a while, he sifts through his Motown Records collection, a throwback to the heyday of soul music in Detroit. I watch as he puts on some Marvin Gaye.

We all know what that means.

Vaginas are stronger than you'd think. They can be stroked. Petted. Filled. Hold on to or expel unwanted objects with a surprising muscularity. They can shed uterus linings and combat disease with the militant efficiency of CD4 cells. They can be locked away, waiting for the love of a good man or even a decent night of romance. They can also be cosmetically rejuvenated, revitalized, or surgically reconstructed after trauma. And I can lock this reconstructed vagina away forever, paid for courtesy of the Canadian taxpayer, or I can finally take it out for a real test ride. Just this once. To see how it takes the turns.

Halfway through, Nate pulls away. "You're not with me."

See, this is the problem when you don't get your lover from the Internet. The expectations aren't clearly spelled out. I want to say: Yes, I am. I'm right here. But he means something else, I guess. And the spell is already broken.

We leave it unfinished, me undone, and go back to the song. We listen to it once more. I want to dislike it now, after what has passed between me and Nate, but it's too good and I just don't have any hate in me at the moment. I'm fresh out of emotions— all of them. The house has gone silent now. The students and activists and hippies have disappeared. I don't know how much time passes, don't even remember moving to the couch and falling asleep. But I do remember the blanket he pulls over me and that, before we stopped, I had been taking the turns okay.

Better than I thought I would, anyway.

30

WHEN BRAZUCA WAKES, a pounding in his head reminds him of the time last year when Nora hit him with a tire iron, but much worse. Curtis Parnell didn't hold anything back, whereas Nora had clearly wanted him to live another day, maybe so that she could use him for sex and leave him hanging.

It's unfair, because he partly deserved what he got for being dishonest with her, but Brazuca isn't in an especially charitable mood. He's in what looks to be a basement, with his hands and feet tied, his knees pulled up to his chest and arms wrenched behind his back. The light in the room hurts his eyes, so he closes them again. He's about to slip back into unconsciousness when he senses someone above him.

Smack. A stinging slap to the face. "You awake, faggot?"

Brazuca groans, but doesn't open his eyes. On principle, because slurs aren't something that he's in the habit of acknowledging anyway.

Another slap. "Hey!"

Brazuca allows his head to loll, the side of his face pressing into the ground.

"Shit." Parnell moves away. There's the sound of a door opening.

Through slitted eyes he watches as Parnell rummages through a hockey bag full of weapons that he's pulled out of a storage compartment under the stairs, carefully selecting an assault rifle before putting the hockey bag back and locking the compartment with a padlock. The assault rifle seems more to make a point than anything else. In close quarters, he could have made do with a good old-fashioned pistol. Like the one he hit Brazuca with, which is now tucked into Parnell's waistband.

Parnell leans the rifle against the wall and reaches for a meat cleaver in the basement's tiny kitchenette. He proceeds to wipe the blade down with a cloth. "You know what I liked about them chinks that used to run around a lil while ago?"

Brazuca gives up the game and opens his eyes. Only because a disgusted sigh won't work if he continues to pretend he's asleep. He once again reconciles himself to the fact that he has a kind of face that bigots seem to trust. Feel open to speak their minds around. It is a quality that he would gladly give away if he could but so far there have been no takers—only an endless line of dangerous losers.

Parnell examines the blade, his dead eyes reflected back at him in the stainless steel. "Yeah, those cats, they knew what they were doing. Puts a kind of fear in a man, don't you think? Hack something off and people will tell their whole life story. So tell me," he says, moving toward Brazuca. "Who the fuck are you and why were you watching my house?"

"Three Phoenix," Brazuca says, on a sudden hunch.

Parnell stops. The name has surprised him, though he tries to hide the quick dart of fear in his eyes. "The fuck did you just say?"

"They sent me to check up on you."

"And who are you?"

"Ask them." Brazuca closes his eyes and leans his head back, channeling an arrogance he hasn't felt in over twenty years. A young man's cockiness.

Parnell yanks his head back and holds the blade to his throat. Brazuca wills himself to keep still. His eyes, when they meet Parnell's, are calm. Though his palms are clammy from the effort it takes.

"This about the chick?" Parnell asks, his eyebrows knit together. He seems nervous, the hand holding the cleaver damp with sweat.

"Of course it's about her. What did you think?"

"Fuck!" Parnell screams suddenly, moving away. A drop of blood beads at Brazuca's throat but there's nothing he can do to wipe it away. "Fuck, fuck, fucking fuck! I told them I got guys in Detroit on it. It's just gonna take a bit longer. That bitch is as good as dead."

"Well, she's not yet, is she?" Brazuca has no idea what Parnell is on about, but whatever it is has created some much-needed distance between them.

Parnell paces the small basement, then swings around to face Brazuca. "Hey, this is a favor, alright? They ask me to get some guys to keep an eye on her and I did. Followed her for months now. I dunno what they wanted from her anyway, never said a word about that. She was boring as shit. Only walking that ugly dog, taking the sick guy to the hospital, and then a couple night classes at UBC—"

"What dog?" Brazuca asks, but Parnell isn't listening.

"—and I was the one who took it upon myself to find out where she went when she skipped town. That wasn't part of the deal. Plus, I'm doing them another favor. I didn't have to call those guys in Detroit to take care of her. They—I offered up an option, on account of our *close relationship,* and y'all said that's what you wanted. Her gone for good. These things take time, you know."

"We did want her gone, but someone's got to be held account-able for the delay." And maybe he's not thinking clearly because, before he can stop himself, he repeats, "What dog?"

This time Parnell hears him. There's a moment of confusion, then he turns hostile. "What do you mean, what dog? The dog that's in the pictures we keep sending." He narrows his blood-shot eyes. Takes a closer look at Brazuca. "What did you say your name was? Oh, wait. You didn't." He puts the cleaver down and pulls his phone out of his back pocket—the same phone that Brazuca picked up from the driveway. Parnell grabs Brazuca by the hair once more, yanking his head back, and takes a photo of his face with the camera on his phone.

When he releases Brazuca's head, he makes sure to slam it on the ground. Lights explode in Brazuca's brain and he lies there gasping. Parnell disappears up the stairs, taking all the weapons with him, even the cleaver, and switching off the lights. The lock turns on a door upstairs.

It takes several long, sweaty minutes for Brazuca to thread his aching legs through his bound arms so that his hands are now in front of him. He just manages to pull himself into a seated position when the door opens again. The light switches on. There's a moment of blindness, then his vision adjusts.

"Jesus," says Stevie Warsame, as he comes down the stairs. "You alone down here, Bazooka?"

"Yeah," Brazuca says, falling back against the wall. "Where's Parnell?"

"Took off in his truck." Warsame cuts through Brazuca's bonds with a penknife attached to his keychain. "Those two assholes I was following were headed for the U.S. border, so I turned back. Good thing I did, too."

Brazuca nods, shakes the kinks out of his limbs.

Warsame glances toward the stairs. "We better go."

"He won't be back anytime soon." If the photo Parnell had taken of Brazuca's face could have been sent via the phone, he wouldn't have left. Which means that he had to go somewhere physically to get in touch with his Three Phoenix contacts. "Got a storage compartment full of weapons down here," he says, rising to his feet. He owes Lee a tip and can't, in good conscience, let a stash of weapons like this go unreported. It isn't strictly homicide related, but it's the best he's got.

It's only much later that Brazuca takes a ride from Warsame from the police station, where they'd given their statements, back to his MINI. Curtis Parnell is officially in the wind, with a photo of Brazuca on his phone, but Brazuca pushes it from his thoughts. He has another worry on his mind.

Warsame glances over at him. "What?"

"How the hell did you find me, anyway?"

"Needed some info for my invoice, so I tried to call. You weren't answering." Warsame shrugs. "Tracked you through the camera. It put you in the house, and I figured you were in trouble when I saw Parnell leave in his truck."

Brazuca reaches into his jacket and pulls out the small Canon that he'd borrowed from Warsame. The lens is smashed beyond repair, but on the underside of it is a dark, almost unnoticeable sticker just beginning to peel off at the edges.

A sticker apparently monitored by Warsame's phone. "You track your spare camera?"

Warsame shrugs. "I don't lend my shit out without some assurances."

Feeling a migraine coming on, Brazuca reaches over to turn off the radio. His head can't take Warsame's house music right now. He'd refused to go to the hospital, because why waste time? It would be a miracle if he doesn't have a concussion. Apparently Warsame thinks the same thing because when they reach Brazuca's MINI he insists on following Brazuca back home.

"I'm not going home," Brazuca says, as he gets out of the car. Down the street, the Parnell house is still blocked off by police. A group of neighbors gather around the police cordon, trying to get a glimpse inside. According to the cops at the station, they'd found a veritable arsenal of guns stashed in the basement, along with bricks of heroin and cocaine, which may or may not be cut with fentanyl and Wild 10. "I'll take it from here. Thanks for the ride." He fishes for his spare key from the magnetic case under the muffler, trying to ignore that Warsame has followed him.

Warsame shakes his head at the muffler key, but Brazuca has his reasons. Last year he'd been stranded at a remote gas station when a woman had thrown his keys into the bushes. He never wanted to experience that level of panic again.

"Amateur," Warsame says. He leans against the driver's door

and stares hard at Brazuca. His famous smile is gone now. "You're being reckless, dude. That ain't like you. You won't let me drive you to the hospital or even back home. There's something you're not telling me. I'm all about the war on drugs and shit, but I'm not your sidekick. I didn't save your ass just to keep on doing it because you're on some mission. You hear? You need to tell me what's going on. Right the fuck now."

In another universe, one where his leg wasn't shot to hell, his head wasn't pounding like someone had taken a drill to it, and a great urgency hadn't taken hold of him, maybe he could have moved Warsame out of the way. But they are in this universe, and Brazuca can't remember the last time he ate anything or where his real keys are. He just doesn't have the strength to keep quiet anymore. A cold fear has been building inside him parallel to his headache, each feeding and giving life to the other. And there's the knowledge that the woman who left him stranded without car keys is once again at the center of his problems.

It's like karma walked up, kicked him in the nuts, and then stole his lunch money.

He tells Warsame about the conversation he had with Parnell, who confirmed the Three Phoenix link. The triad had gone quiet in Vancouver after the disappearance of their head honcho Jimmy Fang but, the last time Brazuca checked, still had a presence in China where, according to Grace's research, there was easy access to those underground chemical labs that produce synthetic opiates like fentanyl and Wild 10.

But that's not exactly what's on his mind.

"Nora's got a dog, Stevie. And she was taking care of Crow,

who's sick. Until she left town a little while ago." He rubs his head, tries to remember the date she left but can't seem to pin it down.

"Where did she go?"

"She never said."

Warsame goes silent for a moment as it hits him. "You don't think Parnell was talking about her?"

Brazuca doesn't say anything. The biker had said he knew some rough people in Detroit. That the woman was in danger. A woman with a dog, who was taking care of a sick man.

He pulls out his phone and dials a number.

He's not surprised when Nora doesn't answer.

31

THERE IS A sound coming from the front of the house. I close the fridge door and am about to duck back into the basement when I realize what exactly is bothering me about the soft creak of a floorboard underneath a foot. The smell of patchouli has dissipated, so I know it's not one of the hippies. And the activists are so loud that I can't imagine them being stealthy in any situation . . .

Stealth, that's what it is.

I move to the back door, but before I get there, I hear Nate on the stairs, coming up from the basement.

It's too late now to run, or to warn him.

I grab the largest knife from the holder on the counter and am moving toward the basement door when Nate steps into the kitchen, rubbing the sleep from his eyes.

A muffled shot rings out. Nate falls to the floor. Not in slow motion, not like in the movies. There is a muted bang and he crumples immediately. Standing behind him is a figure clad in black, hood up over his head. He is the same height as the man in my motel room, but this time I can see his face. His broken nose is taped over and his eyes are on me. He raises the gun again. In the split second I have to think, I upend the kitchen table. It falls to the floor with a loud crash. Another shot splinters the wood behind me, but I'm already out the door.

It is still dark outside, the morning light has yet to filter in. There are so many boarded-up buildings on this street to hide in, but I duck behind a pile of rubble instead. From there I dial 911 on my phone, give Nate's address in a hushed whisper, and say a man has been shot. Come now.

Then I wait until I hear the footsteps careen past me, pause at the end of the street, and continue on.

When I get back to the house, Kev is sitting on the floor with his brother's head on his lap. I can't tell if Nate is alive. Tears stream down Kev's face. Ash is on the phone with emergency services. She's shouting that they need to hurry, none of this bullshit about neighborhood response times. Then she names a soul goddess of the city, one of the many famous singers to come out of Detroit. Do they want to be responsible for her nephew dying?

There's so much blood.

I'm suddenly a child again, walking into a room where unspeakable brutality has been done to a man I know. A kind of sickness overtakes me. One with which I am well familiar. I need my support group, but they wouldn't understand this. I long for Whisper, but she is someone else's guardian angel now. I want someone to give me something to do, but everyone in the room is busy watching a human tragedy unfold. Kev hasn't bothered to wipe his tears away. Nate doesn't seem to be breathing.

Nobody notices me.

I walk out as quickly as I entered and wait out front for the first responders to show up. I wonder how much violence a person can reasonably handle before she goes mad, if she hasn't already.

My fingers are curled around a knife, but I can't remember how I came to be holding it. Am I in shock? I must be. Because I can swear that, once again, someone is trying to kill me.

32

"NORA LIVES WITH Crow now," Brazuca had explained to Warsame on the way to the town house. "She left her dog there. It would be the first place she'd come back to. She loves that damn dog too much to stay away."

When they get to the town house, they find Whisper howling up a racket and an ambulance idling outside. Brazuca leaves the car running. Sprints over to the ambulance. "Hey," he says to the young paramedic who's just about to close the van door. "Who's in there?" He tries to get a look inside but the medic shuts the door firmly.

"Sorry, sir, are you the neighbor who called?"

"No, I'm a friend of that household, though. Is it a woman in there, Nora Watts?"

The paramedic shakes his head. "It's a man. Medication in the house tells us that he was being treated for cancer."

"Was?"

"Sorry, is, but he's in bad shape. Excuse me, but we've got to get going. If you're a friend, can you do something about that dog? Her noise is what got us called over here in the first place."

Brazuca watches as the ambulance pulls away, lights flashing. Warsame makes his way over from a parking spot about a half a block down. "Nora?" he says, nodding to the departing ambulance.

"Crow."

"Holy shit," says Warsame, who had known Sebastian Crow since he and Leo got together. "What's wrong with him?"

"Cancer," Brazuca says. He glances over at Warsame. "Paramedic said it looked bad. Somebody's gotta tell Leo."

Warsame shakes his head and backs away. "Nope. Uh-uh." They are both well aware that Leo hadn't taken the breakup well. Neither of them wants to be the one to share this news with him.

"I gotta deal with this Nora thing. You get Leo to the hospital and I'll take the dog."

"You see why I don't answer the phone when you call?"

"You don't answer the phone when anyone calls."

"Because of this kind of shit!" Warsame says, stalking to his car.

After he leaves, Brazuca goes into the house through the unlocked back door and finds the list of important numbers Nora had stuck to the fridge. Being Nora, she'd also left addresses, physical descriptions, and emails for each of the emergency contacts. She didn't leave an address for where she was going, though, and that's also classic Nora. Brazuca slips the list into his back pocket. Whisper trots up to him and sits at his feet, staring at him expectantly.

"What?"

She whines.

"We'll go to the hospital, okay?" he tells her. "We just gotta see about Nora first."

At the sound of Nora's name, Whisper rises and goes to the door, ready to leave.

33

BEFORE BRAZUCA LAST year, I'd been celibate for over a decade. I avoid intercourse like the plague or, at the very least, some nasty venereal disease. I've had a lot of time to think about why and, besides the obvious events of my past, which I refuse to name, it's simple. Sex represents an end for me. It is never a beginning. It's a wave good-bye, with a fuck-you-very-much thrown in for good measure. It's a breakup song on repeat.

But it has never been a breakup song like this.

As I sit outside Nate's hospital room, I can't help feeling that this has surpassed your average heartbreak jam and has become some country music shit, straight out of a Western. Where the cowboy comes back to his girl, and spends the night, and is ready to settle into a life of raising cattle (or whatever the hell it is that cowboys do). But in the morning his worst enemy rolls into town, guns blazing, and shoots his girl down. Except that this time, it isn't some anonymous girl who has been waiting with her arms open. It's a man named Nathaniel Marlowe. An artist with a voice like Sam Cooke. Who can play the guitar like Buddy Guy. Someone who moves people and is moved by them. Someone with a future, who could have name-dropped at any point that he was related to a soul music deity, but chose to make his own way in life. In his basement studio, he took me to church. I sang again, in a way that I haven't done in as long as I can remember. Without inhibition.

With my heart open.

I want to go into the room to see him, but I can't seem to make myself cross the threshold.

What I'm feeling right now is I'm nobody's idea of a cowboy.

I'm not sure what is happening, only that my worst enemy hasn't come to my town with his ammo in tow. I have inexplicably come to his. And I don't even know who he is. The desire to leave this godforsaken city becomes an itch, just underneath the membrane of my skin. Just out of reach. But I can't go yet because there's something here that I'm not seeing. There is also revenge to be sorted out, if I'm being honest.

There are two hippies waiting with me outside the room, discussing in low tones what will happen to their rally now that the entertainment is out of commission. They have to be quiet because Nate's brother is on the warpath. All talk ceases as Kev steps outside Nate's room and looks at me. "You were there when it happened?"

I stand up, peer past him into the room where Nate lies, still and sedated. He's just had a thoracotomy. The bullet missed his heart, but hit his lung, hit an artery. He almost bled out on his way to the hospital. He is still in critical condition, the blood loss keeping him unconscious. "I was in the kitchen, heard a noise, but Nate came up before I could do anything about it. I saw him go down and saw the man with the gun behind him. He pointed it at me, so I ran. Hid down the block and called 911. You know the rest." In a hushed whisper on the way to the hospital, I'd already told Ash about the man with the tattoo, the broken nose. I left out that I'm quite clearly the target because it's just not something I can put in words to anyone else.

Kev sits on a bench nearby and buries his face in his hands. "We stay out of all the nonsense that goes on around here. We stuck with this city when everybody who could leave left. And for it to go down like this . . . Nate never hurt anybody. Ever."

"He served in Afghanistan."

There's something seriously wrong with me that I would even say this aloud. Kev thinks so, too, by the look he gives me. "You think some Afghani came all the way up here to pay his dues? Come on. I'm talking about the here and now. Black man always gets shot."

"Ain't that the truth," I say, because we're in America, and it is. I've just seen it with my own eyes. The elevator doors open at the far end of the hall. I notice it before Kev does. Spot the plainclothes cops taking their sweet time in the hall, looking at room numbers as they walk. There's not much time left, so I say quickly, "Is he going to make it?"

Kev rubs his jaw, stares at a point behind me, and shrugs. His mind is somewhere else. "I've got a Ph.D. in American history. Did he ever tell you that?"

"No." One of the cops stops to check something on his phone, then discusses it with the other cop. It's a man and a woman, and even at a distance I can tell they're police officers because of the way they are looking at the people they pass in the hallway. Only a cop or a real estate agent looks at people that way. With eyes that seem to say, *It's only a matter of time.*

They still haven't noticed us.

"He wouldn't. Guess he didn't tell you he sent his army salary back home to help me pay for school, either? I am who I am because of him."

But who is he without him? This is the question we leave unspoken. Kev has retreated into himself and his memories of his brother, who is lying there fighting for his life. There is no reaching him now.

I walk away, careful to keep a calm, unhurried pace. From around the corner, I hear the detectives introduce themselves to Kev. I slump against the wall and listen to their questions about the shooting. I could at any point reveal myself and tell them that I was the target, am the target, but I don't. If I don't understand it, how could they?

Nate's still body on the bed, Seb's silence across the continent, the weight of Whisper's need, and Bonnie's last photo. They all add to my confusion. On top of it, I'm in a public place and feeling out of sorts with other people around. A middle-aged couple comes out of the room beside me, deep in conversation.

"Now that's done," the man says, with a great sigh of relief. "Maybe we can get a taxi to take us around, see some of the urban decay."

I give them both a hard look as they pass by me. Urban decay as a notch on a tourist's to-do list is about as insulting as you can get. To want to see the death of a city when it is still so alive. When Nate is, for the time being, still alive. Who are they to talk about death?

The detectives around the corner are speaking to Kev. Their voices travel. ". . . made the first 911 call about the incident at your home. The mobile number was registered to Nora Watts, a Canadian citizen who reported a break-in at her motel room in Midtown a few days ago."

"Hang on," says Kev. I hear another set of footsteps and a cool female voice asks to speak to Kev privately. She begins to explain something to him, her voice fading away as they step into Nate's room.

The two detectives are left hanging. "So what," begins one of them, "is a southwest Detroit thug doing in Midtown and now on the east side?"

It's strange that it has taken me this long to recognize this voice. It is Sanchez, the cop from the motel. The one who told me I should take my tourism dollars to Ann Arbor. He's with a woman cop.

"You sure he's from over that way?" says the woman cop, whose voice I don't recognize.

"The gang ink that Nora Watts saw wasn't from the east side. Base of the neck. It's a new signature going around."

"I've seen that before," says the woman. "What was the tattoo of?"

"She didn't get a close enough look."

"You think he saw it somewhere?"

"Happens. These morons get tats and sometimes they don't even know what they mean. You think they'd heard of Google."

"But what's this Canadian got to do with any of it?"

Sanchez sighs. He sounds a hundred years old when he says, "Dope and bodies. That's the gang scene in Detroit right now. She's got a hit out on her. You can't see that?"

I hear two new voices in the hall now. The doctor speaks to Kev, but I can't hear them clearly. The woman detective says to

Kev, "The witness to the shooting . . . any idea where we can find her?"

"Yeah, in the parking lot, probably," says Kev.

"She's here?"

"She was. Went that way." I have no doubt he's pointing in my direction.

I duck into a nearby room and wait for them to pass. It's the room where the "urban decay" tourists had emerged from. There is an old woman on the bed, staring at me with suspicious eyes, clutching the covers to her chest. She opens her mouth to say something, but I beat her to it. "Your relatives are assholes," I say to her.

She relaxes her grip on the bedsheets and sighs heavily. "Don't I know it. Come all the way here to pay their respects when I haven't heard from either of those bums in five years. They think they're in my will. Ha!" There is a pause as she looks me up and down. "You here to steal from me?"

"Just avoiding someone."

The woman closes her eyes. "Well, in that case, kid, stay as long as you like."

I linger for about thirty minutes, then leave via the emergency exit with my hood pulled up and stray strands of hair tucked into my collar. Walking at a steady pace, neither slow nor fast to attract attention, I still feel like I'm being watched. Just like I did in Vancouver, only this time there's no desire to meet my stalker face-to-face. I've made a mistake coming to the hospital, because this is the first place anyone who's been tracking my movements will look. I have only my phone on me, and my wallet that was in my jeans pocket already when I dressed.

Everything else, including my passport, is in that backpack at Nate's place. Which I can't go back to at the moment because it's now the scene of a crime. I should have never gone there in the first place, but how was I to know that the motel robbery wasn't a robbery at all? How was I to know I was still in danger of being followed, even here. Even in Detroit.

It's tough being a cowboy. You've always gotta be looking over your shoulder.

34

IT'S ONLY WHEN the college kid sees Whisper that the connection is made. He starts running, his backpack slipping off his shoulder and banging against his thigh. Whisper yanks the leash from Brazuca's hand and takes off after him. They're just two streets over from Crow's town house. She snaps at his leg and he goes down. Then stands over the kid, who's just about pissing his pants, with her teeth bared and a sliver of drool swinging above his face, until Brazuca catches up.

"Hey, Sunil," Brazuca says, slightly out of breath.

"Get this thing off me!" Whisper's dog walker is staring at her with fear in his big doe eyes.

Whisper snarls. It's clear the antagonism is mutual.

Brazuca crosses his arms and leans against a streetlight. He's spent the past few hours dozing in the car, waiting for the kid to leave the house. His leg is stiff and aching, but the college kid doesn't have to know that. "Hmm, I don't think you're cut out to be a dog walker."

"You're telling me! I just needed the money, okay? You know what college fees are for international students, man? Then that dog gave me so much trouble and those scary white guys showed up—"

Brazuca suppresses a groan. Barely. "Did you just say 'scary white guys'?"

"Hey, I don't tell you what to be afraid of, dude. These guys . . . you ever seen a horror movie? Who's always the bad guy in a horror movie?"

"A creepy little girl, usually. Did these scary white guys have hockey sticks and masks?"

Sunil blinks up at him. "No, they had guns. What planet are you from?" Sunil proceeds to describe the two idiot assholes Warsame followed from the Burnaby house.

Somehow Brazuca isn't at all surprised. "What did you tell them?"

"They were asking about the lady who hired me. I told them everything. She pays like shit. Went to Detroit. Then they made me call her and find out where she was staying."

"So you did."

"It's not like they gave me a choice!"

Whisper growls at his raised voice, so he lowers it to continue, careful to keep his eyes on her. "Did I not mention the guns? After I hung up with her they told me to forget about everything and just pretend that the whole thing didn't happen. But I couldn't look that dog in the eye, man. I just fucking couldn't do it. It's like she knew what I did."

Brazuca thinks about this for a moment. He drums his fingers against his bad leg. "Where was she staying?" he asks.

"What?"

"The address you gave them."

Sunil shrugs. "Somewhere in Midtown Detroit," she said. "I think it was on Second Avenue—does that make sense? Called Motor Midtown Motel or Midtown Motor—"

"I got it." He moves closer so that he's standing directly over Sunil. "If something happens to Nora because of this, we're coming back for you. Come on, girl," says Brazuca, beckoning to Whisper.

She jumps off her old dog walker and trots after Brazuca without a backward look at Sunil sprawled on the ground. "I'm calling the cops!" Sunil shouts after them.

"Do it," Brazuca says, knowing the kid likely won't. How would he explain this whole mess?

As they walk away, he thinks about putting Whisper on leash, but she seems content enough to walk at his side until they get to the car. Last year, the two of them had combed the wild, rugged coastline of Ucluelet on Vancouver Island. They had been looking for Nora then, too. He's never had a pet, even as a child, so he can't tell if Whisper's instinct for Nora is just the natural way of things, or if the dog has something special. He can't shake the feeling that she knows something's wrong. In her dislike for Sunil, the urgency in her step, her knowing eyes, she's on high alert. After she'd found Nora washed up on a stretch of beach, her body shaded by rocks and trees, Brazuca had a taste of Whisper's love for Nora. He will never underestimate it again. He wonders what has taken Nora away from her dog, and from Seb.

What could possibly be so important in Detroit?

He gets a feeling, a kind of bad omen. Or it would be, if he believed in things like omens. Which he doesn't. Back in the car, he almost heads over to Bernard Lam's place to close his case, but Sunil was right. There's something about that dog that just won't let up.

Like now, for example. She's staring at him from the backseat, a rumble building in the back of her throat. Telling him, without words, that there are more important things to do.

35

AROUND THE CORNER from the hospital, there's a barbecue joint that sells cornbread squares the size of a shoebox and fried chicken to go along with it, if you're curious about what the onset of a heart attack feels like. They also have free Wi-Fi, which is how they get people to stay once they're in the door. I haven't eaten much since yesterday and my stomach reminds me that though I can occasionally make it by on just one meal a day, this is the bare minimum.

The influx of carbs and sugar is saying I need a nap, but the late afternoon sun streaming through the windows keeps me awake. My laptop is in Nate's basement. I can't go back there right now, especially since I know that Sanchez is looking for me. But I still have work to do. I sit cross-legged on a wooden bench with my phone plugged into a charger I bought at the hospital gift shop. A chunk of cornbread obscures my peripheral vision. Ever since I had some on Retta's front porch, I've been addicted to it. Plus, the American motto of quantity over quality is growing on me.

While I eat, I think about sporting logos. The Red Wings jerseys I'd seen at the bar sparked something. They reminded me a bit of the Hell's Angels. Though the enthusiasm of rabid hockey fans is not unknown to me, I'm pretty sure that the man in my motel room didn't get the Detroit Red Wings symbol tattooed on the base of his neck. Not Hell's Angels, either, because I would have recognized it immediately. But, come to think of it, there was something about it that looked like a wing. With nothing better to go on, I narrow my searching of gang tattoos to birds. After an hour of staring at the body art of various gangsters on my phone, I have no answers but have gained a fresh appreciation for finding a good tattoo artist to ink your very original depiction of an eagle in flight. Long story short, it's very important.

I close that search and start another, the search I've been working myself up to since I sat down. The newspaper clipping is somewhere in the bag I left at Nate's place, but luckily I'd taken a photo of it before I put it away. Still, I don't need to look at the photo to remember the names of the people I'm thinking about. Dearborn, Michigan, hosts the country's largest Lebanese community. Many fled after a brutal civil war claimed countless lives. Just like in war zones everywhere, the people who could leave mostly did—and a lot of them inexplicably ended up in Michigan, of all the inhospitable locations they could have chosen. Why they came here is beyond me, but the Nasris seemed to have made a go of it. The bride in the photograph had gone to school in Montreal, so not only is there a Lebanese connection, there is also a Canadian one. Maybe she made a few friends at school and maybe one of them was my mother.

I don't pull up the photo on my phone because I don't need to see it. I don't need to see my mother's unfamiliar face, having been a part of public record for so many years, to know what it looks like. It has been imprinted into my memory since the moment I laid eyes on it. Her name was Sabrina Watts on my birth papers. In Hindi the name Sabrina means "everything." In

Latin, it refers to a river. In Arabic, it has something to do with patience. I think there's also a Celtic origin of the name, but I have forgotten what it could be. Lorelei and I were aware our mother's name was Sabrina. When we were children we would play games, imagining ourselves as princesses of various culturally charged garb. We never took the Hindi or Arabic versions of her name seriously, though, because her surname on our birth papers was Watts and that's as Anglo as you can get. I know a little about what you can get away with on a child's birth documents and the mother's maiden name is always used unless she legally changed it before marriage—which is what she must have done. She must have only wanted to be known, even to us, as Sabrina Watts.

I suppress the desire to call my sister and ask her directly if she found anything about our mother, anything that I wouldn't know. It's not a given, as it might be in other families, that she would keep me in the loop. Her sisterly love only goes as far as it takes to show me to the door. I push Lorelei from my mind, because it is a continuous twist of the blade in my heart that she has excised me from her life. Instead I think about the woman in the newspaper photo. Did she know what happened to my father? Did she know why someone would want to kill him? Lorelei had dug up everything she could on his death before she went off to college. We'd still been talking back then. I know that it was marked definitively as a suicide.

But what if it wasn't? I can't deny that after talking to Kovaks I've stopped thinking about his death as a suicide.

The cornbread obscuring my peripheral vision is getting smaller by the minute, but it's not so small that I can see the doorway clearly. So I'm not aware when Sanchez steps inside and sits down next to me on the bench. "Hi, Nora," he says, eyeing the drumstick that has gone cold on my plate. "I was just walking by and I saw you sitting here. I thought, Hey! There's that Canadian who got robbed at a motel. Excuse me, almost robbed. Remember me? Detective Sanchez?"

"No." It's such a blatant lie, but I'm so angry with myself for letting my guard down that I can't help it. Maybe I can be forgiven because he's now wearing a sweatshirt with the University of Michigan logo on it and has a baseball cap pulled low over his brow. He doesn't particularly look like a cop today, but I'd seen him earlier at the hospital and I should have been paying attention.

"Oh, I think you do. I think you should go for a ride with me."

"Nah. I'm good here."

"Are you sure? Because I'm not. We could have a good time together, you and me. Down at the station. We can catch up. You'll tell me what happened to Nate Marlowe and I'll listen quietly and take notes. C'mon. It'll be fun."

It doesn't sound like fun to me. Though phrased as a request, it's really not. Sanchez smiles, but it doesn't quite reach his eyes. I'm used to cops looking at me this way, so it doesn't faze me. I weigh my options. There aren't that many.

In the end, both Sanchez and I know that I have no choice in the matter.

36

SANCHEZ SEEMS CHEERFUL as he leads me to a Ford Taurus parked illegally outside. He has picked up a brisket sandwich for the road and eats it in record time. His mood only improves on the drive to police headquarters, which I learn has been relocated to a former casino building.

I continue to stare out the window, watching the sun set. The last time I paid attention to a sunset was out on the rocks in Vancouver with Whisper. The Pacific Ocean lapped at the shore and Whisper fell asleep at my feet. Then we picked up Seb from the last rounds of his treatment and all went home to the town house. Thinking of this, I see that the difference between Detroit and Vancouver is more than mere distance. They might as well be two different planets. If there is natural beauty in Detroit, it's so well hidden it might be lost forever.

Sanchez is still chatting about the new headquarters. "There's also a crime lab," he continues to explain. "And the Fire Department has their headquarters here, too." We drive up the multiple-level parking garage to the fifth floor, where we go through various doors opened by Sanchez's key card. There's one hallway after another, then some more after that. I've lost all sense of direction by the time we arrive at a small room with hard plastic chairs arranged across a table from each other.

Sanchez excuses himself. He leaves without locking the door

behind him. I'm not fooled by this, though, because the camera in the corner of the room is on and I know full well that I'm being watched. Have been watched since I sat down. I wonder if, when Sanchez comes back, he'll be good cop or bad cop. I fall asleep thinking about it. When I wake up, there's a cold cup of coffee at my elbow and Sanchez is sitting across from me with his head tilted back and his eyes closed.

I was not prepared for tired cop.

"Hey," I say softly to him.

"Mmm, just like that," he replies. Then he opens one eye to see what my reaction is. He laughs at my irritation. Turns into annoying cop. "I'm just joking."

"Can we move this along?"

"Sure. Want some fresh coffee?"

"No."

"Alright then." He pulls out a notepad and takes his sweet time looking it over. I would wonder why he didn't do this while I was asleep, but I know that mulling over notes is largely an act. He wants me to know that he has notes on me. But I refuse to be manipulated like this. I put my head back down on the table.

"Alright, alright. None of that." When I sit up again, he's back to tired cop.

"Nora Watts," he says. "Canadian citizen, residing in Vancouver, British Columbia." He looks at me over his notes. "Detroit is a long way from Vancouver. What's the purpose of your visit here?"

"Tourism," I say, which is what I told him back at the motel.

"Bullshit. What are you doing here, Nora?"

I think the real reason I'm here is because I have nothing but the past to hold on to. When Seb dies, my life will change again. It will just be me and Whisper and, for all her dedication to our life together, she's a poor conversationalist. I suppose I have Bonnie, but I don't. Not really. She's as much of a stranger to me as I am to her. If she, for example, wanted to know how to follow someone without being detected, we could talk. I could also teach her how to pick a lock or slam her knuckles into someone's throat so that she can buy some time to run away, but I hope to hell that she'll never need to learn any of these things. I hope she doesn't want to know me or my history, but if she ever comes to me to ask about her grandparents, I have nothing to tell her. I have nothing to tell myself.

Sanchez is waiting for an answer. I don't have one, so what I settle for is this: "I'm looking for information about my father."

"Okay, now we're getting somewhere. When was the last time you saw him?"

"Some thirty odd years ago."

He shakes his head sadly. "You're making this hard for yourself."

What he means is, I'm making it hard for him to go home and take a nap of his own. "It's true," I say. "My father died over thirty years ago. I had a visit recently from someone who served with him in the marines. He suggested that something happened to my dad during his military career, but he left before I could ask him more. I wasn't thinking straight. So I came here to see if anyone remembers anything. He grew up in Detroit."

"How did your dad die?"

"Suicide."

He jots this down on his notepad.

"He died in Detroit?"

"No, in Winnipeg."

He frowns. "And you're here now looking for information about a suicide that happened thirty years ago in another country? I gotta tell you, it doesn't seem like a good story. All you need to do is tell me a good story and you're outta here. We get you a nice escort to take you to the airport. Shake hands and you get on a plane. No more harm done. No more people getting shot." He drops the concerned act for a moment, and his voice takes on a hard edge. "Now, when you're telling the story, make sure it's the truth."

It seems a bit rich that he wants a good story that is also the truth. I'm stretched to my limits here just trying for the latter. So I say nothing.

"Okay," he says, going back to his notes. "A couple days ago you reported an attempted robbery at your motel room, but you claim nothing of value was taken."

"That's right."

"You confronted the robber, who witnesses say had a gun."

I nod.

"Your quick thinking got you out of that situation alive. Not a lot of people would have that kind of presence of mind."

"I'm pretty special."

"No kidding," he says, though his tone is less than admiring. "Not even a week later you're involved in another crime. This time a man gets shot."

"A man with an important aunt."

He doesn't miss a beat. "Every man and his aunt is important to the Detroit Police Department. The first 911 call about the incident was made from your cell phone number."

Which reminds me to get rid of my phone.

"Witnesses say that you were being chased by a man with a gun, who seemed to fit the description of the man you encountered in your motel room. We weren't able to identify his tattoo," he says, lying. "But he had a broken nose."

"Oh." My voice is all sugar and spice now. There's nothing I hate more than being lied to. "You think it's the same guy?"

"What's going on here, Nora?"

"I don't know." This is the absolute truth. I'm as upset about it as he seems to be.

"Do you have any idea how easy it is to put a hit out on someone in Detroit? Someone knows a guy who knows a dude whose brother's a gangbanger. It's not sophisticated. These guys are often no more than hired thugs—and they're desperate for the money. Fifteen thousand dollars. That's what human life is worth to some people here. Ten if you catch them on a bad day."

"Might be a lot of money to some."

He's incredulous. "You really arguing that's all your life is worth?"

Someone raps twice on the door and opens it up. It's the plainclothes female officer I'd seen at the hospital. "We gotta get going," she says to Sanchez.

He gets up from the table. Gives me a hard look, then turns to the woman. "Yeah. Actually, I'll do that interview on my own. Why don't you take Ms. Watts here to the detention center? I'm not done with her yet."

The woman is having none of this. "I gotta be there today

and you know it, Sanchez. Don't pass this off on me because all of the female detectives are out. Besides, you got court starting tomorrow," she reminds him. "You won't get a warrant in forty-eight hours for this. Plus, she's just a witness."

Sanchez runs a hand over his shaved head. "Shit. I got the kids this week, too."

"And this is a foreign witness," she says, her tone implying that there may be additional paperwork to account for my Canadian-ness.

"Yeah, yeah." He drums his fingers on the table. Comes to a decision. "Where are you staying?"

"With my uncle." I give him Harvey's address, which he dutifully adds to his notes.

"Who else knows you're staying there?"

"No one." Not even Harvey.

"We'll take my car," the woman says to Sanchez. "Meet me in the lot." Then she is off to begin their secret journey that she won't allow him to cut her out of.

After she leaves the room, Sanchez turns back to me. "Do you know who shot Nate Marlowe, Nora?"

"No."

"Alright. Don't tell anyone else about your uncle's place. Keep your phone on you. You and I both know that Nate wasn't the target."

"I don't know what you're talking about."

"Right. I think you're in danger, lady. I really do." And with that, he leaves.

I'm escorted out of the fancy police station shortly after. I'm not sure how much time has passed since I've been picked up, but I'm as exhausted as Sanchez at this point. The earlier kick from my nap has worn away. I get a coffee from a nearby shop, because my day is far from over. There's still some daylight left. In the restroom of the coffee shop, I take the battery out of my phone. The temptation to throw it away is strong, but I can't just yet. I hate to admit it, but I have become attached to it.

37

DOPE AND BODIES, Sanchez had said back at the hospital.

This is probably the only time in my life I wish that I was a drug dealer, at least there would be some sort of explanation for a gang in southwest Detroit to be after me. In my confusion, I decide to seek refuge with my Arab brethren. The address of the couple in Harvey's article was easy to find. They are upstanding members of the community and the house has been in the family for years.

A woman opens the front door of their sprawling home in Dearborn. Dania Nasri, the bride in the photograph with my mother, must be in her sixties, but looks a decade younger underneath her impeccable makeup. She is stylish and elegant in a way that seems almost effortless—the kind of woman who can make leggings and a tunic look like a fashion statement. "Yes?" she says in a quiet, accented voice.

I introduce myself and show her the photo I'd taken of the newspaper clipping from her wedding.

She takes the phone from me and studies the image on the screen. Her hands are smooth, nails painted a soft gold. "Sabrina Awad. Yes, I remember her very well. I've thought about her often."

Dania Nasri gives me a long look, then steps back to let me in. I follow her into the living room, which is dominated by a beautiful Persian rug in hues of red and gold. "I just made a pot of tea for myself, but there's enough for two. You better sit down, if you want to hear about your mother."

Let me tell you a story, she begins.

A young Palestinian woman lived on the outskirts of a refugee camp in Beirut with some relatives. The last living member of her immediate family, she asked a distant aunt living in Canada to help her get out of the country. She didn't know the aunt very well, but the aunt owed a favor to this woman's deceased father, so there they are. The papers were put in and she took a job as a cleaning woman to pass the time and get some money. The papers came through and she got on a plane to Montreal.

Once in Montreal, she went to university to continue her studies. She wasn't politically active at the time, didn't want anything to do with life back home. When we met through a mutual friend in college, we became quite close. She could be charming when she wanted. I found it hard to believe that she'd ever been a maid. There was just something different about her. She came with me to my wedding in Dearborn. I told her she would get to dress up, meet some other Lebanese, ha. She hated being photographed, though she was beautiful. She's only in one of my wedding photos, and there by accident. It's that photo, the one you're holding now. My father-in-law is an important man in Lebanon. They come from an old family, many of whom are involved in politics. At the beginning of the Western hostage crisis in the 1980s my father-in-law was in Lebanon helping with the negotiations and the newspapers ran a few stories on him and his life here. When they do a background piece on him, they sometimes use that wedding picture because the whole family is in it.

What beautiful woman doesn't want to be photographed?

A journalist showed up when the national papers started profiling my father-in-law's political work back in Lebanon. The journalist wanted to know about the people in the wedding photo. He asked about everyone, but did seem interested in Sabrina specifically. I thought it was because she was so pretty. I called her up after he left, your father answered the phone. I met him once, at the same time she met him. He was quiet, but very nice. It was just like Sabrina to ignore all the rich ones and go for the poorest man she could find. When they met here in Detroit, he was just out of the military and thinking about moving back to Canada, where he was born. She always said there was something about him. He was so kind. She liked the thought of bringing someone back to their homeland because, you understand, she could never go back to hers. Palestine was a dream.

Where was I?

Oh, the photo in the paper. I said to your father I'll send him a copy of the article. He said don't worry, he'll find one. Two days later, she called back and she sounded funny. I tried to ask her about you and about the new baby, but all she cared about was this journalist that was interested in her. She didn't sound like a happy new mother. She sounded . . . I don't know. Dull. Like she was separate from everything. Some women go through that after childbirth—but you didn't really talk about it back then. I told her it was going to be alright. Not to worry about the journalist, he was just doing a fluffy piece on the life of the Lebanese who came over. He said his paper was probably not interested in the ones that went to Canada, but I gave him their new address in Winnipeg anyway so that he could write to her. He was nice. He just wanted to talk about our lives here, not about politics. Sabrina married outside the community so he thought maybe her experience would be interesting. And she married an American veteran—well, one that was *really Canadian. He was interested in that. Like it was some kind of love across borders story or something.*

Your mother—she went quiet for a minute. *I felt that something was very wrong. I've never forgotten that feeling. I kept calling her name, then she asked me what he looked like. I told her, not tall, not short. Blond hair, blue eyes. He was in good shape, though. You could tell. Attractive, except for the scar on his neck he kept touching. Then she hung up. Didn't say good-bye or anything. I haven't heard from her since. I never understood any of it. I told that man only good things. I called your house a few times, trying to talk to her, but finally your dad answered. I remember it like it was yesterday. You know "London Bridge," the nursery rhyme? It was playing in the background. Your father said she was gone. After she talked to me, she packed up and left in the night, while everyone was asleep. That their relationship was under strain and she wasn't handling things too well with the new baby. He thought . . . he thought she was going to come back sooner or later and he'd let me know when she did. He was something, your father. I liked him a lot. He said he understood the impulse to run away, but people usually come back to the ones they love. He believed in her.*

You know what bothered me, though? It was something she'd said when we were in college and had gotten drunk together for the very first time. She said she was tired, so tired of running. That she wanted to live her life like a normal person, without looking over her shoulder. I thought at the time she was talking about the war, but what if she wasn't?

Why was she looking over her shoulder?

The front door opens and closes and a parade of young women fills the room. It is only about five girls, but my standard for what constitutes a parade is low.

Dania smiles at me. "You want to stay for dinner? It's just me and my granddaughters."

Do I want to have dinner with a pack of teenagers and their grandmother hen? I shake my head. "You've been very helpful," I say, holding out my hand.

Her smile is effortless, if a little sad. "You're welcome. I cared about her, you know. Sabrina. She was so independent, so stubborn. She walked to her own beat, that's for sure." She cocks her head to the side as she considers me. "You remind me of her."

With that doozy, she shows me out. I'm a lot like my mother? The woman who left more questions than answers, who abandoned her family at the first sign of trouble?

I knock on the door again, after she closes it. It opens almost immediately. "You change your mind about dinner?"

"No. What you just said about me being like her . . . that's probably the worst thing you could say to me. She left us." I can't keep the anger out of my voice. "My sister and I grew up without a mother. When my dad died, we went into foster care. He was wrong. She never came back."

She nods. "This is exactly what I mean—you coming back here to tell me that. Sabrina, she got into a lot of trouble. You could sense that about her. But she wasn't afraid of a confrontation." She tilts her head slightly to the side. "She came from a place that was hell on earth. One thing you learn about life in war is when to pick up and move on. Maybe she was struggling and she refused to stay with a fight she couldn't win."

My smile has no warmth to it. Not even a little. "Then she was nothing like me at all," I say.

38

WHEN BRAZUCA GETS to the hospital, explaining away Whisper's presence as a service dog, Warsame shakes his head at him from outside the hospital room. Brazuca enters the room with Whisper because he can't imagine keeping her away. She goes over to the lifeless body on the bed and climbs onto the armchair at the bedside. From there she puts her paws on Sebastian Crow's emaciated chest and rests her head just over his heart.

There is a sound from the corner of the room. Leo Krushnik stands there with his fist in his mouth and tears streaming from his eyes.

Brazuca watches as Seb's lover falls apart.

As the expression slides from his face.

And his body follows it down.

As it hits him in the gut that the man he loved is dead and chose to die alone, away from him.

Brazuca goes to his knees beside Krushnik and gathers him into his arms.

"Where's Nora?" Warsame says, much later. He and Brazuca are in the hallway, keeping an eye on the room. Whisper has moved from Seb's body and is now on the floor beside Krushnik, with her head on his lap.

"Detroit."

"So it is her."

"Looks like."

"That chick . . ." Warsame shakes his head. "Might as well paint a target on her back, bro. What's she mixed up with this time?"

"I don't know," Brazuca says, after a moment. Whisper raises her head. She looks toward Warsame, who is leaning against the door, and then back at Brazuca. As if waiting for him to make a move.

"Before Crow passed, he kept telling Krushnik to check the book. You know what he's talking about?"

"Here," says Brazuca, handing over the keys he'd found at Crow's house. "You're an investigator. Find out."

"And you got Nora?"

Brazuca shrugs, because if he says it, it has to be true. He doesn't want Nora. She isn't his problem. But he can't deny that she means something to him. He doesn't know whether it's the sacred bond of alcoholics who've sat meetings together or the fact that she had once trusted him, but it's there and undeniable. As much as he wants to leave her hanging, he doesn't know if he can. As he walks away, Warsame shouts after him, "Hey, you forgot the dog."

"No, I didn't," Brazuca says. When he'd looked a moment ago, Whisper had been staring at him, yes, but made no move to leave Krushnik's side. Last year, before Nora had gone to Vancouver Island to rescue her daughter, she'd left Whisper with Crow and Krushnik. They were still together back then, living in the town house that is now empty. They'd both loved that dog. He can't do a hell of a lot for Krushnik now, but he can do this. Leave him with someone to share his grief with. Someone to be there for him. Someone alive.

He gets in his car but it takes him a full minute to start it. He's too tired to go running to Detroit and has to deal with Lam before he does. But for now, what's on his mind is sleep. Suddenly, he's so damn exhausted.

39

AFTER MUCH DELIBERATION, I put the battery back into my phone, turn it on and send an email I've been dreading since Nate was shot. Describing exactly what has been happening since I left Canada. Then I walk toward the riverfront. I can't go back to the hospital, or the bar, or anyplace I've been since I got to this city, so I sit by the water and look toward Canada. Only a narrow stretch of water, the Detroit River, separates the two countries, linked by a bridge owned by some kind of industry tycoon. If I was to get on that bridge, clear customs, and drive a few hours, I would be just in time for a cup of tea with my teenage daughter. I could send her a photo of where I am but part of me doesn't want her to know that I'm close.

I guess it's enough for now that I know she's okay and getting regular pelvic exams.

I'm not sure how long I stay on the riverfront, but in Detroit time it's about two dozen people on bicycles with speakers mounted on them, playing slow jams. It's impossible to hate on cyclists blasting Luther Vandross and Aretha Franklin, no matter how close they are to running you over.

Hearing Aretha reminds me of Nate's aunt.

It's strange that a place like this could spawn one of the greatest soul legends alive today, but it makes a certain kind of sense. Music comes from shoving open the blinds and letting the sunshine or the darkness in. At least the blues does. Soul music is called that for a reason. If there was ever a place that stripped away the extraneous, it is Detroit. The only city where, after the population expanded to over a million, it has contracted again to far below it in what is America's most famous case study in mass desertion. Detroit isn't pretty, but the people left to pick up the pieces feel real to me. Which is more than I can say for beautiful but distant Vancouver, where there are no cyclists blasting love songs to cheer up the downtrodden. Maybe I'm falling for this city, even though someone here is trying to kill me.

I'm in a stupendous funk, and it's only getting worse.

After my near-drowning last year, my instincts have been off. Though I've at times felt I'd been watched, it took me a long time to figure out that the surveillance was real—that the veteran had been keeping an eye on me and I wasn't, as I thought, going crazy. This would not have happened if I'd been in my right mind, but Seb's illness and the introduction of Bonnie to my life have set me off-kilter.

My phone beeps as several emails from Simone come through. I'm lucky that free outdoor Wi-Fi hotspots exist so that I can be digitally harassed without being charged extra data fees. The first messages are dire warnings about being careful or else. But she never says what the "else" is.

The second contains a list of names and images that she's dug up of marines injured in Beirut during the time my father served. I wish I'd had enough presence of mind when Nate had been shot to recover my backpack from the scene so that I could look at this on a larger screen. I'm reluctant to go back, in case whoever is after me is still lurking around. And I don't want to run into Kev. I'm not sure I can take any more questions from him at the moment. I am still without a change of clothes, my passport, and my laptop. At least I have my wallet and phone on me, but still. I could have been better prepared. Thinking like this is a waste of time, of course. At the bottom of a dark pit is where what-ifs belong. Where you can find Nate. It is also where I put the memory of the time when, as a child, I saw a man bleeding out on the floor in front of me, which is partially why I'm in this godforsaken city in the first place.

I force myself to read through Simone's emails on my phone. The veteran isn't in there. If I'd been smarter I would have asked him his name when I confronted him in Vancouver, but I wasn't so I didn't. Because of this error, I'm here squinting at old records. Out of desperation I begin searching through images of American journalists in Lebanon during the 1970s, because Dania Nasri said that the man I now know as the veteran had posed as a journalist. Maybe there was some truth to that.

My phone rings. It's a blocked number. "Hello?"

"It's me," says Simone. "Did you get my messages?"

"Looking through them right now. Before you say anything about the attack . . ." God help me, but I had to tell her to get her to respond to me right away. And she did, as I knew she would.

"Don't talk to me about the attack, Nora. I've just about had it with you. It's all over the local press that some famous singer is on his deathbed. You're in the middle of a shitstorm. Again."

So she is upset. My strategy for getting her to respond quickly has achieved its aim, but not without some blowback. You can't win them all. And I haven't told her I'm the target. I may have insinuated that someone might be after my new friend Nate.

"Simone—"

"Don't. Just don't. I can't even with you right now."

"Look, I promise that all I've done is gone around asking questions about my dad. That's it."

She's quiet for a moment. I think she believes me, but can't be sure. I'm about to make another declaration of innocence when she speaks. "So you're looking for information about Americans in Lebanon during a very, very difficult time in the history of that country. There's a lot out there. And when hasn't Lebanon had a difficult time of it?"

The vast majority of photographs are from the eighties onward, when the American Embassy and marine barracks in Beirut were bombed. There were also stories about the hostage crisis that held the country in grip for roughly a decade, when foreigners were fair game and would be kidnapped left, right, and center, for as many reasons as there were in the book. The true beginnings of the hostage crisis hit a few years after my father had left the military, after my mother had immigrated to Canada and went to the wedding in Dearborn, but there had been some signs that Beirut wasn't a safe space for foreigners even before then.

"Talk to me about this guy, this veteran. What was your impression of him?"

"He was hard to pin down. His voice was strange and there was a scar on the side of his neck."

"So maybe there was some damage to his vocal cords, or throat, or something."

"That part felt true. When he said he'd been in an attack."

"Okay, this is what you're good at, Nora. This is your strength. Take away all the bullshit, forget that he'd been following you. What else about what he said felt true?"

"When he said there'd been trouble in Lebanon," I said slowly. I'd been looking at my father's life as a whole, looking into his childhood and his military life, but I'd learned nothing about his death from that line of inquiry. "He'd said it in reference to my father, but I can't find anything to support that."

I can hear her drumming her fingers against a table in the background. "So an American who'd had trouble in Lebanon. You're sure he's not in any of the photos that I've dug up?"

"I'm positive."

"Your dad was with the marines on a ship stationed in the Mediterranean, right? And came home in the seventies."

"Right."

"Your mom was a refugee, and had gone to a wedding in the late seventies."

"Yup."

"Sorry," she says, after a moment of silence. "I'm having thoughts about hideous disco outfits. The body type that can pull off a pair of bell-bottoms is so rare . . . Where were we? Your mother goes to a wedding in Dearborn and meets your father—"

"Not at the wedding. Somewhere in the city."

"Right, a few years after they meet, a newspaper article on the groom's family comes out because his dad is some kind of bigwig in Beirut who played a role as a political negotiator for the hostage crisis. The national newspapers pick it up. They use some of the wedding photos to profile his American ties. A journalist shows up at the family's house, asking questions."

"When my mom finds out about it, she leaves. About a year or so later, my dad dies."

"Right. So there's a period after your mom leaves and your dad dies—"

"If this veteran was after her, why did he wait?"

"It doesn't fit." She pauses. Thinks about it for a moment. I hear her cover the phone and whisper something to someone in the background but she's back with me quickly. "Let's leave that alone for a minute. I'm sifting through some other things. I might have some more photos for you to look at, Nora. Hang on."

I am hanging on, alone and in plain sight, as dusk falls around me. A frayed thread is what's keeping me from getting on the next plane back to Vancouver. Any sense of comfort I'd felt being in a crowded public place in daylight has now faded. There's no way I can go back to the motel, or to Nate's place, or Harvey's. But she doesn't have to know that. I sit and people-watch, particularly taken with a man in navy pants, a tan blazer, pink shirt, purple tie, and black shoes who still manages to look more coordinated than me, even though both my jacket and sweatpants are the same shade of dark gray. Some people can pull off color. All sorts of them, and at once.

My phone lights up. There is a photo waiting from Bonnie. Her feet are propped up on the dashboard of a car and, look, there's her forearm at the edge of the shot. Beyond the front windshield is an expanse of water that I assume is Lake Ontario. The sky over the water is a delicate pink. I'm out of Whisper photos, so it takes me a minute to figure out how to respond.

While I wait for Simone's next set of emails, I go over to a nearby streetlight and take a photo of myself underneath it. In the picture, you can see my face and my upper body clearly. It would have been nice for the shot to have been more flattering, but that's a losing battle. I send it off to her quickly, before I can stop myself.

Every girl should have a photo of her mother.

Then I check into a cheap hotel, not far from the waterfront. It's not much better than the motel, but at least the door locks. I pull the mini fridge away from the wall and set it in front of the door—for a sense of homely comfort—and then fall onto the bed with my clothes and shoes on.

I'm asleep when Simone sends a zip file of information through to me.

40

SOMETIMES FOREIGNERS GET hurt in Beirut.

I've given the hotel clerk twenty dollars to let me use the computer in the back office and he has left me alone with the warning that my time will be up in an hour. It is in the third set of Simone's articles that I find the veteran who, as it turns out, wasn't a veteran at all. He wasn't a journalist, either, though he wasn't far off.

He was a photographer who'd been injured in a car bomb blast.

In the photo of the accident, Ryan Russo is on a stretcher, being pushed into an ambulance on the streets of West Beirut. His face is mostly covered by an outstretched arm, but his eyes are wide open and glaring at whoever is behind the camera. The bomb, said the article, had exploded from a parked car that Russo had just walked past.

I skim past the warning of the danger of working in a foreign country until I get to the background information on Russo himself. His family had run a chain of small-town papers in California, and he'd gone to journalism school at Stanford. But photojournalism was his passion. He was working for his family's paper when he'd heard one of his photography idols had been killed in Beirut. The article said he was hoping to write a book about his mentor's work and death in Lebanon. He was a young man, yearning for adventure and was armed with a camera. He had fancied himself a man of the world, said his Beirut landlord. A bit of a daredevil who sometimes hired a "fixer" to help him navigate the city both geographically and politically, but had taken to going off on his own. The landlord suggested this was something of a mistake. According to the report, the blast caused severe burns to Russo's neck, arm, and torso. He'd also fractured a rib and broken his collarbone. After some searching, I find that Russo took photos for the family business for about a decade after returning from Lebanon.

The chain was sold and Ryan Russo dropped off the face of the earth.

"That's him," says Dania Nasri, after I knock on her door a second time. We're sitting in her living room and she is looking at the photo on my phone. It is a head shot taken before Beirut. Russo is looking directly at the camera, unsmiling. But even in this photograph his charisma shines through.

"You're sure?"

She nods slowly, eyes skimming over the article. "But I don't understand. It says right here that he'd been to Lebanon himself and was in an attack. He never said that when he came to see me—and I spent the whole afternoon talking to him." She scrolls back up to the top of the page, looking at the date. "He was in Beirut the same time your mother was there. You don't think that's a coincidence, do you?"

And then he saw her picture in the paper, came looking for her, and when she heard about it she abandoned her family and never looked back?

"No," I tell her. "I don't."

Having five granddaughters must have tuned her to the changes in female posture. Or maybe it's the sudden fear that I'm projecting. She places a hand over mine. "Are you in trouble, Nora?"

"My mother," I say, watching her carefully. "You said she wasn't political in Montreal when you met her. Was she political in Lebanon? Could she have been in some kind of trouble?"

She smiles and pats my hand. "No, I don't think so."

It hurts when someone you trust lies to your face. Even elegant women who love their granddaughters aren't exempt. Maybe that's what makes me hold on to her hand, a little tighter than necessary. I squeeze, not enough to cause pain, but enough for her to know I'm not letting go. Her fingers feel brittle under my grip. She's wearing a diamond engagement band along with her wedding ring. The diamond cuts into my skin, but I barely feel it. I'm so tired that I'm close to being numb. "Tell me the truth."

Dania is looking at me, shocked. She tries to move her hand away, but I don't let her. "You don't want to know the truth."

"Isn't that for me to decide? I need to know." I've come too far now. I sense her weakening, so I loosen my grip.

She pulls her hand from mine and goes to the window. "I heard from a mutual friend who knew your mother's brother from Lebanon . . . She lived on the outskirts of the Sabra refugee camp with some relatives who took her in after her brother was shot in the head. He had refused to provide ID at a checkpoint. He'd joined a Marxist group that fought for Palestine. They were a low-key bunch, but some were involved in petty acts of disturbance. Kidnappings, robberies. This friend said that

Sabrina had hung around them for a while after her brother died, his friends were all she had left of him. It could have been something, or nothing. That's all I know." But I can see the wheels still churning in her brain.

There's something she's still not saying. I wait quietly for her to continue. To realize that she can't fool me.

She turns away from the window and looks at me. I wish at this moment I looked like my mother because maybe it would spark something in this woman. Maybe make her tell me what she's too afraid to say.

I think, at the end of it, it's my stubbornness that wins out.

She sighs heavily. "Your mother lived alone in Montreal. Her aunt who sponsored her . . . she didn't live with her. Never really spoke about her. I just couldn't figure out how Sabrina could afford it all. I always got the sense that she was holding something back. I liked her, loved her at times, even. But I couldn't trust her. It was like she always kept something hidden. You know what her favorite book was? *Catch-22*. She saw herself not as a part of a revolutionary people. In all the time I knew her, there was no struggle in her. She saw herself as a person sick of the world who gets in a rowboat and paddles away. She could be . . . she could be cold. Not always, but every now and then I would see a little glimmer of it. When she didn't want to talk about her new baby, your sister, I felt that coldness again."

I backtrack. I don't want to think about how my mother could look at Lorelei and feel anything other than love. If I do I'll have to confront the fact that, to make up for it, I spent my childhood looking at my sister with nothing *but* love. Even when it hurt so much I could barely speak to her. "She never said how she supported herself?"

"I asked a few times, but she would just change the subject. She was an expert at avoiding conversations she didn't want to have."

A short silence follows. Then something in her breaks. "I always thought there was a man involved, to be honest. We would talk about boyfriends, of course, but she was very cynical. She said there'd been someone, back in Beirut, but she'd seen another side to him. She said he'd just been using her. Something about the way she said it frightened me, I suppose. She was not a forgiving person."

Dania Nasri turns away from me. She looks like she's aged ten years since we began this conversation. I guess that's the effect I have on people.

"Thanks for your time," I say, getting up so that I can put some distance between us. I pause for a moment at the entrance to the room. "How can you remember all of this?"

She hesitates. Looks through me. "My family, when they left Jaffa in Palestine it was supposed to be for a few days. Maybe a month. We had orange groves there, the best oranges in the whole world came from our land. There was an olive grove, too. We had family in Lebanon whom we visited many times in the past, so it was just like another family holiday. And then . . . and then we weren't allowed back. Other people lived in our house. As the years went past, my mother and father used to talk about the house, until they couldn't remember it properly anymore. Then they would argue about what had been on the shelves and the color of this rug or that curtain.

Eventually my mother threw the house keys away because what was the point of keeping them anymore? That part of our history was lost to us, and we will never get it back."

She goes to a bookshelf filled with large albums. Her fingers skip over them and land on one. She opens it up and shows me a certain page. It is the article that I first showed her, the one with the photo of my mother at the wedding. "Everything about us goes into one of these," she explains. "My granddaughters, they think I'm silly for doing this, but it's our history, you know?"

"They'll always know what color the curtains are."

"No, they can forget the curtains, but nobody will throw away any more keys to who we are. The keys are more important. They can look in here if they want to find one. I don't want my family to lose another memory." She pauses here and something like regret crosses her face. It's the first time I've seen her lose her composure. "Like, for example, one of a close friend who has left her family shortly after a conversation with you. I've replayed that phone call in my mind over and over for years and thought about what I said to that man who came to our house. I know I had something to do with her leaving, you understand? I just didn't know what. At the time I was pregnant and preoccupied, but I never forgot and I've thought about it often. I even wrote it down, but destroyed the note afterward. It was so silly of me, giving out her information! When I came to America, I wanted a new life, too. I didn't want to live in fear and suspicion. You have no idea what that does to a person after a while."

Her voice turns soft. Without intending to, I find that I've leaned in to hear her. She smiles the saddest smile I think I've ever seen.

"That time in college with your mother was the freest I've ever been. We would spend nights studying and giggling like we were schoolgirls. When she had something crazy to say, something outrageous, she would grab whatever was handy and hold it up to her ear. 'Who's listening?'—and then she'd laugh with her whole body, from deep inside her belly. In those moments, I loved her. She was my best friend back then. When she left your father, she left me, too."

We don't shake hands at the door because we've come too far for that. She moves in for a hug, but I step back to avoid any attempt at an embrace. I haven't forgotten what happened to the last person I put my arms around. I have no desire to see anyone else lying broken in a hospital room.

"I didn't know your father died when you were a child. I'm so sorry for you and your sister. For whatever role I played in your mother leaving you." Dania Nasri reaches into her pocket and hands me something that she has been hiding there. It is an old, rusty house key from the previous century, warmed from her palm.

"I thought you said your mother threw her keys away."

She shakes her head. "This is your mother's key. We got drunk one night in her room off absinthe and cheap wine, and she showed it to me. Then she laughed and threw it out the window. I saw it on the ground when I left, so I picked it up. I meant to keep it for her if she was ever ready to have it back. She never brought it up again. I've been waiting for some kind of sign of what I should do with it but now you're here and you know everything I know about your mother. So it's only right you should have this, too."

She looks at me expectantly, waiting for something. Understanding. Forgiveness, maybe. She may even settle for acknowledgment, but she'll have to do without it because I leave without another word to her, feeling like I'm being watched. Well, that's nothing new. Watched. Hunted. Just like my cold, distant mother, who I guess I really am like.

My mother's old friend was wrong. I do know what it's like to live with fear and suspicion hanging over my head. That it's an inherited trait makes a kind of sense. My mother was a migrant, a refugee—one of the many. A sad song that would be played on repeat for years to come. A broken record that left a trail of despair that would see the migration from country to country, shore to shore. And the trail would keep moving, along with the bodies. As changeable as the political arguments for and against intervention, keeping in mind the protection of various economic interests in the region.

As fluid as the world's capacity to give a fuck.

41

I SIT IN a café in Dearborn Heights, drinking Arabic coffee and thinking about what Dania had said. Maybe I'm here because I'm trying to connect with my heritage, but, as always, it's an exercise in futility. My heart isn't in it. I'm distracted. There are too many windows in this place, so I have chosen a seat at the back of the room and proceeded to glare at anyone who comes through the door. I have commandeered the single electrical outlet in the seating area to charge my phone. The staff is unhappy with my presence, but there are few customers this time of evening and they're no doubt thinking about their day's take.

Simone sends me an email. I open it up to find a Chicago police report from nearly forty years ago for one Ryan Russo, whose girlfriend had taken out a restraining order against him.

I think about asking Simone how she got access to this, but she has never spilled her secrets before and I'm betting this case will be no different. That she's remarkably well connected in the hacker world isn't exactly news to me.

There's no other information in the email. Simone has signed off with "more soon" but soon isn't specific enough for me. I order a second piece of baklava and let my mind wander while I wait for it to arrive. Seb's phone is going straight to voice mail now, but his voice is still in my head. Still asking me to take a minute and try to sort through the threads. Dania had asked many rhetorical questions when discussing my mother, but the one that I focus on is this one: What beautiful woman doesn't want to be photographed?

A woman on the run, obviously. From her past, from a man who had seen her photo in a newspaper and come looking for her. A man who has kept tabs on her daughters throughout the years. He'd followed me in Vancouver and set me on this course. Now I'm looking into my father's history, looking into my mother's life, and what do I find but this man who'd claimed to be a marine?

And who wants me dead, apparently.

Dania Nasri talked about coincidences. No matter how I turn it over in my mind, I can't see it as a coincidence that my mother disappeared when that article on Dania's father-in-law was printed. A photo of my mother emerges, right before Dania spoke with a man who might have been posing as a journalist and who would, many years later, pose as a veteran. And then a man shows up at the bar to spread the news of my father's death to Kovaks, while also trying to find out more about my mother's whereabouts. I've sent Russo's picture to Kovaks, who confirmed this looked like the concerned friend, but he can't be a hundred percent sure.

But it's enough for me.

All roads lead back to Ryan Russo, a man of hidden motivations. Who lived through a car bombing—which had been common in Beirut at the time.

When I look at my phone again, I see multiple messages from Brazuca, asking me to call him. I'm about to do just that, when a text comes in from Leo. Leo hasn't attempted to reach me since he thought I betrayed him by going to work with Seb after their breakup.

I open the message. *He's gone. I have Whisper.*

There's no answer when I try to reach him. I know he's in Vancouver, staring at his phone, because a few minutes later he sends another text.

I've read the book.

Which means he knows everything now. I can feel his pain palpitating over the miles separating us. There's nothing more to be said than what's in Seb's memoirs. There's only forgiveness to be granted, if Leo can find it in himself to give it.

Harvey Watts told me that my aunt wasn't my father's birth sister, said it like it was something that I didn't already know. When I tried to run away from foster care the first time, this was made perfectly clear to me. She wasn't kin to me, was too sick to raise us alone, but she loved my father. It didn't matter to either of them that they weren't blood relations. What those made-for-TV movies that come around at Christmastime to bludgeon you with the restorative power of family reconciliation don't want you to know is that there are connections stronger than blood.

Sebastian Crow needed help with some research once and he took a chance on me. I helped find him a handful of interviews some years ago.

After that, we never looked back.

I may not have much to call my own in this life. I live in a city I can't afford. Close by is a sister who is embarrassed by me and an ex-sponsor who has betrayed me. My mentor has just stepped off death's doorstep and his lover may never forgive me for my silence on the subject. There's a town house I have no right to stay in now that Seb is gone and a dog who will punish me for my absence.

It may not be much, but what I do have I owe to Mike Starling and Seb Crow, who are both gone now. Both lost to me, and the fragile world I'd built for myself around them.

Dope and bodies.

Dope and I haven't had a relationship since high school, but I can't deny that I've got a line on bodies. And they seem to be piling up.

There's no point in calling Brazuca, because I already have the news. Besides, I don't want to bring him into whatever it is that I'm facing now. The men around me have a short life expectancy and, even though I haven't forgiven him for his past betrayal, Brazuca deserves a bullet-free life filled with a healthful smoothie on the side. Also, a life free of mysterious figures from my mother's past who have been showing up periodically throughout the years, searching for her. I don't know what she did to bring this upon herself, upon us, but I wouldn't ever underestimate the hatred that someone can hold tight for years. Decades, even.

In Detroit there's a man who bought the house next door to his ex-wife's and erected a giant statue of a middle finger in the yard. He made sure it was positioned front and center and lit up at night. It was a visual monstrosity, designed to scandalize the entire neighborhood. An expensive representation of his outrage, mild compared with what I seem to be dealing with now.

They say hell hath no fury like a woman scorned. Yeah? Try a man.

42

"SO YOU WANT to hear about that old boys' club, do you?" says the woman on the bench.

This morning I had still been in bed when a woman named Jules Dubois called me, told me that Mark Kovaks had cashed in a favor on my behalf, and if I wanted to talk to her about what it was like in Lebanon some thirty years ago, I'd better not waste any time getting to Forest Park. Which is where she spends her midmornings. I thought she chose the location because it's a place where little old ladies can take their daily constitutional and watch over the kickball field, but Jules Dubois is a little old lady who has something different in mind when it comes to her constitution.

We're on a bench and she's rolling a joint with meticulous precision. She lights it, lingers over a long pull, and offers it to me. I take a small puff and hand it back to her. I'm not above peer pressure when my defenses are down.

"I have cancer," she says. She watches me as I close my eyes briefly against the instant high. "When was the last time you smoked a joint?"

"Maybe twenty years." I think. The pistons aren't all firing this morning, even without the weed factored in. I've spent another night at a cheap hotel in downtown Detroit—a different one this time. I slept for more than eight hours, too, but it's hard to feel rested when you're on the run.

"It's good, isn't it? Get sick and they give you a prescription. I've got it in the tits."

"Excuse me?"

"The cancer," she says, as though I'm slow. "It's in my tits. Man, I thought I was so lucky with these things." She adjusts her bra, heaving it up by the straps. "You shoulda seen me in my heyday. Small everywhere but the chest. It was like I won the genetic lottery. Now look at me. It's the opposite."

"You look fine to me," I say, determined not to give her what she wants, which is for me to look at her breasts and offer up an opinion for the sole purpose of her knocking it down. Living with Seb these last months has been an exercise in sidestepping these kinds of subjects with the terminally ill. Their bodies have changed with the illness, noticeably so. They know it, but they want their body image reaffirmed. Problem is, they can't accept this kind of affirmation. They know it's a lie. And it makes them angry, bitter, or worse. Sad.

"It's because I'm wearing a prosthetic. Ever seen one?" With her free hand she plucks at the opening of her flowered blouse. Over the blouse and a pair of dark sweatpants, she wears a long pink trench coat. She reminds me of the man on the waterfront, except he was more coordinated. Jules Dubois looks like she threw on whatever happened to be on her floor before coming to meet me. This is probably why I liked her immediately. She seems like my kind of woman.

"Nah, I'm good. Thanks."

"Just as well," she says, sighing heavily, before going back to her spliff. "You should really look into getting a prescription. This stuff does wonders. I waited until I had cancer before I partook, but you don't have to."

She offers me the joint again, but I shake my head. The first toke was enough for me to question my reasons for being here, suffer the longing to be with Whisper since I'm enjoying the outdoors, and consider the purpose of my existence in general. I'm not sure I can handle what a second will bring. "I live in Vancouver. You can get a prescription off the streets there." You can walk into any cannabis clinic, fill out some paperwork saying you get panic attacks, and boom: access to reasonably priced marijuana and its various derivative products. I know this because Seb had one for his condition and I often went with him for his refills.

"Lucky you. So what do you want to know? As I said on the phone, I might not have much time left. Got rid of the tits, but not the cancer. Ain't that something. It's metastasized—what a word. *Metastasis.* You heard the phrase 'spread like cancer'? Well, what happens when it's your cancer that's spreading? You lose more than your tits."

I'm once again under that microscopic stare as she waits for me to explain myself.

"When you were in Beirut, did you know an American photographer named Ryan Russo?"

Her response is almost instantaneous. Whatever is happening to her body, and even on what I personally know to be some very potent bud, her mind is razor-sharp. "Never heard of him. When was he there?"

"Seventies. He was there to work on a book, but he might have been a freelancer also."

She shakes her head. "I was there as an AP correspondent in eighty-two, right before the massacres at Sabra and Shatila, the Palestinian camps. Most awful thing I ever saw, those bodies on the streets. Right now we've got a global refugee crisis happening with Syria, Jordan, Somalia. I've visited a lot of camps in my time, but walking through Shatila after all those people were butchered . . ." She shrugs. "Probably the worst day of my life."

Dubois takes another long pull of her joint and stares through a couple walking their massive pit bull. They give her the stink eye as they pass but she is beyond their censure.

I've been told that some things actually do improve with age, and one of them is the ability to communicate to people that you give no fucks without fear of reprisal. Dubois has embraced this fully as she extends her middle finger to the couple.

When they're out of earshot, she turns back to me. "First of all, let me tell you I left Beirut more confused than I'd been before I got there. I was asked to write a tell-all book about my experience after the hostage crisis became a hot thing in the eighties, but the truth is that I left because I could no longer write dispassionately about human suffering. To continue to live in Beirut I would have had to do like the Lebanese and keep adapting. Play psychological games with myself so that all of the death and destruction didn't really matter. Keep moving forward and never look back, or even look around too much. I'm not ashamed to say I didn't want to do it any longer. Maybe your Ryan Russo couldn't either, because I was there for two years living in West Beirut where all the foreign correspondents lived and I've never heard of him. And I would have, if he was anybody. We all hung out at the Commodore Hotel. Heard of it?"

I shake my head, which sends it spinning.

"No? It was a very famous watering hole for journalists and spies. Some decent businesspeople, too, though I can't imagine how they stayed among all the ruckus in Beirut."

"Spies?" Something about what Kovaks said back at the bar hits me. Some people were obsessed with conspiracy theories, but this is the second time it's crossed my mind in relation to Beirut.

She looks at me sideways and stubs out her joint. "It was the Cold War. Besides that, there was a civil war and the Syrian invasion. Also the Israeli invasion. There was so much intrigue that people blamed every little thing on some plot or the other. That's the story of Beirut. There were plots and counterplots everywhere. In every group of people, there were a hundred different stories used to describe the same event. It was madness. It was the national pastime."

"Right." This had seemed to be relevant to Kovaks, too, but Dania Nasri never bothered to talk espionage. Maybe she no longer indulged in the national pastime. Clearly, though, it had made an impression on Dubois.

"Sorry I couldn't be of more help, but I wish you luck with your search." She smiles over at me and communicates silently that I'm the one expected to get up and leave. I do, glad that she didn't give me the look that she'd given the couple with the pit bull.

It should be no surprise to me that she's talking intrigue and espionage. I come from people who attract secrets. The silky wings of a moth ensnaring them, holding them, daring them closer to the light. That part of me comes from a place like that . . . well, it explains a lot.

43

THE BUS TO Chicago takes four hours, maybe five. I should be counting, but I've effectively been on autopilot for the last four hours. Maybe five. What matters is the woman I find at the end of this road. But I still need to keep myself occupied somehow. I've tried to read *Catch-22*, which I picked up at a secondhand bookstore by the bus station, but I can't seem to make heads or tails of it.

I call Lorelei and tell her what I think happened some forty years ago. Our mother moved to Montreal and went buck wild. At university she made friends, let down her guard. Went to an American wedding and met a man in Detroit. Fell in love, legally changed her name to Sabrina Watts, got married, had kids . . . and eventually took off again.

I leave out my suspicions about her being pursued. Still, Lorelei refuses to believe any of it. She hangs up on me.

I call again. She doesn't answer. I wait another ten minutes until the next try. I've got nothing but time to kill. On my third attempt, she is so frustrated that she picks up. I suppose it hadn't occurred to her to turn her phone off. "She was an Arab," I say, when the line connects. "A Palestinian refugee who lived in Lebanon before she immigrated. You should add that to 'mixed heritage' on your website bio."

"You're an asshole," she says, to cover up her surprise that I have been on the website of the environmental nonprofit she runs. As though I'm not interested in antipipeline coalitions also. The mixed-heritage description is a new gem displayed on her public profile. Before this year, Lorelei hadn't been comfortable speculating openly about our family's background, especially when it comes to our father. Her private life was full of day-dreams about where he might have belonged once upon a time, but in her public life she was less open about her confusion.

I can't give her what she wants to know about Sam Watts, but I've discovered who our mother is. We had given up on her a long time ago, but now we have some information. Maybe it will mean something to Lorelei. Maybe I'm hoping she can tell me what it means for me. "Her name was Sabrina Awad," I con-tinue. "Remember we used to wonder about where she came from? Before she married Dad she legally changed her name in court to Watts. That's why she never had her maiden name on our birth papers. It's the only way you can get away with not having a maiden name listed. But she was Palestinian." I use the past tense because that's what I know of her. Her past.

"Palestinian?" Lorelei repeats slowly.

"From Lebanon."

"But . . . why would she change her name before she got married?"

Because she was running from something—or someone. I want to tell her this, but her skeptical tone puts my back up. I can feel, even separated by thousands of miles, that she doesn't trust my information. If only because it's coming from me. "Maybe she was testing the legal system here," I say instead. "For fun."

"Huh," is her reply to this.

I can feel her thinking on the other end of the line. Softening, even. "She had a big belly laugh," I say quietly. Remembering the love in Dania Nasri's voice. "When she was going to say something outrageous she'd—"

"I have to go, Nora." Her voice is small. I can't remember the last time I heard her so unsure of herself. Before I have time to adjust, however, she remembers herself, and that she is unsure of nothing. "I don't have time for this right now."

"Wait. Remember that veteran you talked to? He's dangerous. I mean it. If he ever approaches you again—"

There's a click as she disconnects the call.

I must, for a moment, examine my motivations for telling Lorelei about our mother. They are not inspiring. I guess that I still, after all these years, want to keep her in the loop about what's happening with me. If one day I, too, might be useful on her website bio, I'd like her to get the facts straight.

I'm aware that this is mean-spirited, but I can't help myself. Thinking about Lorelei has always brought out the worst in me. Perhaps because she is so obvious in her hunger for belonging, so shamelessly transparent in wanting to know what is in her blood and what it must say about her. I think I should feel that way, too. But I don't. Wanting to know where you came from doesn't make you weak . . . but it can make you vulnerable. It can make you crave answers about people you should belong to and places that call to your heart, answers that you're never going to get, from questions you don't have the courage to ask.

This desire is buried so deep in me that I can only bring it out when I sing. Which I do now, softly and to myself, in a seat at the back of a mostly empty bus, on my way to meet a frightened woman who is not expecting me. Amy Winehouse is what I settle on, which speaks to what kind of mood I'm in. You can't listen to Amy without a sense of terrible foreboding. I've decided to embrace it. Wallow in the sense of impending doom.

From the bus station, I take a ride share using an app on my phone to the address in a wealthy suburb. The street is tree-lined, the homes stately and beautiful. The people who live here are clearly not aware that they live in a perpetual global recession, because they seem to be okay with spending vast amounts of money on gaudy Halloween decorations. I knock on the door of the corner house on the street and wait by a pair of devilish jack-o'-lanterns.

A lovely gray-haired woman opens the door. She looks at me, at my outfit, then at my shoes. None seem to pass muster, but she is far too elegant a lady to comment. She and Dania Nasri have taught me that a classy woman should always be dressed nicely to answer the door. For some reason.

"Yes?" the woman says. "If you're here for the food drive, I left a shopping bag out this morning. I thought you'd already picked it up?"

"I'm here about Ryan Russo, Gloria."

Her reaction is unmistakable. Gloria Tate sags against the doorway. A look of panic crosses her face. Her fear is a living, tangible thing. Even though her restraining order was dated almost forty years ago, she is still not over it. "What? What has he done? Is he back in Chicago?"

"Can I come in?"

"Yes, yes, of course." She holds the door open for me to enter. There is a room just off the entryway that she leads me to. A half a dozen bags of Halloween candy sit on the coffee table. "Sorry for the mess. I'm just getting organized here."

I perch on the edge of an ivory armchair, across from an ivory sofa, separated by an ivory rug. "Where's your tower?" I say.

"What?" Her fingers grip the edge of the sofa.

I gesture to the room and am about to explain the joke when she gets up and closes the spotless white curtains. I have a sudden insight. Only a certain kind of woman has furniture this pristine. One who is, of course, hiding something behind the facade. My joke disintegrates.

She looks at me. Clears her throat. "Ryan . . . has he hurt someone?"

It's not surprising that violence is what she thinks of first. A woman doesn't take out a restraining order for nothing. "Not recently, that I know of."

"Is he in Chicago?"

"I don't think so. I'm here because I think he might have known my mother, Sabrina Awad. Back in Lebanon. I think she might have been running away from him, but I don't know why."

Gloria Tate's hand trembles. She disappears into the kitchen without a word to me and comes back about a minute later with two glasses of white wine. I accept the glass she holds out but am careful to set it on the table. A glass of wine for me isn't the same thing as a puff of a joint. It is a slippery slope, at the bottom of which lies my self-respect. Gloria handles her wine differently. She finishes her glass in four long gulps. I push my own glass toward her and she accepts it with the grace of a lady who knows how to keep her habit under wraps. A functioning alcoholic. I know them well, mostly because I used to be one.

She holds this glass in her hand, swirls it around. I get the sense that she's deciding whether or not to confide in me. I see the moment when the fear wins out and she decides against it. It's when she puts the glass back down and stands. "I'm really sorry, but my husband will be home soon. I have some errands to run before he gets here."

I stand, too. "I'll come along."

"That's not possible."

"I could just follow you," I say. "Like Russo did."

She clutches the neckline of her blouse, her fingers convulsively closing over the buttons. The signs of abuse are impossible to ignore. "Please don't joke about that. He—he made my life a living hell! Even after I took out the restraining order, I used to feel like someone was watching me."

She goes quiet, but I can't let her stop now. "Tell me about him," I whisper, going to her. I don't touch her, though, because you don't dare touch a woman in this state. It occurs to me that I should leave her alone to her fear, but I have come so far and am closing in on something. I can feel it. "Tell me and I'll be gone."

Her eyes narrow and her voice hovers just barely above a whisper. "He was obsessive, alright? We dated for two and a half years. I was his physiotherapist. That's how we met."

"Why was he in Lebanon?"

"His family had some connections in the publishing world and he'd gotten a small advance to write a book about his hero, a friend of his father's who was a French photojournalist who died in Lebanon. One day outside his apartment in West Beirut, two men shoved him into a car, attacked him, robbed him, and left him on a street a few blocks away. He was walking back to his apartment when, ten feet away from him, a car bomb went off. It was a Mercedes. He used to bring it up whenever we passed one together. He had second- and third-degree burns along the right side of his body. It was a long rehabilitation process for him."

"He was kidnapped and robbed? Are you sure?" Because none of those details had been in the article on him after the blast.

"I heard that story so many times while we were together. Yes, I think I'd remember that."

"Did he ever talk about another woman? Someone who stood out."

She blinks at me. Her eyelashes are long and thick, with a delicate coating of mascara sweeping them upward, giving her a startled appearance. "Well . . . yes. Now that you mention it. During therapy he told me about a woman he'd met in Lebanon when he was reporting there. They were together for a while, then she somehow got the wrong idea about him and ran off one day."

"What wrong idea?"

"I don't know. He never said. Maybe she thought he was cheating. He said he just wanted to clear the air. To let her know that he only wished her well. She was a Palestinian woman and he wanted to make sure that she didn't face any repercussions from being with him because he was a white man. He wanted to help sponsor her to come to the States. I thought . . . I thought it was considerate. He was so worldly and charming at first. I'd never been out of the country at that time so his adventures were quite fascinating to me."

She pauses here and drinks some more wine to steady her nerves. The effect is one of total relaxation. She is so calm now that she loses the trail of the conversation.

"And then?" I say.

"And then he wasn't charming. He was hooked on morphine after it was prescribed to him for the pain management. It messed with his head when he tried to keep off it. He would follow me if I forgot to tell him where I'd be going. He was violent some-times. I don't know what his trigger was, but every now and then we would just be having a regular conversation and I'd say some-thing to upset him. Then I'd be on the floor, bleeding. I'd wake up in bed an hour later with him holding my hand and pouring me tea . . . Please can you go? I can't talk about this anymore."

"Okay, I understand. I have one more question, though. Did he ever seem like he had anything to hide?" I say, on a hunch.

She frowns at me. "Other than his temper and his habit? I don't know. I heard from a friend of a friend that he might have had a gambling problem after we broke up. I think she men-tioned that he filed for bankruptcy. I wasn't surprised that he played cards, but I was surprised he lost. He was a really good liar."

"No kidding." He sure fooled me back in Vancouver.

"Ryan had a way of telling you a lie that was so close to the truth that you wondered if you were crazy. About conversations or events that you were present for. Sometimes I got the feel-ing that he enjoyed it. He liked the idea that he was making me crazy. He was a political junkie and we'd have these bizarre debates. Whatever my position was on this event or the other, he'd spin it around later and make me think I said something else. He thought it was fun. I don't know. Does that help? Can you leave now?"

There is no excuse for frightening a woman like this, not really. In my defense, there's a man lying in a hospital bed because of the danger I'm in. I'm about to thank Gloria for her time, maybe even apologize, when the front door opens and a man walks in. He looks to be in his seventies, but his age does nothing to detract from the vitality he projects into the room. Vitality and something else, something that I can't quite put my finger on.

"Honey?" he says, looking from Gloria to me.

I give him a crisp nod and move to the door. "Sorry to interrupt your evening, I was just going. I'm from the food bank. Your wife donated to our Halloween food drive and I came to personally thank her."

"Gloria is wonderful that way, isn't she?" He beams and grabs my hand, giving it a firm shake. "I'm Frederick Halpern. Please let us know if you need any more help this year. I could probably organize something with my club." He smiles at Gloria until he notices the two wineglasses on her side of the coffee table. His smile takes on a tense edge. Gloria's brightens in response. It is so awkward in the room that there's only one thing to do now.

"Have a nice evening," I say to them both. On my way out, I pass a set of family photographs in the hallway. They are mostly of Gloria and Frederick holding hands in various vacation destinations, but one above the potted palm in the entranceway stands out. It is of Frederick alone at work. I see now what I had tried to understand back there in the living room about Gloria Tate's husband. It was the sense of authority that he embodied.

On the porch I pass the two jack-o'-lanterns. Maybe it's just my imagination but they seem to be judging me for pushing an obviously distraught woman past her limits. Well, I'm not proud of it, either. As I walk away, I mull over what I've learned. Gloria Tate kept her maiden name even though that had made her easy for Simone to track down—but she was a lot more clever than I had initially given her credit for. For a woman who lived in fear of an ex, she managed to find a way to put herself squarely out of his reach. She married a man whose station in life was so high and mighty that it was enough to keep her safe as long as he was alive. Frederick Halpern isn't just above the law. He is the law.

Gloria Tate married a judge.

44

THE CAR FOLLOWS me down the street.

I turn the block.

It also turns.

I stop to tie my boot laces.

It slows to a halt.

I take off running, and reach a crescent at the end of the road. A god-awful semicircle of death, lined with picture-perfect brick houses and white picket fences. Who are these people and don't they realize that the 1950s are over?

The car that has been following me idles nearby. Frederick Halpern rolls down the window on the driver's side. "Get in," he says.

I weigh my options. A car from a private home security company pulls up behind us. Halpern sticks his head out the window and waves at the driver. "Hey, Joe. No worries. She's with me."

The car flashes its high beams in response and waits for me to get in Halpern's car. I do. The other car pulls off. Halpern smiles at me. "Gloria has her problems, I'll give you that. But deception isn't one of them, at least with me. You want to know about Ryan Russo?"

I nod, speechless for the moment.

"You came to the right place, then. I've got something I want to show you."

We drive for about twenty minutes. I'm not familiar with Chicago, so I can't tell from our surroundings where we're going. I'm just grateful for the heated seats and dual climate control. Halpern's BMW is a lot nicer than Sanchez's Taurus, that's for sure. Finally, Halpern pulls into an apartment complex across the road from a strip mall. I have no idea where we are, but it looks like the suburbs. He hands me a set of keys. "Big key is for the front door and the little one is for 309. I'll wait for you here."

I look at the keys. "Whose apartment is it?"

"Russo's. About ten years ago Gloria thought she saw him at a coffee shop, but chalked it up to her imagination. I had a PI I know look into it. Russo sold his family paper years ago and invested in real estate. He's got a few investment properties in California where he lives mostly, but I found out that he keeps a little place here. So I had my guy make keys. I've never been able to catch him checking up on her so I can't prove it, but I know he does from time to time. I've taken the liberty of informing my PI that you'll be here. Happy hunting."

I get out of the car without another word. I'm still confused as I head into the sleepy little building. Nobody stops me on my way in. The elevator is broken so I take the stairs up. Apartment 309 is just off the stairwell, perfect for someone who doesn't want to be friendly with neighbors in elevators.

I hesitate at the door.

What if Russo is in here? But if I don't go in, I'll have to face Halpern and tell him I was too scared. This is not an option. Unless he has planned some kind of ambush. But deep down inside I know that he hasn't. He had no idea I was coming to visit his wife, nor time to formulate an organized response even if he were so inclined. I don't question a possible motive for this to be a setup because, truly, I am beyond understanding human beings at this point. Why they do what they do is as much of a mystery to me as anyone else.

I enter the apartment as quietly as I can and wait in the dark while I listen for sounds or movement. Nothing. So I turn on the light and see some more nothing, but in a lit space. I walk through the tiny apartment, which is empty but for a few dishes and utensils in the kitchen cabinet and a single bed underneath a window in the bedroom. There's a small bedside table with a lamp next to it. I open the drawer of the table, but find it empty. When I slide the whole thing out I see there's nothing taped to the underside, either. I walk through the apartment again. It's sparsely furnished, but doesn't feel abandoned. I wonder when Russo was last here. If he's been hanging around Chicago, then it would make sense he might have some connections to Detroit, which is not far at all. And could he have resisted having a peek at Gloria while he's been trying to get me killed?

Under the kitchen sink there's a bucket and some cleaning supplies. In the bucket there's a knotted-off plastic bag with some used paper towels, an empty bottle of whiskey, and a manila envelope. It's one of Stevie Warsame's steadfast rules. If in doubt, look through the trash. Inelegant, but I can't question his instincts. Especially now.

I close the door of the bathroom while I use it, by force of habit, and when I come out there is a man lounging on the bed.

"Now don't go yelling and screaming just yet," says the man on the bed, who sits up with a slow, easy motion. He's got the manila envelope from under the sink in his hand. "I'm Fred Halpern's PI. He told me to meet you over here because you're looking for Russo. Fred has been waiting for years for that asshole to slip up so that we can put him behind bars."

"For Gloria's sake." I look toward the front door of the apartment. It was closed and Halpern's keys are still in my pocket. So this man must have his own set.

"He loves the hell out of that woman. I'm Jeff Samson. You can just call me Samson, if you want. Most people do."

"Nora." We don't shake hands and he doesn't attempt to reach out to me. I like a man who respects a woman's personal space. I lean against the wall for some emotional support. It's got none to offer. I must be desperate. Samson and I eye each other for a moment. A mild showdown that gives me enough time to get a good look at him. He looks as world-weary as any detective out of an old Hollywood noir film, with all the grace of an exhausted Sidney Poitier.

"What you got on Russo, Nora?" he asks, getting straight to the point.

"Not a hell of a lot." I tell him what I know so far. He has a trusting face and, since the wall isn't doing what I'd hoped, I've got to find my support from somewhere else.

"Sounds just like him," Samson says, when I'm done spreading my confusion and unfounded allegations around.

"Yeah?"

"I owe Judge Halpern a favor or two from back in the day and the only way the man asked me to repay him is to keep an eye on this guy. I've been on Russo for a long time. Ever since Freddie found out about him from Gloria. Russo's unpredictable as all get-out, except in one way. He's a gambler. Sometimes it's money and sometimes it's other things. Digs himself into a hole, gets desperate, and lies his way out of it again. That's the pattern of his life. At the beginning, I looked into Beirut. Don't have my files with me, but I can get them to you if you want."

"I'd be okay if you just tell me what you remember," I say, trying not to let my excitement show.

"Not planning to stick around for long, huh? I understand that. What I remember is sitting with him at a blackjack table for a couple hours straight, watching him pretend he wasn't a morphine junkie while he lost what I made in six months. Told him I was a vet and I'd served in Vietnam. Wasn't a lie. He told me about when he was in Beirut. Started talking about all the crazy shit that went down in that country. How everyone turned on each other all the time. How a man could get a little side cash if he had the right kind of information."

"He was a spy?" I ask, again remembering what Kovaks and Dubois seemed to both be obsessed with.

"He was an asshole. No kind of real intelligence operative would have opened his mouth like that. I got this feeling that I couldn't shake. I've known bullshitters like him my whole life. I think he got in trouble and somebody had something on him. Used it as leverage to get a favor or two out of him, maybe. I don't know how long this lasted, but I do know that for a while in Beirut the Soviets used to use a foreign flag cover to recruit people. Recruiters would pretend to be from other countries or lead unwitting agents to think they were working for the American government sometimes. If you're looking for excitement, you'd be an easy mark. Add a debt owed and, boom, you got yourself an agent."

"A debt . . . like from gambling."

"Seems the likeliest story to me, Nora. Been on domestics for longer than I can remember and if a husband ain't cheating or doping, he's gambling."

"That's sexist."

"It's the truth. It's a curse. An addiction. But the thing with Russo is he likes to think he's smooth as shit, but he really ain't. I think if he got mixed up in something, it didn't go over well. He started talking all kinds of smack about the Arabs down there in Beirut. I knew he was injured when a car bomb went off near him, but I got the feeling this was something else. Something personal."

I know whatever happened in Beirut must have been personal—or else he wouldn't have spent all this time looking for my mother. "He didn't strike you as competent, huh?"

Samson laughs. "Not even close. I think he's the kind of idiot who goes around scaring women and acting reckless to show people he's some kind of big man, because deep down he can't control himself and never could."

"Harsh."

He acknowledges this with a smile. "But true. That kind of attitude don't change with age, which is why I'm here talking to you. You can't change a reckless man." He gets up and hands me the envelope. "Things start to heat up and guys like Russo come unhinged. I've seen it a thousand times."

Me, too. I have seen enough people crack to know that it only takes that extra little push.

"When I was sitting with him at that table, he got pretty close to unhinged. Gloria said he'd tried on and off to kick the morphine habit. Looking at him I could tell he was jonesing because when he started losing, it hit him hard. Went off about how he was working for the CIA. I said yeah, sure, buddy, and let him keep going. Didn't believe a word of it. He got worked up like that with a stranger. Don't want to imagine what he'd do with someone he knew well. Maybe I don't have to imagine, because of what Freddie told me about him and Gloria. I know Freddie wants him to mess up somehow so that we can put that bastard behind bars for good, but I wouldn't want a nice lady like you to get caught up in the crossfire."

Seems like this so-called nice lady is already caught up. But I don't say that. "I appreciate that. But you don't actually think he worked with the CIA?"

"Not a chance. And I don't think he believed it, either. But it was pretty clear he was working for someone. You take care now, Nora." He goes to the door. I see now why I had no idea he'd come in. He could teach a course to a cat burglar on how to move silently. Maybe he already had at some point in his past. He's that good. Before I know it, he's gone, leaving behind no trace that he'd ever been here at all.

When I get back to the car, Halpern is listening to classical music with his eyes closed. He's drumming his fingers against the steering wheel to the tune. I have the feeling that he already knew the apartment was mostly a dead end. He showed it to me to reveal what, exactly? I don't ask him outright because I don't trust his smiles. They remind me of Sanchez. Brazuca, too. They belong to men who know what it's like to wield power.

I have no experience with that.

We are mostly silent on the drive to the bus station. He doesn't mention a thing about Samson. Chopin plays in the background. I only know it's Chopin because Seb used to have some classical music on his computer that he listened to when he thought I was asleep. Chopin was Leo's favorite.

Halpern pulls up in front of the terminal. He nods to the manila envelope. "Samson showed me that already. Do you know what's in there?"

"Lab results of some kind." I'd taken a peek before Samson showed up.

"That's right. We've already made copies and I had a doctor friend I play golf with take a look."

"And?" I ask, playing along.

"What it shows is that over time, his creatinine levels are high. Dangerously so. And so is his potassium."

A smile crosses his face. The Chopin dies away. I sense he's waiting for me to say something, but I'm not in the mood to play his games anymore. So I return his little smile and keep quiet. He can't help but fill the silence, because this is why he's brought me here. To show me Russo's little crash pad—and be his captive audience. We've come too far for him to stop now.

"Which means that his kidneys are failing and he needs to be on dialysis immediately. Three hours a day, three times a week for the rest of his life." His smile turns satisfied. "He thinks he can just terrorize my wife for years and that he won't get what's coming to him? Well, life has a different idea about justice. May not be in the courts, so little justice is served there—and I'd know—but things have a way of coming 'round. He spent years in recovery after the bomb in Beirut. Years. And he didn't learn his lesson. So guess what? He's going to spend the rest of his life in excruciating pain."

And Halpern's going to enjoy it. Hell, he seems to be loving it already because he's still smiling.

I nod, to show him that I've heard all this. I'm about to say good-bye to him, but the look on his face tells me there's no point. He's somewhere else. Maybe he's still thinking about how much he's going to love watching Russo die painfully—whatever it is, he's already forgotten me.

I leave the envelope behind when I get out of the car.

There's a bus going back to Detroit in half an hour, so I buy my ticket and sit on a hard bench to wait for it to board.

This has been the strangest night.

Ryan Russo may be something of a mystery, but he'll soon be a dead mystery. It explains the renewed interest in my family after all these years. Like Seb, Russo is getting his affairs in order because pretty soon he'll have to deal with a debilitating illness, one where he'll spend the rest of his life tied to a dialysis machine. So, naturally, he's got to get all his stalking done now. Find the women he blames for his shitty life. Murder people like me who are getting a tad too close to some of his deep, dark secrets.

You know, the usual.

45

SOME PEOPLE HATE hospitals for their smell. Some won't go near them because they can't stand the sight of blood. Or illness. Or death. Personally, I stay away because of the waiting. Like now, for example. Sitting by Nate's side, waiting for him to wake up so that I can say good-bye. He is fast asleep, though, because recovery takes rest. This is what I hope. He has never lied to me and, even now, his silence leaves much to be desired on the subject of hope. He's not promising anything he can't deliver.

The room is filled with flowers from well-wishers. There's a particularly large arrangement in the corner of the room. The name on the card leaves no doubt that this bluesman who goes to open mics for some pin money has connections that I would have only dreamed about back while I was trying to make it as a singer.

Scentless flowers in a riot of colors watch over us as I give him the update on my search for information about my father's death. How it clearly wasn't a suicide, but I can't prove it. How my mother was involved.

Just as I'm nearing the end of my explanation, a doctor comes into the room. He looks at Nate. Then at me.

"Family?" he says somewhat doubtfully, taking a stab in the dark.

I do have one in the form of Whisper, if no one else, so I nod and try my best to look like someone's fiancée or a long-lost cousin. "Yes. How's he doing?"

He hesitates, assesses me for signs that I might not be able to handle the truth. Then he checks Nate's vitals. "Too soon to tell. He lost a lot of blood, and he's very weak. There's a high risk of infection and he's still bleeding internally. He's scheduled for a second thoracotomy to suture the remaining blood vessels."

He is about to leave when I hold up a hand. "Before you go. Just a quick question. I have a friend who served in Afghanistan. He was . . . a bomb went off and he had second- and third-degree burns to the right side of his body. What can I expect?"

"You can expect someone who is deeply traumatized. Someone who will be in a great deal of pain. Your friend will need all the support he can get because recovery will be a slippery road. Not just medical support to treat his burns, either. Burns like that can have an extreme effect on a person's mental health, especially if it's regarding explosives. He might be sensitive to fire, to loud noises. They may trigger something for him."

"But do you think he can heal and be perfectly rational, pay his taxes, walk his dog, and tuck his kids into bed at night without us worrying about him having a break?"

The doctor smiles gently. "Yes, of course," he lies.

I'm willing to let that one slide.

"Okay, but what if my friend was a little psychologically unstable to begin with. For example, if he liked to follow women around, that sort of thing?"

The doctor stops smiling. He edges away, using Nate's chart

as a shield. "In that case, you should probably find another friend. Have a good day." Then he slips out the door.

I sit by Nate's side for a long time, staring at the article about Ryan Russo on my phone. I don't dare touch Nate, or look at him for too long. It's too painful. Something Seb taught me is penetrating the fog of confusion in my brain. *But what are they deliberately not saying? What are they dancing around?* It's here that you'll find the truth.

I look at Nate. He has no answers. I want to tell him what singing with him has meant to me. What he has meant to me. In the end, all I can manage is a butterfly kiss on his lips and one above his brow. I don't want to leave, but I know I have to. Seb is gone forever but Nate is still here. My presence isn't going to help his chances for survival. The hospital isn't a safe space for me. I think about calling Sanchez and telling him everything I know, confessing my sins and everyone else's. Making my problems his for the moment, just to unburden myself.

I leave the hospital. I'm not sure where to go, so I catch a ride share to town. The driver turns up the music when I get into the car, which suits my mood just fine. I have him take me to a casino in Greektown. The security guards eye me, but don't move to bar my entry. They want everyone's money—not just the people who can afford to give it up. I wander around the tables and watch people lose more money than I'll ever have in my bank account. There are no windows in this place. No way to mark the passage of time if you refuse to look away from your cards.

A woman in a red dress walks by me and makes a beeline for a man seated at a blackjack table. She goes right up to him and slaps him hard. The man rubs his face. He tries to ignore her. She's upsetting his concentration. She bursts into tears and pulls at his arm. He pushes her off. A security guard comes to take her away. She shouts at the man, screaming, pleading, but he has forgotten that she's even in the room. Nobody else blinks an eye. They keep playing, pretending that the woman and her tears don't exist.

What's missing here is their humanity.

The article says Russo was badly injured by a car bomb on his way home to his apartment in West Beirut. But not that he'd also been kidnapped and robbed. It's not the kind of detail that a reporter would leave out unless Russo chose to keep that little tidbit to himself. But him being something of a journalist himself . . . he would know the value of adding this to the story.

So it is clearly something that he wanted to keep under wraps.

A car bomb in Beirut during the civil war, and after, was an everyday tragedy. But a kidnapping suggested he was being targeted. For what, and by whom? And why didn't he want anyone to know about it?

This is what's been eluding me.

46

BRAZUCA WAITS FOR Lam to finish a conference call. The call is on speaker and the language spoken is rapid-fire Cantonese. Lam's participation is minimal. Just a word here or there to fill in the gaps.

He's in Lam's study, taking in the fine furnishings while he tries to disguise his impatience. It has been a couple of days since he discovered that Nora is being targeted. He's tried to reach every motel in Midtown Detroit and come up empty. Nora isn't answering his calls and her phone seems to be switched off, for the most part. She's never been easy to get in touch with, so he's not sure if she is just ignoring him or if there's something else behind it.

"Sorry," says Lam, as he disconnects the line. "My father's on the warpath."

"What did you do this time?"

Lam runs a hand through his thick dark hair and then rubs at the back of his neck. A platinum watch glints from his wrist. "Doesn't have anything to do with me, thank God. He expects nothing from me now that I've married the woman he chose. He's got great hopes for the grandkids, though."

"Is your wife pregnant?" Brazuca doesn't even know her name. Lam barely mentions her, or talks about why she's never around. Where she is, this ghost wife, is something he doesn't particularly want to get into.

Lam smiles grimly and shakes his head. "The only grand-child he'll ever have died with Clem. Let him deal with that."

Brazuca lets that go. Lam's anger still overshadows all reason. Suddenly he's tired of it all, and has especially had it with this man he's given up his new leaf for. The only upside is the money, which isn't holding the appeal that it once had. He reaches into his pocket and hands Lam a flash drive. "My report." It had taken him two days to compile all his notes and extract the usable photos that he and Warsame had taken. The links that made up the supply chain. The Triple 9s at the Lala Lair. Curtis Parnell at the port. The Three Phoenix connection in Hong Kong—the mysterious players that have some bizarre interest in Nora Watts.

Lam opens the file on his laptop and reads it through. After he's done, he steps away from the screen and pours a drink. He pours one for Brazuca as well, remembering to include Brazuca this time, but forgetting that he's an alcoholic. "Last year, when your friend came to that conference at the chalet up north . . . she was looking for a missing girl. She thought Ray Zhang, one of my father's colleagues, had something to do with it."

Brazuca is startled by Lam's sudden shift to Nora, who has been on his mind almost nonstop these past few days. When Lam had met Nora during her search for Bonnie, he had been thrown off by being in the presence of a woman who wasn't in love with his money.

"That's right." Brazuca eyes the glass of scotch in front of him but makes no move to touch it. It hasn't gotten any easier to push the glass away, but he manages to keep it together.

"I told you then that the Zhang family had a security guy

who they used quite frequently and it's been said he has triad ties."

Brazuca nods. "Dao. Worked almost exclusively with Zhang for years."

Ray Zhang was the patriarch of a wealthy family that was connected to Nora and the events of last year when Nora's daughter, Bonnie, had gone missing, but the details were fuzzy. The only people who would know what had actually happened were Nora, who has a selective memory about the events, and Ray Zhang and Dao, who have both vanished. It was hard to forget the spectacular mess Nora had found herself in, though he had made a point not to talk about it with Lam. Nora's privacy had been on his mind then. Her personal connection to the Zhangs, and that the deceased Kai Zhang was Bonnie's birth father, was something that only she could discuss.

Lam continues, unaware of Brazuca's sudden coolness. "Ray Zhang had some stink to him, but nobody questioned him about Dao when he was alive."

Brazuca stares at him. "Nobody has seen Ray Zhang since last year. How do you know he's dead?"

Lam, once an open book, becomes cagey. He looks at his watch. Takes a sip of his scotch and smiles without a trace of mirth. "I've heard rumors." Lam turns the laptop screen to face Brazuca. He points to a photo of a shirtless Chinese man displaying his tattoos in his living room. It was a very famous photo in the Anti-Gang Unit, according to Grace's research. "Jimmy Fang. He's connected, through Three Phoenix, to the umbrella organization that Dao is affiliated with."

Brazuca's headache is back, now that the pieces have fallen

into place. In one fell swoop he has gained his financial freedom and learned of a startling connection. Now he understands why Nora has become a target. Last year, when she went looking for her missing daughter, she made a powerful enemy in the Zhang family—and the head of their security detail: Dao.

Out of all the players involved in Nora's drama, Dao was the most dangerous. A ruthless killer, with an alleged background as a mercenary.

"Are we good?" Brazuca says, standing. "This is the supply chain you were looking for?"

"Yes," says Lam. "Thanks, buddy. I'll take it from here."

Brazuca opens his mouth to ask what Lam means by this, but decides that he doesn't really want to know. It is obvious to him now that his friendship with Lam was always based on this, the fact that he is and has always been an employee to this man. A trusted employee, but one that is there on the payroll nonetheless.

"I'll have your wire transfer ready in the morning," Lam continues. He begins talking about his plans for vengeance against his father, drug dealers, and the world at large. But Brazuca has stopped listening. Men like Lam can afford to go on about personal vendettas and the like. Their wealth and connections will always protect them from danger. The every-day business of survival hasn't touched them.

For people like Nora, on the other hand, that seemingly mundane task of making it through a day without someone trying to murder you isn't as simple. Especially now, given what she's up against. A personal vendetta by someone much more powerful than she is. A dangerous enemy, like the one he has now in Curtis Parnell, the biker who has gone to ground with a photograph of Brazuca stored on his phone.

Brazuca leaves without another word. There's nothing more to be said. His exhaustion hasn't left him. It has simply morphed into a kind of anxiety. In a perverse way, it hasn't settled on him or the danger he might be facing with Parnell—if the biker hasn't already skipped town. His own survival isn't even on his mind. It takes him a long time to get to his car. The first reason is that he's still in recovery. From a blow to the head, being threatened with a meat cleaver, having to chase college kids down streets, and the emotional weight of Crow's death and insecurity about his own personal safety.

The second is sheer confusion.

He had tried, hadn't he, to leave the past behind? There's nothing he wants more than to get in his car and drive to Whistler. Book a cabin in the woods for a few days, test out the telescope that he's been eyeing out there. Sleep. So why, now, does this feel like a distant dream?

47

RULE NUMBER ONE of fleeing the country: get your passport.

There must be other rules, but it's not like I know what they are. I would ask my mother, except she has turned out to be so good at fleeing that nobody, not even her dedicated stalker, can find her. In any case, the first rule is proving hard enough. Nate's house is full of do-gooders. There is a meeting in full swing. Groups of people linger outside, dressed in matching neon orange T-shirts on top of their outerwear. It now occurs to me that my concept of time has yet again slipped out of my grasp. Tonight is the night before Halloween and the do-gooders are preparing to counter Devil's Night assholery with color coordination and astonishing faith in humanity.

A group of teenagers eyes me as I linger too long on the street, debating whether or not stealing a T-shirt from someone outside will help gain me entrance to the house without anyone remarking that I'm the woman who was there when Nate got shot. "Hey," says one of them, walking over to me. I tense. She holds out a shirt. "You got your group yet?"

I shake my head.

"That's alright. You can walk with us if you want," she says brightly.

"Um, I'm waiting for a friend," I say, but put on the T-shirt to blend in better.

"Okay, good luck tonight. It's not even sundown yet and it's been the worst we've seen in years. Warning went out to be extra careful tonight. People are riled up and some of these guys just want to do some damage." She gives me a grim smile and walks away. I wait for another twenty minutes, watching as the house empties out and several groups head off. A young man rides by on his bicycle blasting music. He's wearing one of the neon T-shirts, but doesn't seem attached to any particular group. It takes me several seconds to recognize the song. And even then, only because it's my own voice pouring like dark honey from the speakers. He's playing our song. Mine and Nate's. Hearing it shakes me to my core. The last time I listened to it, I was in the basement of the house I'm standing in front of now, being cared for by the man whose voice is now trailing away. The man on the bicycle rides off down the street, taking the music with him.

In this state of internal chaos I enter the house and, surprisingly, am able to do it without being seen.

My backpack is not in the studio downstairs, the door to which has been removed. Nate's recording equipment and guitars are also missing, but whoever has taken them has thoughtfully left behind the love seat for whoever wants to sit and contemplate an empty room. There are no takers except for me.

Another hour passes before all the voices die out. The makeshift soundproofing has been stripped from the room for some reason, so I can hear everything going on upstairs. The house goes quiet and I am finally able to search it properly.

I reach an upstairs bedroom toward the rear of the house, protected by a lock that any amateur lock picker who has access to Internet tutorials can pick. It takes me about a minute to get inside what I presume to be Kev's bedroom, from the framed photos of Malcolm X and Assata Shakur on the wall. Perversely, there is also the Lord of the Rings trilogy on the desk immediately to my right, and the *Game of Thrones* collection as a hard juxtaposition. I move past these quickly. I've never been much of a fantasy fan myself. Reality is hard enough for me to wrap my head around.

I'm tempted to salute the photos on the wall when I find my pack in the closet. People who don't trust the police are predictable. I know, because I'm one of them. Somehow I figured that Kev must have taken my pack away before the authorities came. Still, I wonder if Kev knows that he has buried a tangible link to his brother's attack under some T-shirts and a pair of pink sweatpants with the word *ANGEL* stamped on the seat.

I take my passport out of the bag and slip it into a zippered pocket of my jacket, next to my wallet. As I'm about to leave, I pause, hearing a noise from inside the house, and retreat farther into the room. There's not far to go. Damned if I'm going to hide in a closet, so I step behind the door and listen carefully. I slip the backpack off my shoulder and rest it carefully at my feet. I hear only footsteps on the stairs. Quiet footsteps. More than one set, maybe two. My phone is in my hands, so I dial the number on Sanchez's card, the one that I'd put on speed dial, just in case. I don't listen for him to answer, I just turn the volume down and slip the phone into my pocket.

There is no way to listen for intentions, so I'm going to assume the worst.

When the door eases open and a hooded figure enters, gun first, I shove the door back toward him. He shouts and his hand gets caught in the frame. I open it and slam it back again until he howls in pain and falls back into the hall. I grab the gun off the ground and follow him into the hallway where a stomping kick to the groin doubles him over with a groan. Another hooded figure bursts out of the first bedroom by the staircase with his gun drawn. I have only a split second, so I grab his hand, tug it toward me at the same time that I extend my lower leg. He trips and falls toward the stairs, and a push with my free hand sends him flying down. His gun goes clattering past him. I run down the stairs and grab the gun on the landing just as his hand closes around my ankle, pulling me down.

I twist, turn the gun on the hoodie upstairs and take the second out of my waistband. I'm on my ass now but I've got the two weapons in my hands. I turn the second pistol on the hoodie on the stairs. The bandage is still on his nose. It's my friend from the motel. The one who shot Nate. I'm furious enough for my finger to hover over the trigger, but what I need now are answers. "Who hired you to kill me?"

"Like I fucking know," he says. His voice is strangely high-pitched and nasal. His leg is twisted behind him and a look of intense agony crosses his face as he tries to move it.

"Was it Ryan Russo?"

"Who's that?" He seems to be in so much pain, he can't be lying. But I have to know.

"Tell me who hired you." My eyes flick from him to his friend at the top of the stairs. I've been told that a full contact blow to the groin is the worst possible feeling for a man. I hope so, and that it keeps him down for a while.

My old friend on the stairs grimaces. "Order didn't come to me, bitch."

"Who does know?" I say, when I've finally got my feet under me.

I crouch next to him and put the gun to his head. My hand is steady, like it always is when handling a weapon. Truth is, I used to like guns.

Gun control is a big deal in Canada, everywhere but at my friend Wallace's house. Wallace had a dad who not only thought the name Wallace was appropriate in the twentieth century, but also drank Tennessee whiskey, wore a cowboy hat, kept a large gun collection locked away in his basement, and gave Wallace the key. After we'd fooled around and drank some of the whiskey we would take one of the guns out for target practice. For a couple of years during high school, I lived at Wallace's house when his dad was away on business. I shot a lot, too, because Wallace got itchy being inside too much and I can be competitive even when the stakes are low. I'm a good shot. I had a lot of practice in a previous life.

The young man at the other end of the gun laughs. He presses his temple deeper into the muzzle. "Yeah? You go ahead. Do it. Ain't no hell that's worse than Detroit. *Do it*." His eyes are dead serious. He's not lying and there is no bluster to him now. This kid with a broken nose and a broken leg isn't afraid to die. His friend upstairs gets up on his hands and knees.

The desire to exact revenge is overwhelming. There's a man lying on a hospital bed because of these desperate young men. Because one of them is a terrible shot who should never have had his hands on a weapon.

I see my father's face in my mind. His quiet smile. And I remember that this is how he died.

I can't pull the trigger.

Dania Nasri spoke of hell, too. In relation to the place that she was from. I guess hell is a matter of perspective. "I hope this was worth fifteen grand, asshole. Don't move."

Then I take off out the front door and run as fast as I can. I run as though I'm being chased. Which, of course, I am. For what seems, truly, to be a paltry sum. I had shrugged it off when Sanchez mentioned how much it costs to drop a body in Detroit.

Fifteen thousand dollars isn't nearly enough.

48

MY PHONE IS dead again. I don't know if Sanchez caught any of my little chat with the young men inside the house, but it doesn't matter now. What does is that I get the hell out of here as quickly as possible.

I run past a group of neon shirts without stopping to warn them about what's back at the house. "There's a fire that way!" one of them shouts to me, so I veer off to a side street. I smell the smoke from the fire, and for a brief moment wonder if I'm back in Vancouver. A crescent moon hovers above me, giving more illumination than the meager streetlights. I can see flashes of revolving light in the distance and hear the squeals of fire trucks or ambulances. It would make the most sense to head in that direction, toward the people, so I don't. There's a loud crack in the air. Fireworks blaze across the night sky. I am unsure of what to do with the two guns I have on me now. I'm sick of seeing guns everywhere in this open-carry state. They even make appearances in my dreams.

I shy away from the crowds that may or may not be armed, like I am. I am done with human beings right now and long for Whisper to be at my side. But she is busy with Leo, who I refuse to think about because then I'd have to spare a thought or two about Seb. And if I'm off people right now, the death of one of my favorites isn't going to help much.

Soon enough, the problem I run up against is that there's no place to go. Every time I see smoke or a neon shirt, I veer in another direction—but this isn't much of a plan. I don't blame myself, though, because I don't know this city well enough to have any kind of strategy. I'm doing what I have been since I got here. Running around in circles. Where there are no circles there are dead ends, and this is no exception.

Soon enough, there's nowhere left to run.

I reach the bottom of the street. On one side is a field of tall grass. On the other, and to my right, is a boarded-up warehouse, one of the few buildings on the block that's been left standing. I have come to the end of the road, and am regretting my earlier decision to run away from the sounds of civilization. I feel exposed. Coming off the adrenaline rush I'd felt back at Nate's house, I'm now shivering.

In the distance there is a figure at the top of the road, backlit by a streetlight. The figure pauses, looks in my direction. This could mean nothing, but after running into my would-be executors at Nate's house I don't want to chance it. The need to be indoors, have my back against a wall, is urgent. The building to my right doesn't look that old. I wonder if it's only been recently abandoned and begin to think that it might give me a moment to stop and think. To burrow for a while, just until I collect my thoughts.

There is a door around the side that is slightly ajar. I slip in, making sure to close it behind me. The quick glimpse that I've gotten before shutting the door showed a large room, one that once served as a lobby maybe, with two corridors branching off from either side.

There are only a few short seconds of blessed silence before footsteps approach from the corridor farthest away from me. So the building isn't abandoned after all.

"Who shut the door?" says an angry voice. A young man, by the sounds of it, one who has been kicked out of several prep schools before taking up residence here. It's amazing what you can hear in people's voices when you are frightened and in the dark. Somebody slightly less articulate mumbles something in response about another door being around back. I pick up my speed, hoping to get to the back door before them. Now I know that the building isn't empty, I no longer crave the comfort of walls around me. I just want to escape. I go down the corridor closest to me, and away from the voices. I have no desire to make conversation with a couple of frat boys in an abandoned warehouse on Devil's Night. Their presence here isn't exactly comforting.

Since Nate brought it up, I've spent some time looking into it. Its roots are in the Detroit race riots, three of which were so devastating that the army had to be called in to put a stop to the fires that blazed through the city. Detroit became an arsonist's playground, the situation escalating in the eighties to the point that the city had to take action. Angel's Night was created to counter the worst of the vandalism and violence, but pyros still flock here to set things on fire. I have a feeling that these young men, whoever they are, don't have the city's best interests at heart. Funny, sneaking around in an abandoned warehouse at night can leave that impression.

A faint, acrid scent reaches my nostrils. A trace of something that requires a moment to place. It's odd that it takes me this long to notice the smell of gasoline, then I'm running back down the hallway toward the door I came in through. It's shut firmly. The scent is stronger in here now, making me think they doused this room last. I can't get the door open. I bang on it with my fists and shout "Help" until I'm hoarse. If I shout "Fire," well, that's just what they want to happen, isn't it? To use the cover of Devil's Night as an excuse to watch things burn.

Maybe it's because I cried wolf back at the motel, but this time nobody comes to my rescue. I stop pounding my fist against the door and am about to go back to the corridor when I hear movement from the opposite end of the room. I freeze.

"Hey there, Nora," says Ryan Russo.

49

VISIBILITY IN THE room is zero. This could be a metaphor for my life, if I was the kind of person who read horoscopes and believed in life metaphors. What's affecting me now is more than just the absence of light. That voice in the darkness is a weighted thing, almost heavier than the smell of gasoline. I trip over what seems to be a plastic container, sending it skating across the floor.

In the darkness, I can feel Russo turn his attention in my direction. He's not an owl. He can't possibly see me. But I feel his stare nonetheless. One of the guns is in the waistband of my jeans, but the second is in my hand. I cock it. It sounds like a clap of thunder in this echo chamber of a building.

"Oh, you don't want to fire a gun in here," says Russo. "I think those kids doused this place with gasoline and set a fire in the basement. They're probably aiming for it to be a slow burn, but you don't want to take any chances. You don't know if they have some compressed gas canisters or something around, just to make sure the fire spreads. A single shot could send this building up in flames. So how about you and I just put our guns down and have a talk."

"How about we get out of here, then?" I have no idea if what he's saying is true, but it sounds like bullshit to me. In any case, I can't see a target to fire at. "We should grab a coffee," I say. "What's your schedule like next week?"

"Me? I'm free as a bird."

"Got a lot of time on your hands to stalk women, do you?"

He laughs. "You know, it's funny you bring that up. I've been thinking about your mother a lot lately," he says, making the leap from me to my mother. I hear him move in my direction. I can't see him, but I can feel his gaze. Hear his slow, measured step on the ground. "It's hard for women to start a brand-new life. They're so emotional. They always let something slip through."

What strikes me is his confidence. This is something he clearly has given a lot of thought to.

"Bitches be crazy," I say. There's something bothering me, but I can't quite put a finger on it.

"You have no idea how true that is. I saw you with Dania Nasri. You found out about your mother, did you? About who she was. After all these years she left you and your sister in the dark . . . Any idea where she is now?" he replies, a peculiar, soothing softness to his voice.

There's something different about the way he sounds.

The last time we spoke, we'd been in Vancouver and he'd seemed lost. Unsure of himself, even. It's a marked difference from what he sounds like now. When he talks about my mother, his tone takes on a completely different quality. Something that all the softness in the world can't mask. Something bordering on hatred.

I'm so distracted by his shift in tone that it takes a moment for the question to sink in.

Do I know where she is? The woman who abandoned me as a child?

I have a stunning realization. My stomach clenches, like I've been hit. I guess this is how it feels when you figure out you're bait.

Back in Vancouver his comments about my father started me down this path. What I find at the end of it is not about his military career at all. Part of me was expecting the plot of an airport thriller, to be honest. Some kind of vast military conspiracy that had ensnared Sam Watts and pushed him to his death. But this is not that kind of a story. For Sam Watts it was as simple as a man falling in love with the wrong woman. Full stop. The end. Because he was exactly as he seemed. A veteran who had transitioned into civilian life. One who went back to the country of his birth to search for his roots—even though, to my knowledge, he never found them. Maybe the road was bumpier than I knew, but he'd been trying. He was a devoted husband. Loving father. The kind of man who was nice to mean old ladies and gave houses away to fawning siblings. Could it be that he was wonderful and died anyway? Could life be so cruel?

Could I have been gaslighted this whole time in order to unearth my mother?

"You showed up in Vancouver because you knew I'd come looking for the truth about my father." I keep the gun in my right hand and walk as silently as possible with my left arm outstretched to the nearest wall. Then I use it to guide me, searching for any unseen doorways. The going is slow, because the floor is covered in debris of various kinds. I step on something gelatinous, but refuse to think about what that might be.

"No. You took me by surprise with that. I thought I'd find you girls and see if your mother had made contact after all these years. I wasn't prepared when you confronted me, so I impro-vised. But when I saw you pick up the trail, I thought, What a perfect way to provoke her! You going around, asking your questions. Nobody would deny her long-lost daughter informa-tion if they had it. Especially if that cunt is still alive and in touch with anyone from around here."

There are certain things I've lost patience for over the years. Every time I hear the word *cunt* it's like a slap in the face with a wet fish. One that's just come off a bed of ice at the market; a cold, empty carcass that hits right where it hurts the most, meant to remind me that I'm just a gaping hole, an empty space where a person should be.

An empty space, it seems, that fills now with uncertainty.

Something doesn't make sense here. "So, if you're not trying to cover up my father's death, then why did you hire those guys to kill me?"

Russo pauses. "What are you talking about?"

I don't answer. He sounds genuinely confused. But then who has been after me?

I can't afford to linger on this thought, because now I can smell smoke. Not heavy smoke, but it has become more no-ticeable than its accelerant. Russo was right. There is a fire somewhere in this building, one that's probably being eagerly observed by the frat boy arsonists who have left in a hurry. They are most likely outside, far enough away that they can watch without getting hurt. Too far to hear me scream, if that would matter to them at all.

If Gloria Tate was right, and Russo had been burned badly in a car bomb attack, shouldn't he be terrified?

He uses my silence to inch closer. I have a rough idea where he is, but I can't pinpoint it exactly. What I'm hoping is that he's experiencing the same thing. I should stay silent because my life might depend on it, but I can't help speaking. I've come too far to stop now. I tried to leave this godforsaken city and he somehow found me, this man with the answers to the questions I have about my parents.

"When I was a little girl you came looking for my mother. When the coverage of the hostage crisis started ramping up, you saw the picture of her at the Nasri wedding and you recognized her. Dania Nasri told you where she'd been living but when you went to Winnipeg she was long gone. Why did you wait to go find her?"

There had been a gap of about a year after my mother spoke with Dania Nasri, and my father's death. The answer dawns on me before he can speak. "Because you were a junkie. You couldn't handle it."

His anger is like a blade, cutting through the darkness. "I was still in recovery from that car bomb. Do you know what they did to burn victims back then? They put you in a tub, cleaned off the burns, and scrubbed the open wound to get rid of the dead skin and ward off infection. I never felt pain like that. Ever. So yeah, I had a problem, wasn't ready to deal with the bitch but I knew where she was. My mistake was I thought she'd stay put."

"You thought you knew her."

He snorts. "You can never know a woman."

"Hmm, that's so interesting. I wonder if you hate her so much because she knew you were a gambler and it got you in trouble in Beirut." There's a pause, so I continue on to the plot, which is what I've finally realized this is. There is something of my mother in me, after all. I remember what Samson said back at the apartment in Chicago about him being the kind of man that could be seen as a mark.

"Maybe you owed some people money and they asked you to do a couple favors for them. Maybe it didn't matter who they were, you just liked the thrill of the thing. Or it could have been just about the money. Who were you working for in Lebanon? The Soviets? It was the Cold War." My throat feels like it's being scraped from the inside. I wonder how he can stand speaking through this smoke, but maybe he's simply used to excruciating pain.

"Was? The Cold War never ended. It's just on a different playing field now," he says, but I can tell that I've shaken him. His confidence is slipping. He's sounding more like he did in Vancouver when I confronted him. On his back foot, playing defense.

For a moment there is a heavy silence as what has been just a hunch now takes a different shape. I'm guessing that his relentless pursuit of my mother hadn't just been some kind of lover's quarrel. Kovaks had said that Beirut had been a place of intrigue. Russo had been known for his sense of adventure, his desire to be in the thick of one international crisis or another.

As wild as it is, it hits home. I'm hoping that there's some truth to the theory that even the baddest of the badasses feel the need to gloat sometimes—or unburden themselves in light of a terminal illness. Something Dania Nasri said comes back to me. That there had been a man, and my mother saw a different side to him. Maybe it was more than just figurative.

"She saw something, didn't she? Something that she wasn't supposed to see."

I think I'm going to suffocate before he speaks. He doesn't make me wait long. We both know we don't have much time left. Somewhere, within sight, is the end. For me, it might be this warehouse. For him, it's those lab results in that manila envelope. A life sentence.

A moment passes and I think he's going to laugh it all off, but then he speaks. Urgently, as though he's been waiting his whole life for just this moment. This is the problem with secrets. The internal conflict they create. There's always a part of you that wants to give them up.

"She was a maid," he says, the words coming quickly, the gravel in his voice more pronounced. "Did you know that? Every week she cleaned a certain apartment in Beirut. It was leased by an American and it was . . . of interest to the Russians. It was supposed to be some kind of CIA safe house. They wanted access to it but never told me why. My handler just said she might be more likely to let a young American in. When I met her, it changed the game. He thought—"

He hesitates here. "When we met, I made it look like an accident. There was a connection between us. She wanted to work on her English, so we kept meeting there on her cleaning days. We had a relationship, if you must know. He wanted me to put something in the apartment one day . . . I had a feeling she saw me do it, but I wasn't sure until after."

The conversation with Dania Nasri is still in my mind. My mother would ask who's listening and then laugh a deep belly laugh. She had also seen a different side to a man who'd been using her. I know, though I can't say how, that this is the dark, beating heart of the matter. "Put something? You mean a bug?"

My hands skim over something that feels like plywood. Behind it might be a window. If I can pry it away, there could be an exit point.

He's silent for several excruciating moments. "I don't know how she knew. How she put it together. She was . . . devious. Yes, I was asked to put a bug in that apartment and she saw me doing it, but I wasn't sure she had. I guess she figured everything out. Why I was at that apartment in the first place. About a week after, right before we were supposed to meet again, I got jumped coming home."

"Coming home from the casino?" It's just a hunch, but as soon as I say it, I know it's true. So does he. Samson said no one is as predictable as a gambler—and maybe my mother knew that as well.

"Look at you," he says in a perverse kind of admiration. "I did win big that day, was just going home when I got kidnapped and robbed. It wasn't an accident. Life doesn't work like that. They'd been watching me, whoever she'd told about me. Knew my habits. Robbed me, then kicked me out of the car while it was still moving. I had no idea where I was."

"And you walked into the path of a car bomb."

I thought the visibility in the room couldn't get any worse, but it has. It's so hot now that I want to strip and leave my clothes behind me in a headlong rush to an exit. Any exit. The only thing stopping me is what has brought me to this city in the first place. Despite everything I've been through, I still want to know the truth. I've dug my hands into the outer edges of the wood panel and have pulled so hard that I feel my nails break and blood drip from the splinters lodged in my hands. But the plywood doesn't budge.

"I underestimated her. She was the only one who could have figured it out. I don't know who those guys were, but it didn't really matter. All you sand niggers are the same. Can't trust one of you." He spits this, his breathing coming out in harsh gasps. Whether it's from the lack of oxygen or something else, I can't tell.

This isn't the first time a slur has been directed at me, but it's the first one that has come about from my mother's background. Not that I'm too surprised. You can't be a virgin forever. "She outsmarted you. And you killed my father because you were angry at her."

Russo pauses here. Like he's trying to calm himself. I hear him moving, but not in my direction. "Look, it was an accident. I was there to talk to your mother. Way I saw it, she owed me some money. At least. He had a gun. I tried to grab it and we struggled. It went off."

Now I'm more angry than frightened. In the dark, everything recedes but the overpowering smoke and the sound of his voice. I can hear everything clearly, even what he doesn't know he's revealing.

He just lied to me.

"You killed him with his own gun and made it seem like a suicide."

What I said about Russo being some kind of spy was mostly a bluff. A theory that makes sense, given what I learned from Mark Kovaks, Jules Dubois, and Samson. Until he confirmed it, there was no proof, and nothing to lose by trying it out. The truth is, I don't care about listening devices, Cold War espionage, or his reasons for pursuing my feckless mother to the ends of the earth. If there was any space in my heart for her, it disappeared the day Lorelei and I were sent to foster care and forced to fend for ourselves.

But my father is a different story. Whatever my mother had gotten herself into in Beirut led to my father's death. This man murdered the only parent I've ever really known, and my sister and I never recovered. No, maybe Lorelei did. In my exhaustion, brought on from days of sporadic sleep, of constantly looking over my shoulder, I realize that she recovered and moved on. It's why she is able to hang up on me with such authority. I'm her past and it doesn't matter to her anymore. But I have never been able to let go.

"I didn't think she'd abandon her family," he says. "Shows you what kind of woman your mother was. Do you know what my greatest fear used to be?"

I'm breathing now through the sleeve of my shirt. The smoke is stinging my eyes. They've narrowed to slits and I can barely keep them open.

"The thing about life is, you're supposed to have figured it out by the time you're my age. You're not young yourself, so you must have some idea of what I'm talking about."

Now it's my turn to not speak. He continues anyway. I can feel him moving closer. "I used to be terrified of fire. It got so bad I couldn't even be near a fireplace in the winter. Or hear a match strike. The scars . . . you have no idea about the scars." He sounds calm. How can he sound like this when we're about to be burned alive? "But now all I feel is relief. Maybe this is what should have happened back in Beirut."

A kind of horror builds now inside me. He has no plans to make it out of here alive, to live a life full of pain and on dialysis. This is his last stand. Maybe it would have been different for him if I'd known where my mother was. Maybe he wouldn't have trapped us both in here because he'd still have some revenge to live for. But I've never been that lucky and neither, it seems, has he.

I can feel him getting closer, but I can't see much now. I reach a doorway and start to run through it when I feel him grab the back of my jacket and pull me to the ground. He's stronger than I expected. The gun in my hand skids away from me as I fall. I feel the brush of his fingers on my arm.

He puts a gun of his own to my head. Like I had to the young man I'd threatened back at Nate's house—like Russo had to my father before me.

The air is thicker here. I can barely breathe. The hallway is filled with smoke. "You said . . . explosion . . ." A harsh, racking cough shakes my body. The only thing keeping me grounded is the cold metal against my temple. I almost turn into it, it feels so good. I can't see him. He is a voice in the dark, at the other end of a gun.

His voice, when he speaks, is muffled. Like he's talking into his sleeve. He gets very close, right up to my ear. I feel him now, feel his hatred. It's on his breath, raising the hairs at my nape.

"I lied."

Of course.

"I keep waiting for your mother to pop out to save you," he

whispers, taking up what must be the remaining oxygen in the building. "But I guess she just doesn't care."

I think of the test results found back at the apartment. And I see now why he has kept me here all this time, endangering himself. He doesn't care, either. He's prepared to die on his terms, and take me with him. Because he's come too far to die alone.

I laugh. Choke, and laugh some more. "You're . . . another loser. L-like me." The last word is nothing more than a whisper dragged through my ragged throat, just as it seizes up, but I know he has heard. That he knows as well as I do it's true.

He pulls the trigger. The gun jams. The building does not explode.

The second gun that was in my waistband is now in my hand. I cock it and brace myself against the wall. Russo knocks my hand away just as I pull the trigger.

There is a loud crashing noise. A part of the ceiling slams into my shoulder. I try to crawl away, but I can't get enough oxygen in me. Maybe there's just none left. I think I'm in the doorway. I don't know where Russo is, but does it even matter?

When Dania Nasri said she heard "London Bridge" playing in the background as she spoke to my father, it sparked something. Memories of a little red music box. I remember that my father used to wind it up for me and it used to make me happy. I think that's what love must be.

There's another rumble over my head and then it all falls down.

50

BRAZUCA IS REGRETTING the amount of coffee he's been drinking. It should have been kombucha, he thinks. He's been cautious about his kombucha consumption because of the steep cost, even though he can afford it now. But now is, as always, too late. He's already fallen off his health wagon and his stomach lining is paying for it. On his way to the airport, he tries Nora's number again. The call goes straight to voice mail, but the mailbox is full. Most likely with dire messages from him. He's also been texting her but, again, no reply.

On a whim, he pulls into a residential neighborhood in Richmond and parks in front of a two-story house. The lights are on inside and he can see shadows crossing behind the curtains. A man about ten years younger than he is opens the door. He's dressed in a button-down shirt and tailored slacks, and his thick dark hair is swept off his brow.

"What's wrong?" the man asks, upon seeing him.

Brazuca raises a brow. "I'm here to see Grace. I'm a friend."

"Oh, I thought you were a cop. Sorry," he says. "You just have that kind of face, I guess." The man leads him into the house and toward the adjacent living room. "Grace didn't tell me she invited friends, but welcome."

Grace glances at them from the couch. There are a handful of people with her, whom he assumes are relatives since she didn't invite friends like him. The grin on her face dies. She excuses herself as she makes her way over, dragging him back out the door. It's not subtle.

"Nice to meet you!" calls the man who'd let him in.

"That your boyfriend?" Brazuca says when they are alone and the door is firmly shut between them and whatever festivities are taking place inside.

She glares at him, hands bunched at her hips. Tonight she's wearing a dress that fits her, but is not as interesting or sparkly as her sister's blue number. "Are you stalking me?"

He puts his hands up. "No. I'm leaving for a bit and I wanted you to have something." He hands over the flash drive that he'd taken from her earlier.

She reaches for it automatically, turns it over in her hands. "My research?"

"And my report on your sister's death. Everything I have is in there. You said you wanted to know?"

"Yeah, I guess I did." Her hands unclench. She leans against the railing. "You look like hell."

"Had a rough couple days." Which is a massive understatement.

"I've been busy, too. Finally finished cleaning out my sister's place. This is my first night back since she died. We're celebrating my fiancé's new job. He's a lawyer."

"The guy who answered the door?"

"Yeah," she says, twisting the ring on her left hand, a ring that had not been present in any of his previous interactions with her.

He takes her hand, passes the pad of his thumb over the cool metal band. "How come you weren't wearing this when we met?"

"I didn't have it when we met. After my sister died, we decided to take a break. But I guess he thought it was time to move forward. He said he didn't want to be away from me anymore. He proposed last night."

"Congratulations."

She looks at him, surprised. "You mean that?"

"I do."

She hesitates for a brief moment, then comes to a decision. She hands the flash drive back to him. "You did all this work, tracked down who her supplier was, staked out that stupid bar, and figured out where that woman got her stuff and then who her boss was and then his boss. You know what I think? What the hell was the point of any of it? My sister is gone. She was miserable, she got high, and then she died. None of this explains why she did what she did, why she didn't ask for help for her problem."

"Would you have listened?"

She is quiet for a moment. "Maybe, maybe not. But we'll never know now, will we? I gotta go now, Jon. But thanks for . . ." She loses her train of thought. Maybe she just can't think of anything she'd like to thank him for.

"Yeah. You take care."

"You, too." She presses a quick, furtive kiss to his cheek before disappearing inside.

He watches the living room window from his car for a while, then drives to the long-term parking lot at the airport. There is no moon out tonight. No stars to look at. It's just as well. Apparently the Tim Hortons across the road doesn't carry kombucha, so he's back to drinking coffee. There's a flight to Atlanta with a connection to Detroit leaving in a couple of hours. But he makes no move to get out of the car.

A call comes in on his speakerphone. A Toronto number. Relief flares for a moment. Toronto is close to Detroit. Maybe Nora made it there and she has finally decided to call him back.

"Hello?" says a young female voice, when he answers.

"This is Brazuca."

"Um, listen, I don't know if you remember me. I saw you in the hospital last year when they found my mom . . . um, my birth mother I mean. Nora? You gave me your card and told me to call you if I remembered anything from . . ."

"From when they took you," Brazuca says to Bonnie, Nora's estranged daughter.

"Yeah. Look, I remember something. It's a tattoo I saw on my—on his arm. My—"

"I understand," he says softly. It was her own father who had kidnapped her last year when she'd gone missing. That's what she almost said. *My father.* "Kai Zhang."

"Yeah. I've been drawing his tattoo without realizing it. It just came back to me, really."

"What was the tattoo of?"

"Talons. I can send you a sketch if you want?"

"Yeah, please."

She goes quiet for a moment, then Brazuca sees an alert message on his screen as the text comes through. "There's something else," she says, when she gets back on the line. "The other guy, the bald one who was sometimes in charge of watching me?"

"His name is Dao."

"Oh. Dao. Well, he got real mad when he saw it. I thought maybe my . . . Kai . . . he wasn't supposed to get this tattoo. They fought about it for a while, but I didn't understand what they were saying."

"Okay, that's good that you remember it all. Thanks for telling me."

"Yeah, it's just . . . I'm worried about Nora," she says. "She sent me a photo. Of, like, her face. She took a selfie. Usually it's of Whisper and now . . . it's just weird. I have this feeling . . ."

"I'm sure she's fine," he says lightly, even though he can't imagine Nora taking a selfie to save her life.

"It says on your card that you're an investigator? Can you find her and get her to call me? She's not answering her phone and I would do it, except I'm in Toronto."

"I'm retired, love."

"Don't call me that," she says, her voice going high. "I'll pay."

Last year at the hospital she'd been recovering from her own trauma, her own captivity at the hands of her biological father—a man that she'd never met before he'd kidnapped her. Bonnie had just gone in to see Nora, who was in and out of consciousness, talking nonsense when she woke. Bonnie came out of the room looking devastated. Her adoptive parents, Lynn and Everett, had their arms slung around her shoulders and there were tears streaking her face. Nora hadn't recognized her.

Bonnie had looked up then, and met his eyes. So he gave her his business card and muttered something about getting in touch if she remembered anything.

After a moment of silence, she sighs and says in the most aggravated tone, one only a teenager would have the balls to use, "Whatever. I'll just find someone else."

After she hangs up on him, Brazuca stares at the sketch she's photographed and sent. It is riveting. A sinister talon with what looks to be blood dripping from it.

If he was the kind of man to make charts, there would be a line connecting the Triple 9s to Parnell's bikers, and another connecting both the bikers and the Triple 9s to the disappeared Jimmy Fang and his Three Phoenix group, based out of Hong Kong. Representing Three Phoenix would be a symbol of three bloody talons. Like the one that he'd seen on Lam's laptop, in the photo of Jimmy Fang. The three-talon tattoo was Fang's most prominent ink. Bonnie had only seen part of the design—but it was enough to send Dao into a fury. Dao, a man so dangerous that even Bernard Lam had looked like he was about to piss himself when talking about him. A man who, like Jimmy Fang, could disappear without a trace. He was that connected.

Brazuca has no doubt that Dao is still alive, and holding a grudge against Nora. She is, after all, the woman who killed his employer's son Kai, and was somehow involved in the death of Kai's wife. If she'd been involved in Ray Zhang's death, however indirectly, would that have sent Dao into a rage?

Could it be that when Nora left the country, keeping tabs wasn't enough anymore? That maybe he'd seen an opportunity to exact revenge—in a city that was so notoriously dangerous that a murdered Canadian woman wouldn't raise eyebrows?

The longer Brazuca thinks about it, the crazier it seems.

As he sits in his car watching a plane approach, another photo comes through from Bonnie. It's of Nora's face. Tired, drawn, a lock of hair falling over her brow. Her mouth tilts up at the corners, a shadow of a smile there, though her eyes are direct and without any semblance of light. As usual.

He looks at the photo for a long time, not able to place why he is so disturbed by it. Then he finds it. What haunts him, what makes him get out of the car and onto the shuttle to the terminal, is that she tried.

51

IN THE DISTANCE I hear a woman ask, "She alive?"

A man replies. "Found her in a doorway. Wall collapsed all around her."

"Squatter?" says the woman.

"Nah, Angel's Night volunteer."

I have visions of a neon shirt. I'm on my back, being wheeled somewhere. The stretcher continues its journey but it's rough going. The ground beneath the wheels is uneven. They catch on something and refuse to budge. Near my head I hear the man curse. "Shit," he says. "Goddamn piece of junk."

I hear him move away. There are bright lights flashing beyond my eyelids. I don't want to open them, but I suddenly remember that I'm in Detroit and I seem to be strapped onto a stretcher. Images of exorbitant American medical bills float through the air. Going to a hospital in America on my budget isn't an option. My hands instinctively undo the straps holding me down. I get off the stretcher and immediately fall to my knees. My legs don't want to work. I see the smoldering wreckage of a building nearby and everything comes back to me.

I wonder where Ryan Russo is.

When I blink the heaviness away from my eyes, I find my answer. To my left is another stretcher, but this one has a body bag on it. The image of medical bills is replaced by jail bars. With it comes the realization that although Russo is gone, I have a very powerful enemy in this world. My imagination makes a few connections that appear unlikely at first, but I can't seem to let go of them. A kind of certainty blossoms within me. All along I was thinking that I was being pursued because I was looking into my father's past but this has nothing to do with him. I've brought this on myself. There's only one person who would want me dead badly enough to put a hit out on me, who would even have the resources to find me here in Detroit. I was responsible for the deaths of two people last year, both belonging to the spectacularly wealthy and well-connected family he worked for. Dao. Only, a man like Dao, if he was back stateside, would do it himself. So he's not here in North America, but he is alive. This is the only explanation I have, crazy as it seems. But it feels right. It feels true.

The lights from a car coming down the street remind me that I called Sanchez back at Nate's house. But I don't know where my phone is.

I have to get out of sight.

My legs are useless, so I crawl on my hands and knees to the end of the lot where the grass is near waist high. The un-marked car pulls up to the curb and Sanchez gets out. He's on his cell phone. Hidden from sight, I watch him shake his head at the empty stretcher and look around, confused. He calls something to a fire fighter in the distance, then moves cautiously toward the warehouse. The back of the building is still on fire.

From the grass outside I watch it burn. There's something

so wrong, and so beautiful about it. In the distance there is the wailing of another fire truck.

I begin to laugh. Something has come apart inside me.

For me hell is cold. What is happening here is a cleansing. Soon this building will crumble and something new will take over. I close my eyes, and wait for it to happen.

52

THE LAST TIME Brazuca searched for Nora, it was in the wilderness of Vancouver Island. His limp had been so bad he was hardly able to walk the trails without slivers of pain slicing up his leg. He'd been prompted by Simone to go looking and aided by Whisper in his search. He would not have found Nora if not for the dog and now he wishes he'd thought to bring her with him to Detroit, if only for the company. It had been blind, stupid luck that he'd managed to get a tip from the first motel in Midtown Detroit he'd visited. The squinty-eyed woman at reception was much more talkative in person than she'd been over the phone. A business card led to a detective who'd talked to Nora about a robbery attempt in her room. An overworked detective who, Brazuca discovered, thought Nora's life was in danger but who also believed that she was no longer his problem.

Sitting beside Sanchez on a hard bench in a Detroit hospital, Brazuca listens to a recording of Nora confronting two armed attackers in a house that belonged to a young blues singer. The message cuts off abruptly to her running footsteps.

After the recording ends, Sanchez glances over at Brazuca. "This was last night. At first we thought she was injured and would seek help. We think the fire that burned down the building she was found in was started by a couple of kids a witness saw in the area, watching. They poured gasoline all over that building, used a candle to ignite the fire, and put metal drums of paint thinner around to heat up, explode, and keep the fire going. Crude, but it worked. Whole place went up in fucking flames. There was debris all over that dump. The paramedics we spoke to said she was lucky to survive—she'd crawled into a doorway and part of the ceiling collapsed around her. They thought she'd find her way to a hospital eventually."

"But she didn't," Brazuca says, because it's Nora, and she wouldn't.

Sanchez shrugs. "Not her style, I'm guessing, to seek help. We got the guys who were responsible for the attack on Nate Marlowe from a tip. One of them confessed and gave the other guy up as the shooter. So that case is closed."

"But."

"But whoever put the hit out on your woman is in the wind. These guys won't talk about anything higher up. They know they're dead if they do."

Down the hall there's a man fighting for his life because of this mess. Brazuca had been reluctant when Sanchez arranged to meet him here, seeing how he can't get the image of Seb Crow's still body out of his head. Can't forget Krushnik in his grief. But he understands now this choice of location. Sanchez is likely hoping this will give Brazuca a dose of clarity of what someone like Nora can do to a man who lets his guard down. As if he doesn't already know.

The Detroit detective could also be hoping for some insight to tie up loose ends.

They watch a nurse wheel a sleeping boy down the hall and disappear around the corner. "She's not my woman," Brazuca says eventually. Even the thought caused a certain amount of anxiety. "I'm looking for a triad connection here. Ever heard of Three Phoenix? Based on the west coast, but tied to Hong Kong."

Sanchez shakes his head. "Not that I can think of, man. I can tell you one thing, these guys weren't professional enough for triad, especially one that operates internationally. They missed Nora going on three times now. It was sloppy work."

Brazuca gives him a thin smile. From what Sanchez has explained, it seems that Curtis Parnell had contracted the hit out to the wrong people. And that there would be hell to pay for a fuckup of that magnitude.

"Maybe, but you don't know Nora."

He isn't surprised that she found a way to escape. He'd once called her a survivor and that's exactly what she is, but not without consequences. Proof of her uncanny ability to avoid death lay on a hospital bed down the hall from them. The detritus she left in her wake.

"Is Marlowe going to make it?" he asks Sanchez.

Sanchez seems to weigh his words carefully. "I don't know. That's what I'm here to find out. I'm not even supposed to be on this case, you know. I'm with Robberies. This whole thing is now out of my hands." He pauses, seems to wrestle with something internally. "So you have no idea where she would go now?"

"No."

Nora on the run wasn't something Brazuca wants to think about. Nora scared, alone. With a powerful enemy at her heels, one who has underestimated her yet again. But she is alive.

This, at least, is something to hold on to. Something that he can tell her daughter.

With an abrupt farewell, he leaves the Detroit detective on the bench and follows the path taken by the nurse and the sleeping child. Making sure to avoid the room where Nate Marlowe lies in critical care with a perforation in his lung. A stark reminder of a life in the balance.

He's not sure about Marlowe's relationship to Nora, never bothered to ask Sanchez, but that he was almost killed because of her dangerous past is enough to make Brazuca move quicker. If he was a different man, he'd stop to think about why . . . well, he'd stop to think, period. His new leaf is withered by the coffee he's been downing like it's the elixir of life. Then buried under a mountain of calories from a cheeseburger an hour ago.

So he doesn't stop.

Knows that if he does, a troubled young woman might lose her mother. He has seen so much loss in his life that he can't bear that thought.

He's surprised to find out that the sun has set while he'd been in the hospital with Sanchez. The night sky is so heavy that not a single star can be seen. Which seems about right, but is ominous as hell. The sound of Nora's footsteps pounding the pavement haunts him all the way back to Vancouver, where Bonnie had seen a tattoo that she wasn't supposed to see, and where the Three Phoenix trail went cold.

53

SOME OF THE details are fuzzy but I remember waking up on the ground, just before dawn. Was it yesterday? Seems like ages ago. In my jacket pocket, I found my passport and my wallet, with a brass key tucked inside it. It took me a full minute to recognize it. It belongs to a house, somewhere far away. Maybe it unlocks nothing—I don't know.

I don't want this key, but I know who to give it to. I crawled away from those ruins until I felt my strength returning, then I got to my feet and started walking. Left my identity back in a smoldering building. Nora who? That woman has enemies, some that still pursue her. Maybe those enemies will think that she has perished in that fire. Maybe they will give up now.

Even if they don't, I can't be bothered to care right now. They will have to catch me and I won't make it easy for them—now that I know they're still looking. Dao, the man I'm convinced is after me, has shown his weakness—and if he thinks revenge is anything but weakness, he should take a look at Ryan Russo.

For now, I keep moving, staying to the shadows. Staying low. Gathering my strength. Death is all around me here in Detroit, but I won't be here for long. Maybe it's wishful thinking, but I have a key to pass on.

I yearn for Whisper by my side, as I always do, but she's with me in spirit. I'll see her soon enough and we'll sit by the rocks and look out at the ocean. We'll think of Seb and I'll eat pad thai while she gnaws on a fresh bone. We'll get nice and fat, the two of us, and maybe there will be no more secrets between me and Leo.

In the burning warehouse I was ready for it to be done, but it's not nearly over yet. I'm like the hero in an absurd war novel. Look at me, in a canoe. Paddling away. Except I'm on yet another filthy street in Detroit, and I can barely put one foot in front of the other.

There are no canoes in my future, but there's a great big bridge. A few hours past it is a girl I have to see. To hand over a relic of the past, one that has crossed continents and come through fires. Someone should have it, but that someone isn't me. I'll tell the girl about my father, who was a good person, a decent human being who fell in love with the wrong woman. She'll also hear about my mother, who was a cold bitch who walked away and never looked back. She's got an aunt in Vancouver who hates me, but may not hate her. It's not a perfect story, but it's ours if she wants it.

The key is warm to the touch, so I hold it in my palm. I need as much heat as I can get for the road.

I have a bridge to cross.

ACKNOWLEDGMENTS

I'M GRATEFUL FOR the support of Miriam Kriss, Lyssa Keusch, Kate Parkin, Katherine Armstrong, and the wonderful people at William Morrow and Bonnier Zaffre.

Many thanks to the generous individuals who gave me their time and expertise: Sunni Westbrook, David Pledger, Nadeen El-Kassem, Munir El-Kassem, Jim Compton, Linda L. Richards, Sarah Yu, Aysha Alkusayer, PH, Tiffany Morris, Debra Malandrino, and Andrew Mockler.

A great number of texts shored up my research, too many to list in full, but I wanted to acknowledge three in particular: *Sabra and Shatila* by Bayan Nuwayhed al-Hout, *Spy Handler: Memoir of a KGB Officer* by Gregory Feifer and Victor Cherkashin, and *Pity the Nation* by Robert Fisk, which introduced me to The Plot, as it applies to Lebanon.

A special thank-you to my police consultant, Ira Todd, who pulled out all the stops for me in Detroit. My friend, this book wouldn't have been the same without you.

ABOUT THE AUTHOR

SHEENA KAMAL holds an HBA in political science from the University of Toronto, and was awarded a TD Canada Trust scholarship for community leadership and activism around the issue of homelessness. Kamal has also worked as a crime and investigative journalism researcher for the film and television industry. Her academic knowledge and experience inspired her debut novel, *The Lost Ones*. She lives in Vancouver, Canada.